the deep dark descending

ALSO BY ALLEN ESKENS

The Life We Bury

The Guise of Another

The Heavens May Fall

the deep dark descending

allen eskens

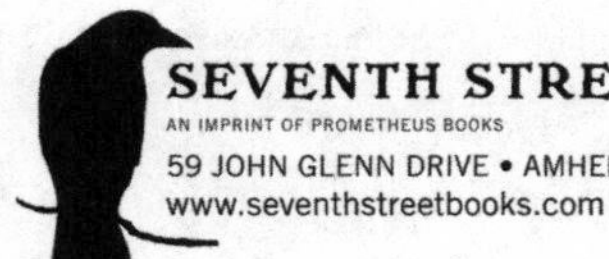
SEVENTH STREET BOOKS®
AN IMPRINT OF PROMETHEUS BOOKS
59 JOHN GLENN DRIVE • AMHERST, NY 14228
www.seventhstreetbooks.com

Published 2017 by Seventh Street Books®, an imprint of Prometheus Books

Cover image © Maarten Wouters / Getty Images
Cover design by Jacqueline Nasso Cooke
Cover design © Prometheus Books

Inquiries should be addressed to
Seventh Street Books
59 John Glenn Drive
Amherst, New York 14228
VOICE: 716–691–0133
FAX: 716–691–0137
WWW.SEVENTHSTREETBOOKS.COM

21 20 19 18 17   5 4 3 2 1

Library of Congress Cataloging-in-Publication Data

Names: Eskens, Allen, 1963- author.
Title: The deep dark descending / by Allen Eskens.
Description: Amherst, NY : Seventh Street Books, an imprint of Prometheus Books, 2017.
Identifiers: LCCN 2017019514 (print) | LCCN 2017023729 (ebook) | ISBN 9781633883567 (ebook) | ISBN 9781633883550 (paperback)
Subjects: | BISAC: FICTION / Mystery & Detective / Police Procedural. | GSAFD: Mystery fiction.
Classification: LCC PS3605.S49 (ebook) | LCC PS3605.S49 D44 2017 (print) | DDC 813/.6—dc23
LC record available at https://lccn.loc.gov/2017019514

Printed in the United States of America

To all the teachers I've had who have led me (and sometimes pushed me) in the right direction. Thank you.

CHAPTER 1

Up North

I raise the ax handle for the third blow and my arm disobeys me, stiffening above my head, my hand tangled in knots of shouldn'ts and shoulds and all those second thoughts that I swore wouldn't stop me. My chest burns to take in oxygen. My body trembles with a crystalline rage, and my mind screams orders to my mutinous hand. *For Christ's sake, get it over with. This is what you came here for. Kill him!*

But the ax handle doesn't move.

A surge of emotion boils up from somewhere deep inside of me, building to such a violent pitch that I can't hold it in, and I let loose a howl that fills the spaces between the trees and whips through the forest like an artic wind swirling skyward until it fades into nothingness.

And still the ax handle doesn't move.

Why can't I kill this man?

He's on his back, unconscious, his eyes rolled up behind the slits of his eyelids. His arms are bent at the elbows, hands sticking up in the air. His fingers curl into sharp hooks, as if clawing at something that's not there. Maybe in the dark corners of his senseless brain he's still fighting with me—grabbing for my throat or plunging his fish knife into my ribs. But the fight is over; he'll realize that soon enough.

My chest is on fire, the frozen air scraping my lungs with white-hot bristles. Exhaustion kicks at my knees until I tilt back, planting my butt in the snow, the ax handle sinking to rest at my side. It's maybe five degrees out here, but I'm burning up under my coat. I pull the zipper down to expose myself to the winter air, and it chills the sweat that clings to my flannel shirt. I lift my collar to cover my mouth and breathe through the material, letting the dampness of my exhale moisten the cloth, smoothing down the serrated edge of my inhales.

The man just beyond my feet should be dead, but that last strike didn't land true. Excuses line up on my tongue, bitter seeds waiting to be spit to the ground. I was tired from the chase, and I was off balance when I hit him. I started the swing of my ax handle ready to send a hanging slider into the upper deck, my aim zeroed in on that soft plate beside his left eye. But he lunged at me with a fishing knife. Dodging the blade caused me to tilt enough that it changed my swing from a death blow to a knockout. Such is the difference an inch can make.

The man's head twitches, and his right hand jerks and falls to his side—a mean dog having a bad dream. A tiny trail of blood trickles from beneath his stocking cap. It follows a path down the side of his head to where it has been dripping off his left ear, creating a red blossom in the snow. I watch his torso slowly rise and fall. He breathes, and that irks me. I should have killed him in the heat of the fight; that's how it was supposed to happen—no contemplation, just action and reaction. He had a knife. I had a headless ax handle. A club verses a blade, that's about as fair as it gets, isn't it?

Fair. Why do I care about fair? If things were reversed and I was the one scratching at the dead air, he would not hesitate to kill me. He doesn't deserve the courtesy of fairness. Yet I remain ensnared by childhood notions of right and wrong, impressions as thin as tissue, but layered so thick in my memory that they have become walls of stone. I am somehow tethered to the black-and-white world of my youth as I struggle to pull myself toward a shadow of gray. I'm not that boy anymore.

I try to clear the tar from my thoughts. One more hit will put him to rest. One more swing of the ax handle is all I need. My fingers tighten around my weapon.

It's then that I hear the whisper of her words, faint, mixing with the breeze that's whistling through the nettle. She's speaking with that same tsk of disappointment that she sometimes used when I was a child. *Is this what you've become, Max Rupert?* Nancy asks. *Is this who you are?*

I loosen my grip on the ax handle. I hadn't thought of Nancy in years, and now when I need her least, the goblins of my subconscious find it necessary to summon her memory from the dust. I don't want her interference. Not today. I squeeze my eyes shut and her ghost disappears.

The man starts to move, rolling like some newborn larva, blind to the world but coming to understand that something has gone terribly wrong. I had hit the man hard—twice—but not hard enough, because he didn't die. The gurgle of each exhale lifts up from the back of his throat like a snore. He'll be waking soon.

I climb to my feet and square up like I'm getting ready to split a log. This time, it's not a random whisper of Nancy's voice in the breeze that stops me. It's a memory that took a full day to create, but comes back to me now in a starburst so brief that I can barely blink before it's gone. I was in fifth grade and had just left the cafeteria on my way to recess, racing at a pretty good clip. As I neared the entrance to the playground, a couple of sixth-grade boys came around the corner, walking toward me. I didn't know either one of them, but I would learn later that the bigger of the two was a kid named Hank Bellows.

As we passed each other, Hank threw his shoulder into me, sending me careening into a wall. I bounced off the brick and went sprawling across the asphalt, the ground chewing up a good chunk of skin on my forearm. I looked up to see both boys laughing as they continued their walk to the cafeteria.

When my father heard the explanation for my wound, he lit into me like it had somehow been my fault, as if my weakness brought this on. "You can't let that stand," he said. I could smell the beer in his words. "It don't matter that he's a sixth grader or that he's bigger than you. You have to call him on what he did. He'll never respect you as a man if you don't stand up for yourself. It's up to you, and no one else, to make this right. That's what a man does—he makes it right. You want to be a man, don't you?"

I didn't need his encouragement. I already had plans for Hank.

But later, after my dad fell asleep watching TV, Nancy came to my room, carrying a first-aid kit. She had moved into our house when I was five and, as near as I could tell at the time, she was my dad's girlfriend. Her touch was gentle and her words soft. She asked me to go through the incident again as she washed dried blood from the wound. I told her what had happened from beginning to end.

"You're pretty mad at Hank, aren't you?"

"I'm going to kick his—" I stopped myself because Nancy didn't like profanity, even though profanity seemed to be half of my dad's daily vocabulary.

"Being mad doesn't feel good, does it?" She lifted a dollop of salve to spread on the abrasion. I braced for the sting, but it never came. "All that anger you have inside you?"

I gave a shrug.

"I've been angry like that before. For me it felt like I had a stone pressing down on my chest. Can you feel that?"

I don't remember if I could feel a stone, exactly, but I could feel something, so I nodded.

"There's an old saying that a person who goes looking for revenge should dig two graves. Have you ever heard that before?"

I shook my head no.

"It means that you're not solving the problem by getting revenge. You're only making it worse. You're making it just as bad for yourself as for the other person. You see what I'm saying?"

As she spoke, I relived getting thrown into that wall and I could feel the anger crawling up my throat. My eyes began to tear up, and I wanted Nancy out of my room. I didn't want her to see me cry. She didn't say anything more as she cut and taped gauze to my arm. I know now that she was letting her words sink in.

When she'd finished, she returned her supplies to the kit. Then she turned to me and said, "Tomorrow, when you go to school, you do what you think is right. But don't do it because your father told you to do it or because I told you not to. You're the one who has to live with what you do."

The man at my feet moans again and I'm pulled out of my thoughts, Nancy's words fading into silence. I curse myself for letting that memory find daylight. I'm not ten years old, and this isn't about a skinned-up arm. It's about much more.

But what if he doesn't understand? What if the man at my feet doesn't know which of his many sins has brought him here? What if I kill him and he doesn't understand why? He needs to know why. Her name must be his last thought—its echo should be the last sound he hears before darkness chokes him.

Snow, thin like fire ash, is falling on the man's face, pulling him back to consciousness. I tap my leg with the ax handle. It would be foolish to let him wake up to continue our fight. But I'm not ready to kill him yet. I know that now. I knew it back when I couldn't strike that third and final blow, only I didn't understand it then. I need something from him—something more than just his death. I need to hear him admit that he killed my wife.

CHAPTER 2

Minneapolis—Three Days Ago

It was only three days ago that I first listened to the two men as they planned my wife's murder. Their conversation, a slow, drawling phone call that bounced off of satellite towers four and a half years earlier, had been preserved on a compact disc—insurance against faithless co-conspirators was my guess. Now that disc spun inside my laptop, their small words filling my house, their cold, rusty voices ripping into me, gutting me, leaving me hollow and weak. These were the men who killed my wife.

When the recording ended, my house fell silent except for the sound of my own breath billowing through my nostrils in short bursts. My mouth watered as though I were going to throw up. Maybe I *was* going to throw up. Chaotic thoughts broke against my skull, words careening off bone and leaving behind a twisted muddle. These two men were talking about Jenni. They were discussing how they were going to end her life, and they were doing it with the nonchalance reserved for weather chitchat or reading a lunch menu.

I stood up from the couch because my legs demanded it. A sudden burst of energy sent me walking in circles around my living room. I wanted to hit something. I wanted to kick and tear and destroy things. I wanted to scream at the top of my lungs, anything to purge the anguish from my body. I raised my hand to punch the wall, but stopped short, grabbing my head instead, my hands squeezing into my temples. I clenched my teeth and swallowed the explosion that fought to get out. I pressed everything inward, holding fast to a rage more pure and more acrid than anything I have ever before tasted. I kept it all in. The time would come for that to be unleashed, but not yet.

When I opened my eyes, I was myself again, calm, steady, thinking, breathing. I stepped to my front door and opened it a crack to let in some cold air. Eighteen degrees below zero. Not unusual for Minneapolis on December 31st, but this winter seemed colder than normal. I breathed in, filling my lungs with what felt like raw ice, and then slowly exhaled. Outside, the afternoon sun had already started its slide toward the horizon. Evening came so early this time of year.

I had no plans for that night. Even before Jenni died—before she was murdered—we rarely went out on New Year's Eve. We had refined our tradition to a simple evening of popcorn, old movies, and a kiss at midnight. That was my idea, or my fault, depending on who you asked. Jenni, the free spirit, loved to dance and dress up and enjoy a well-prepared meal at a nice restaurant. She was the one who found significance in the small squares on the calendar. I once told her that I didn't see the need to celebrate the arbitrary end of another rotation around the sun. On this score, she ignored me completely, and we celebrated birthdays and anniversaries and a plethora of lesser occasions.

After Jenni's death, those occasions, even the lesser ones, remained my connection to her. I found her thread woven through almost every part of my existence, a tapestry once vibrant and alive now in danger of fading away. But it didn't fade. I wouldn't let it. Every turn of the page brought some new reason to remember her: our first date, the day I told her I loved her, the day I proposed, birthdays, holidays, the day she died.

I didn't watch old movies that first New Year's Eve without her. The wound—a mere five months old—was still too fresh to relive such a tradition alone. Instead, I drank scotch until I threw up on myself. I did a lot of drinking that year—not the steady drip of sneaking shots into my coffee cup. No. My drinking came in torrents—binge sessions that amplified the tiniest memory into a mind-numbing cacophony. I could go from breaking the seal to bed spins in less time than it took to play one of her favorite CDs.

I probably would have continued down that path had it not been for the scene I'd made at the cemetery on the first anniversary of her death. It was whiskey that night, enough that I passed out hugging the grass above Jenni's grave. Security guards had kicked me out of the cemetery when it closed earlier, but I wasn't done talking to my dead wife, and I still had half a pint of Jim Beam. I retain a vague recollection of climbing back over the wrought-iron fence, relying more on luck than skill to keep from impaling myself on the railhead spikes that surrounded the cemetery.

I was found there by my brother, Alexander, and a friend by the name of Boady Sanden—at least he'd been a friend back then. They managed to drag me out through a side gate, with no security guard being the wiser. That night had become a solemn memory, but that memory—that friendship with Boady—went up in flames, the way tinder is supposed to, I guess. We were a pairing that should never have been, a homicide detective and a defense attorney. Other cops told me that it was unnatural. I probably should have listened.

As I contemplated the start of another year without Jenni—my fifth now—I held no thought of Boady Sanden. I had planned to spend that New Year's Eve sitting alone in a house that hadn't changed its mood since the day she died, watching black-and-white movies until sleep took me. That plan fell away with a ringing of a door bell. I wasn't expecting company; and when I answered the door, I saw Boady Sanden standing before me, his back braced against the cut of the frigid wind. It was all I could do not to punch him in the face.

"Can I come in?" he asked.

Images of our friendship passed between us like a train speeding by. There had been some good times. But then I remembered the day our friendship ended.

Two months ago, I'd been testifying in a case for which I was the lead investigator and Boady the defense attorney. It wasn't our first time playing that game, although it had been several years since I had to face one of his tough cross-examinations. But that day, Sanden blindsided me. He brought out a reprimand I'd received for digging into my wife's death, an act forbidden of a detective like myself. Sanden, *my friend*, accused me of playing loose with my investigation, of worrying more about Jenni's death than about his client's case. He paraded that reprimand in front of the jury, telling them that I had lost my mind from grief and had not done a proper job.

Boady Sanden torched our friendship in defense of a worthless piece of garbage, and in doing so committed, what was for me, an unforgivable sin.

"Five minutes of your time," he said. "That's all. After that, I'll leave and never bother you again. Just five minutes."

I was about to shut the door in his face when I saw the briefcase in his hand and the serious look in his eye. Against my better judgment, I let him in.

More words went unspoken in our brief meeting than were actually said. He had something that he needed to give to me, an olive branch, or maybe this was his way of clearing his conscience. When he left, I held in my hand a criminal file with the name Ray Kroll written on the tab—a stolen file that I was never supposed to possess. Inside that file was a CD that Boady said I should listen to, a CD that might hold the secret to Jenni's death.

After Boady left, I played the recording and felt my world tilt.

Hello?

Yeah, it's me.

The boss said you'd be calling. What's up?

We have a job. I need you to lift a car. Keep it clean. No fingerprints. No DNA. Wear gloves.

I know what I'm doing.

We have to deal with someone right away.

Send a message?

No. Extreme prejudice. Hit-and-run.

Great. Another drop of blood and we do all the work.

This is serious. It's a cop's wife.

A what?

You heard me. She stumbled onto something she shouldn't have. If we don't move fast, we'll all be fucked. I don't like this any more than you do.

When?

Today. 3:00.

Where?

Hennepin County Medical Center. There's a parking garage on the corner of Eighth and Chicago. Meet me on the top floor. I'll fill you in there. I'm not sure if they have cameras at the entrance, so cover your face when you drive in.

The voices belonged to two men. The first to talk answered the phone with a thick "hello" and was likely the one who recorded the call because his voice, deep and throaty, came through more clearly than the other. He spoke with that kind of permanent slur that I've heard in men who spend their lives around bars, his words dragging like he'd just woken up.

The boss said you'd be calling, he said. This man had a boss; he was an employee—a henchman. He understood that he was expected to follow orders, even if it meant killing a woman that he apparently didn't know.

It's a cop's wife.

A what?

I could hear an edge of surprise, maybe even concern in his voice. The Henchman didn't know Jenni. He didn't know the target.

The second man's voice was a little harder to hear, like he was talking through wax paper. Despite the bad connection, I could make out the professional tone, the steady calm of someone who handled stress well, someone who could plan a murder and not trip on his words. This man, the Planner, came across more clipped and trimmed than the Henchman. Educated, I would say. Concise. No chitchat. There was something about his voice that struck me as familiar, not like an old friend or relative, but familiar as though maybe we had met once—chatted at some point in our lives. That was probably just wishful thinking.

The Planner knew who I was. He knew that Jenni was *a cop's wife*. When I heard those words the first time, my breath knotted up in my chest. It had been my fault, just as I believed. Jenni died because she was my wife. She died because of my actions, because of my sins. They were going to kill a cop's wife to get even with the cop. I had suspected that for some time, and the Planner's words now confirmed it . . . at least that's what I thought.

But then he continued. *She stumbled onto something she shouldn't have.*

I missed that line the first time that I listened to the recording. After he said they were going to kill a cop's wife, the next words fell behind a thick hum of rage. It wasn't until I played it a second time that I heard the reason for Jenni's death, and it made no sense to me. Who would want to kill a hospital social worker? She did nothing but help people. I must have heard it wrong. I played it again, and I heard it again: *She stumbled onto something she shouldn't have.*

I stopped the CD and backed away from my laptop as though it had turned venomous. It had never occurred to me that Jenni died because of something she did or something she knew, no more than it would occur to me that the sun might, one day, set in the east. I was supposed to be the target. I was supposed to be the reason. I was a homicide detective. I was the one who had enemies. Not her.

I couldn't stop pacing. I couldn't sit down. I went to the front door and opened it again, letting another wave of frigid air slap me in the face. I left the door open until my eyelashes began to frost over and stick together. When I closed the door, my head was quiet, and the world no longer spun backward.

I returned to my laptop and played the CD again and again, writing down every word they said, listening for accents and sounds in the background. After listening to it for the tenth time, the words held no sway over my blood pressure and I saw the CD for what it was—a gift. All these years, I'd been looking down when I should have been looking up. I had discovered more about Jenni's death in one hour, on that bone-chilling New Year's Eve, than I had learned over four and a half years of digging.

I closed my laptop and looked down at the pad of paper in front of me, my eyes focusing on one line: *The boss said you'd be calling*. I turned to a blank page and wrote three words: *Boss*, *Planner*, and *Henchman*.

CHAPTER 3

Our home in Logan Park was the kind of house you'd drive by every day and never notice. Blue siding. A modest front yard cut in half by a sidewalk. A fenced-in backyard with a garage off the alley. Small by most measures, it had always been big enough for the two of us. After Jenni died, the house seemed to expand and contract depending on the strength of her memory, inhaling and exhaling, breathing deepest when I missed her the most.

Jenni's china figurines watched me from the fireplace mantle as I paced around the living room, mumbling to myself, debating my next move. The file that Boady had stumbled upon, the stolen file that now lay on my coffee table, had to be the key. Boady didn't know how important his single contribution might be. How could he? He didn't know about the other puzzle pieces that I was hiding in my house.

I went to a drawer in my bedroom and brought out my other file, a file I had secretly copied from the archive room at City Hall. I put it on the coffee table next to its new sister. As I stared at the two files, I became swept up in the hope that somewhere in those pages lurked the secret that would lead me to my wife's killer, one file filling in the gaps left by the other, consonants and vowels finally joining together to give meaning to the noise.

My thoughts settled as the path ahead of me became clear. The time had come to toss aside half measures and shadow investigations. Like a base jumper committing to the leap, I would either succeed spectacularly or fail spectacularly. What I would no longer do, though, is waver.

With our master bedroom on the main floor, we rarely went upstairs, which held two small bedrooms and a bathroom. We kept one of the upstairs bedrooms nice for company to stay in. That room was also going to be the nursery when—if—that time ever arrived. Even before the wedding, we talked about having children, a plan that fell behind careers and the daily pressures of life. Then, one day, Jenni called me up to the guest room in the middle of a spring afternoon. When I walked in, I found her lying on her back, completely naked except for a bracelet on her left wrist. It was a piece of jewelry she had never worn before, her great-grandmother's bracelet, an heirloom that carried over a hundred years of history.

Jenni had shown me the bracelet back when we were still dating, a simple chain with six golden charms on it, each about the size and shape of a dime. On each charm had been inscribed a name. Three of the names were those of Jenni's grandmother and her grandmother's two brothers. Two more names belonged to Jenni's mother, Alice, and Jenni's aunt, Helen. The sixth charm carried Jenni's name. Great Grandma Mary had started the tradition of inscribing the names of her children on the bracelet, adding a new charm with each new birth. Now the tradition had fallen to us.

Jenni's nakedness surprised me and was a happy interruption of my afternoon. When I had lain beside Jenni, she told me that she had made a decision. The time had come to have a child. We'd been risking the possibility for a while, but now, she said, it was time to get serious. She wanted to make me a father, and she chose to begin that journey in the room that would become the nursery.

I slipped the bracelet off of her wrist and hooked it on a nail above the headboard where a picture of ducks once hung. And there the bracelet would remain—for years, a symbol of what we lacked. We never made love in that room again, and, over time, we both stopped visiting the guest room all together. I think neither of us could take the daily reminder that not all trees bore fruit.

The second upstairs bedroom had been turned into a storage room, filled with everything from old textbooks and unused exercise equipment to boxes of clothing. I don't remember being inside either of those rooms since Jenni's death, but now, that time had arrived. I needed a war room, a place where I could immerse myself in Jenni's case with no distractions, a place where I could release my inner Mr. Hyde and indulge in my own form of masochism, like those penitents who flog themselves into religious ecstasy. In this room, I would purge all other thoughts from my head and focus on one task—hunting down the people responsible for my wife's death.

With that inspiration, I went to the guest room to begin my work.

Before anything else, I wanted to remove the bracelet from the wall. I didn't need the weight of that history distracting me. When I went to pull it from its nail, it was gone. I hadn't noticed before. Jenni must have packed it away with all of the other reminders of our broken dream. If I had looked for the bracelet, I probably would have found it in the storage room, in a pink sewing kit that also came to us as an heirloom, a box that held Jenni's bronzed baby shoes and the hospital band they wrapped around her wrist on the day she was born.

I took a moment to let the memory pass and then went to work.

First, I took apart the bed, hauling its slats and rails out to the garage and leaning the box spring and mattress against the wall at the top of the stairs. I dragged the dresser to the storage room and emptied the bookcase of its books, throwing them into the dusty bathtub of the upstairs bathroom. Within a couple hours, I had emptied the guest room of all of its contents other than the bare bookshelf, which I figured I could use.

I would need lots of table space, which I didn't have, so I popped the hinge pins off the doors of both bedrooms and the bathroom. They were cheap, hollow-core doors with flat, smooth surfaces. Laying them on boxes I'd taken from the storage room, I created three tables, which I arranged into a horseshoe.

Satisfied with my effort, I brought up my laptop, a dining room chair, and the two files. As I began organizing my investigation, I heard the pop of firecrackers in the distance, their lonely clap offering proof that, even in subzero temperatures, people can't resist bothering neighbors when it's New Year's Eve. I looked at my watch and saw that midnight had just passed.

Thus began my fifth New Year's Day without her.

I opened the first file, the thicker of the two—the file that led to my reprimand last year. Swiping it from the archive room was an act that would not have garnered a second glance, much less a reprimand, had it not been my wife's case. I made a copy of the file, kept the clone, and returned the original to its home. The case was originally assigned to Detective Louis Parnell, who was given instructions not to pass anything along to me. There were rules against such things. I was the victim's husband. If Jenni's death had been anything other than a hit-and-run, I would be the top suspect. Nothing personal; that's just where most spousal murders ended up.

I knew Louis well, and it didn't take long for him to break his silence about the case. It also didn't take him long to conclude that Jenni's death was nothing more than what it had appeared to be—a hit-and-run. Just as that man on the CD, the Planner, had intended.

Parnell's final report concluded that Jenni had been walking through the Hennepin County Medical Center parking ramp and had been hit by a yellow Toyota Corolla. He knew the make, model, and color of the car because of paint transfer on Jenni's clothing and part of a headlight that remained behind. I don't think Parnell spent all that much time looking for the car, and I don't believe he lost too much sleep over not finding it. I didn't fault him for that. His efforts didn't matter, because I had been looking for that car. Nights and weekends. An obsession at first, but as months turned into years, it took on the pattern of a hobby—walking through junkyards and randomly stopping by body shops, leaving my card wherever I went.

Then, four months ago, I found the car—or rather the car found me. An anonymous envelope with a cryptic note and storage-room key sent me, once again, into the night in search of the yellow Corolla. And, by God, this time I found it—me—the husband. I was responsible for the break in the case. I was the one moving the game pieces forward. And still, I was the one who was once again frozen out of the investigation—reprimanded for sticking my nose where it didn't belong.

Like a dutiful Boy Scout following the rules, I turned my evidence over to my commander—well, maybe I didn't follow all the rules. I had come too far to pay attention to needless roadblocks. So, I kept the clone file. I got my ass chewed when Commander Walker found out that I'd taken the file home; he had to do it, but he never asked if I'd made a copy. I always figured Walker didn't want to know. He was a good man that way.

The second file, the Kroll file, was another story all together. When he handed the file to me, Boady told me, flat out, that he had secreted it out of the office of a dead attorney named Ben Pruitt. Boady had been placed in charge of resolving the dead man's cases and client funds. Sanden would lose a great deal if his deed ever came to light. Friend or not, that would be a line I'd never cross.

I turned my attention first to the Ray Kroll file and read that he was a small-time criminal who graduated to the big leagues by bashing a guy's head in with a brick. I had never heard of Ray Kroll, nor could I remember Jenni ever mentioning the guy's name. Yet his file held the key to Jenni's death. It was in Kroll's file that Boady found the CD of the telephone conversation.

I laid the contents of the two files out across the tables, separating stacks of police reports, witness transcripts, pictures. There were some pictures, however, that would remain tucked away in a sealed folder. When I took Jenni's hit-and-run file to the copy center, I gave the clerk instructions to place all the photos of her body into a special folder and tape the edges shut. I had never looked at those pictures, and I never would, unless it became gun-to-the-head important. I had enough nightmares without having to wrestle with those images.

There were nights when I dreaded closing my eyes, knowing how my Freudian cup had runneth over. Usually, those dreams didn't start off all that bad. In fact, they often began in a world where Jenni and I had been happy, sitting on the porch and playing gin rummy or wading through the shallows up at the cabin. I liked that part of the dream, but that part never lasted. Soon the sky would grow black and the air cold and Jenni would be ripped away from me. The dream that came to me most often involved a pack of wolves, their eyes glowing, their teeth long, silver, and dripping with appetite. In their snarls I could hear the whisper of Jenni's name, and in their eyes I saw my condemnation for having failed her.

But now I had Kroll's file and the CD. I knew about the Planner, the Henchman, and the Boss. The time had come to go on the hunt.

I did an Internet search for *Raymond Kroll* and *Ray Kroll* and *R. Kroll*. The man had done a pretty good job of living under the radar.

I had his date of birth and address, so I could weed through the Ray Krolls who had nothing to do with my investigation. I found his mug shot; but, more than anything, I wanted to hear his voice, compare it to the voices on the CD. If only he had made a YouTube video or something. But I found nothing.

I went back to the paper reports on my table, poring over them until my eyelids became heavy and my mind thick. I fought to keep sleep at bay, as though calling a halt to my work that night might make it all disappear, nothing more than a hallucination born of my desperation.

When I finally went to bed, I found myself floating in an unfamiliar calm, a strange concoction of equal parts wariness and excitement. Yet one final thought kept me from nodding off. Everything I had in my possession, all of my evidence, had been pilfered. None of it came through legal channels. None of it would be admissible in a trial—a small detail that would undoubtedly grow into one of those insurmountable problems.

How would I explain the CD? I had the voices of the men who killed my wife, but no jury would ever hear them. I couldn't say that a friend of mine stole a file from another attorney's office. Boady would lose his license to practice law, and that would only be the start. In the end, the evidence would get kicked out and the killers would walk away free. I may end up uncovering the truth about what happened to Jenni, but those men who plotted and carried out her murder would never be convicted in a court of law.

I tried to put that minor wrinkle aside and get some sleep. I felt oddly hopeful as I meandered between wake and sleep, ready to take on those demons that prowled in the darkest fissures of my subconscious. Maybe tonight would be the night that I would stop the wolves. Then, as I was about to fall asleep, a new thought brought me back from the deep dark. This thought was not calming; it made my heart thump inside my chest. Fear? Excitement? I wasn't sure, to be honest.

Yes, it was undeniable that this evidence would never be admissible at trial. But it struck me that there would be no trial if the wolves were dead.

CHAPTER 4

Up North

The man is stirring. He's trying to speak, but the garbles that stumble from his mouth make no sense. I should tie him up while he's still in this state of tranquil befuddlement. I take off my gloves and unbuckle my snow pants to get to the belt on my blue jeans. I'm on my knees, pushing through the snow, shuffling around him until I'm above his head. I lift his shoulders to sit him upright.

He mutters something unintelligible.

I pull his arms back and wrap my belt around his elbows, buckling them behind his back.

"What are you . . ." His head flops on top of his neck as he speaks.

I let him fall back into the snow, and I move to sit across his hips, yanking the drawstring from the waist of my coat, three feet of cord a quarter of an inch thick. I tie one end around the man's right wrist, cinching it tight enough that I don't have to worry about him slipping free. He tries to pull his hand away, but with his mind in a fog, his efforts are meaningless. When I grab his left wrist, he yelps in pain. Through the coat sleeve, I can feel that his forearm is swollen from where my ax handle connected. I'm pretty sure it's broken, and, if it's not, it won't be of much use to him.

We're in a small clearing no more than twenty feet in from the shore of a large, frozen lake. The clearing gave the deceptive appearance of a portage, which must have drawn him in like a lost man stumbling toward a mirage. But only a few feet into the clearing, he became tangled in a patch of pin-cherry scrub. Our chase had come to an end. He had no choice but to face me and turn his flight into a fight.

By the time I'd caught up to him, I was so exhausted that I could barely stay on my feet. I lumbered up the embankment, my shaky legs driven forward by a rage that had been on a slow burn for years and was now erupting—my ax handle raised and ready. I didn't see the knife in his hand as he turned to make his stand. It wouldn't have mattered if I had seen it. I lunged at him with the ax handle arcing down from above my head. He raised his left arm to block my attack and took the full force of the blow. I swear I heard the sound of the bone breaking.

He started to go down onto one knee, a half-assed genuflection, but caught himself and struggled to get back to his feet. I swung again. This time, just as the ax handle reached the top of its arc, I saw the glint of the blade in his hand. He fell toward me, the knife aimed at my stomach. I jerked to the right, my feet tangling in the scrub and snow as I drove the ax handle into his head. The jolt reverberated through my palm, and the man went down hard. I raised the ax handle for a third blow, the one that would end his life, but there would be no third blow.

He's gaining strength as he resists my effort to tie him up. I grab his broken arm, and the stab of pain wakes him. He speaks with clarity, almost yelling at me, "What the fuck are you doing!"

He tries to pull his arm free, but I use my knees to push his wrists together. He bellows and curses as my leg presses against what I suspect is a broken ulna. That's got to hurt something fierce. I bind the cord around his left wrist, then double it back again to his right wrist and tie it tight. I turn around to sit on his knees so I can untie the laces of his boots. He kicks, but his legs barely move under my weight. I pull the laces tight, knotting them so that the collar of each boot pinches into his calves. Then I tie the loose ends of the boot laces to one another, binding his feet together.

I stand up to inspect what I've done. Behind his back, the belt has his arms trussed at the elbows, and his wrists are tethered in front of his stomach with my drawstring, his hands far enough apart that his fingers can't touch. I pick up his fillet knife and slide it into my boot. He is at my mercy.

Mercy. I repeat the word in my head. The irony. A wisp of a chuckle escapes my lips and dissolves into the breeze as my thoughts retreat back into darker corners.

"What's going on?" he asks. "Who are you?"

I stand, brush the snow off my pants, and I look around, thinking maybe I can get a fix on where I'm at. Although I had done my best to commit this part of the Superior National Forest to memory, I lost track during the two-mile chase, and I'm not sure if I'm still in Minnesota or if crossing that frozen lake brought me into Canada. My mind begins calculating arguments of jurisdiction and law, and I drop my head to laugh. Still thinking like a cop. I'll have to get over that.

I zip my coat shut, now that the cold morning air has found its bite again. The lake looks to be about half a mile across and wide enough from east to west that I cannot see those shores through the haze. A jaundiced sun seeps through low clouds, and the thin veil of falling snow obscures the southern shore, where I can barely make out the smudges of green pine mixed with streaks of white aspen and birch.

"I think you broke my arm," he says. "It hurts." There's a salesman's sincerity to his words, which fall barren upon my ears. "Why are you doing this? I don't understand. Who are you?"

I walk down to the edge of the lake to clear my head, my gaze lost in the murky distance. We are alone. The closest semblance of civilization is the cabin where the chase began, some two miles away. He started on a snowmobile and I ran on foot. Had he not been in such a hurry, he'd have gotten a better head start. Instead, he wiped out early on a hairpin turn.

Even if he hadn't wrecked it, his machine could only take him so far. The snowmobile trail turns into a foot portage where Superior National Forest butts up against the Boundary Waters Canoe Area, well before the Canadian border. From there, he had to run on foot. I would have followed him to the end of the earth, if I had to. He had fear to feed his effort. I had revenge. I was willing to bet that my fuel would burn hotter and longer than anything he could muster.

But what to do now? If I was back in Minneapolis, there would be procedures to follow—a step-by-step blueprint of how to treat a suspect. *Suspect*. That's the wrong word. This isn't an investigation. I'm not looking for the truth; I know the truth. I need to hear him say what he did. I want him on his knees, blubbering his confession through tears of remorse so sincere that I have no choice but to believe him. I want an act of absolute contrition from this man, and even that might not be enough.

I'm thirsty. I don't have water, so I take off my gloves and scoop some snow into my mouth. It melts quickly on my tongue, but it does not quench my thirst. I lift another small handful of snow and for a moment allow myself to take in the beauty of the forest around me.

There is very little wind, and the man has stopped his yapping, which allows a sense of tranquility to descend on our little corner of the world. In the quiet of the woods, my thoughts turn to what I have lost—what he has taken from me. Jenni would have loved it here, sitting in the middle of nowhere, listening to the snow feather its way through the trees. She loved the woods, and she loved winter.

I close my eyes, and the smell of pine takes me back to our little house in Logan Park and the Christmas trees we put up every year. Jenni always insisted on the real thing, its scent filling the house, its branches decorated with a hodgepodge of ornaments that we had collected over the years, ornaments that held a special meaning for us: our first Christmas together, souvenirs from trips, and art fairs. She had ornaments from her childhood that she'd made from as far back as preschool.

Our last Christmas together, we spent the whole day bedecking the house and baking cookies. That night she poured wine and led me to a blanket that she'd spread out in front of the fireplace. There, we made love, her soft skin warmed by the fire, her eyes sparkling with the gentle twinkle of Christmas lights. I looked at her in that moment and wondered, how had a man like me ever gotten so lucky? How had I come to be with a woman so beautiful? So loving?

"Are you still here?" The man's words pull me from my memory and I hate him for it. "Hey, are you out there?"

He is lying on his back with a jack pine between us, so he doesn't know whether or not I've left him. It occurs to me that leaving him is an option. This forest is teeming with wolves. I'm no expert, but I would think that a pack of wolves would delight in such meal. I smile at the thought, even though I know that I won't allow chance to decide his fate. There is no penitence in that. No, this man will not die until he understands the gravity of what he's done.

But there's something else that scratches at the back of my mind, something faint and mercurial, a wisp of disquiet that dances just beyond my grasp. I try to understand why I hesitated, why that ax handle froze above my head, and the only flicker that makes it through the murk is that I need something from this man, something more than just his death—something more, even, than his confession. But what? Vindication? I don't think so. Such a sentiment seems petty to me, unworthy of her memory. No, I think this has to be about more than common revenge. This can't just be about me. This man's death must set right a universe beyond my own personal desires. That's what he has to understand. That's what I need to see in his eyes.

I contemplate what to do with him and keep coming back to the notions of time and pressure—forces that can build mountains and tear them down. In my experience, repentance comes neither quickly nor easily. I let my mind wander through a field of ideas, looking for the one that suits my needs. I try to keep the darker thoughts at bay, thoughts of torture and pain, thoughts so delicious to me that I can almost taste them on my tongue. But I set those impulses aside.

What I need is a countdown, a cadence that would let him see the end coming. His time on this earth is dwindling, his fate marching to a drum beat that he cannot alter. His only choice will be in how he meets that fate.

I like that idea. And if I'm being honest with myself, then I have to admit that I need that countdown for me as much as I do for him. I need it in the way a child on the high dive uses the fall of numbers to summon his resolve to jump. I know what I came here to do, yet, when I raised that ax handle for the death blow, I froze, my will to act caught in the cross fire between lesser gods of virtue and vice. I don't want to think about that, because I don't want to believe I can't go through with it. But that's the case, if the truth be told—and in the end, truth is what this is all about, right?

I sit on the bank of the lake, trying to come up with a plan, my feet resting on a shelf of ice below me, a crag sticking up through the snow that had been pushed there by expansion in the middle. I tap the edge of that ice with my toe just to hear it crack. That's when a thought pops into my head. I remember a case I once had where a man tried to hide a body by cutting holes in a frozen river and slipping the body through. The ice on this lake has to be at least three feet thick—maybe four. But back at the cabin, before the chase began, I had peeked into a shed to make sure he wasn't hiding in it. At the time, nothing piqued my interest, but now I remember the ice auger hanging on the wall. A plan begins to form in my mind, details falling into place. *Time and pressure.*

"Help!" the man yells. "Somebody help me!"

I stand up and walk back to where the man lies.

"Oh, thank God. I thought you were going to leave me. I knew you wouldn't—"

I plop down on the man's thighs and begin to undo his snow pants.

"What the hell?"

Beneath his snow pants, as I expect, he's wearing blue jeans, held up with a belt. I undo the belt.

"Get off me!" the man yells. "What are you doing?"

Did he really think I chased him for two miles in knee-deep snow just to molest him? I suppose, had I been in his position, I would have been questioning this conduct as well. Or maybe he thinks I'm going to relieve him of his man parts. I pause for a second when that idea flashes across my mind. But then I go back to my task.

I pull his belt from around his waist and toss it to the side. Then I stand and lift his torso until he is in a sitting position, his legs straight, his feet bound together by his boot laces. I pull him down the hill until his back is resting against the pine tree.

"Thanks," he says. "My arm really hurts. Could you—"

I pick up his belt and wrap it around his neck.

"What are you—?"

I pull the belt tight, cutting off his words, but not his breath. The belt is just long enough to close around both his throat and the tree. I buckle it on the last hole.

"What the fuck are you doing?" His voice is raspy against this new binding. "Why are you doing this?"

I take a moment to inspect my work, to make sure that, after I leave him, he won't be able to escape. His eyes are large with fear—or is it rage? I can't really tell. Either is fine by me. Satisfied with my handiwork, I put my gloves back on and pull my coat hood over my head, cinching it for the walk. As I step out onto the frozen lake, I can hear him yelling, or at least trying to yell past the belt around his neck.

"Where're you going? You can't leave me here. There're wolves out here. Come back here. You can't leave me like this."

As his voice trails off behind me, I find satisfaction in his fear, in his belief that I'm leaving him to be eaten by the wolves. But I will return. And when I do, he'll regret that he wanted me to come back.

CHAPTER 5

Minneapolis—Two Days Ago

My first case of the year came a mere seven hours after the New Year began; at least, that's when I got the call. Niki and I were next up on the rotation and, quite frankly, I kind of expected to spend my New Year's Day on the job. It's a curious thing how early-morning homicides are so often born of late-night partying—back-slapping and high fives mutating into punches and blood as the alcohol digs its way down to those darker passions. And with all the alcohol dispersed on New Year's Eve, the odds go way up.

I arrived up at the scene of a burned-out minivan parked on a turn-around at the end of First Street North, a lonely stub of blacktop that lay between a line of railroad tracks and the Mississippi River. Smoke still rose from the tires, and the exterior of the vehicle looked like the peeled skin of a bad sunburn. Three squads and a fire truck had arrived before me. The display on my dashboard warned me that the air temperature was –21 degrees Fahrenheit, which explained why no one was standing outside of a vehicle. I put on a stocking cap and got out of my car. When I did, a car door opened on one of the squads and Sergeant Richard Martinez stepped out. Rick and I started as patrol officers the same year. Unlike me, however, he loved the streets and bucked any attempt to move him off patrol.

"Rick," I said as I reached out a hand.

"Hey, Max," he said returning the handshake. "You're going to love this one."

"It's twenty fucking degrees below zero. What's not to love?"

"You gettin' soft behind that desk?" Martinez puffed out his rib cage and slapped his vest with both palms. "This is why we live in this fucking state, ain't it?"

"It's days like today that make me root for global warming."

"Haven't you heard? That's all a hoax. Besides, I hear we're in for a warm up—above zero in two days."

"I'll break out my sunblock."

As we approached the vehicle, the smell of the burned rubber was overwhelming in the light breeze, and behind that I could smell gasoline.

Rick walked me around to the side door of the minivan and pointed to a lump of charred flesh and muscle lying on the back seat. I leaned in and took a whiff, slow and deliberate, like a wine expert looking for the oak in a glass of chardonnay. The smell of burned flesh reminded me of a hog roast I attended in college. And again, the gasoline was heavy behind the punch of the burned car.

The body appeared to be a woman, lying in a fetal position, her arms and wrists twisted and curled into a pugilist's pose, a condition caused by the shrinking of the tendons as they bake. There may have been pieces of clothing still covering her, but I couldn't tell which patches were cloth and which were skin. She had the remnants of boots on her feet; the soles had melted away. I pulled on latex gloves and lifted up enough leather around the ankle to see light skin. Caucasian.

With the sun not yet cresting the horizon, the van was primarily lit with the headlights from the squad cars, where the rest of the patrol personnel waited in warmth for instructions. The air, when it gets that cold, is something sharp that you can almost hold in your hand. It can be inhaled, but breathe it in too deeply, and it will feel like a blade in your chest.

Another car pulled up to the edge of the circle and parked beside mine. I could see my partner, Niki Vang, putting ear muffs and gloves on before stepping out into the frigid morning air.

"Did someone call the ME?" I asked Martinez.

"Yeah, they've been notified. They're probably drawing straws to see who has to come out here."

Niki carried a hot coffee in her hand as she made her way to the minivan.

"Did you bring enough for everyone?" I asked.

"I thought Boy Scouts always came prepared," she said, handing me the paper cup. I took a sip, the hot dark roast warming my throat and chest as it made its way down.

Niki wore more layers than Martinez and me combined, and she had just left the comfort of a heated car, yet it was Niki who marched in place to keep warm. Martinez and I, on the other hand, had that stupid man code to live up to. It would have been unsightly to have us hopping around with other cops and firefighters watching. I could already feel my toes starting to grow numb inside of my shoes.

"One victim," I said to Niki. "Female, likely Caucasian."

"Do you think the firemen would mind if I lit one of these tires back on fire?" Niki said. "This cold is ridiculous." She edged past me, leaned into the van, and inhaled. "Definitely gas, or some accelerant."

"A killer wanting to hide their tracks," I said.

"Either that or they just wanted to get warm," Niki said.

Martinez said, "911 got a call from some guy who was screaming his bloody head off. Said he was on fire. Wanted someone to put him out. We found ol' Fireball over there." Martinez pointed to a scuff of ash in the snow where the caller had been rolling around to put out the flames. "And take a look at this." Martinez walked us around to the other side of the van and pointed to a small BIC cigarette lighter on the ground, directly beneath a partially opened window.

Niki looked at the open window and back at the lighter. "So Fireball reached his hand through the window, flicks the lighter and . . . kaboom!"

"I'm not a detective, like you guys," Martinez said with a grin, "but if I was in Vegas, that'd be my bet."

"That's about as stupid as they come," I said.

"I know, right?" Niki said. "If he'd used a Zippo, he could have just tossed the lighter through the window instead of sticking his arm inside."

Martinez said, "He was still smoldering when we got here."

"Where's he now?" I asked.

"Ambulance took him to HCMC. One of my guys is there watching over him to make sure he doesn't leave."

"Do we have a name?" Niki asked. I could tell she was trying to hide her shiver as she spoke.

"We do," Martinez said with an exaggeration that suggested that he was enjoying himself. "The EMTs dug his wallet out. The guy couldn't talk by then, and they wanted to see if they had medical records on him—you know, blood type and that sort of thing. Well, I happened to be standing outside the ambulance. You ever heard of Dennis Orton?" he asked.

"Dennis Orton?" Niki repeated. "As in deputy chief of staff to the mayor? That Dennis Orton?"

"I only heard the name." Martinez said. "His face looked like the overcooked ham my wife baked on Christmas, so I couldn't make an ID, but, again, if I was in Vegas—"

"Fireball has connections," I said. "Keep his name off the radio. I don't want the scanner crowd getting information before we're ready to release it."

"I'll do what I can," Martinez said. "But you know as well as I do, there's a lot of guys in blue who don't like Orton."

"I know," I said. "Just keep a lid on it for as long as you can. As far as I'm concerned, it's just another homicide, no different than any other, and I don't want the press or the brass interjecting themselves."

"What about the plates on the minivan?" Niki asked Martinez.

"Comes back to a Pippa Stafford. I'm guessing that's her in the back seat."

"I don't see any gas cans," she said.

"Hey, Max," Martinez had his gloved hands on his face to warm his cheeks. "If it's all the same to you . . ." He gave a slight nod toward his squad car.

"Yeah, that's fine," I said. "Maybe, if one of your officers doesn't mind . . ." I reached into my pocket and pulled out my wallet and withdrew a couple twenties. "A round of coffee on me. No sense sitting out here being any more miserable than we have to be."

"Thanks, Max. I'll get someone on that."

I turned toward Niki. "Why don't you go to the hospital and check on Orton. We'll need a warrant to dig through his clothing, and if he made a 911 call, he has a cell phone."

"Thanks, Max, but it's my turn to be the lead. That means I stay here with the ME and Crime Scene."

"It's too cold. You go to HCMC. I can stay here."

"Max? Do we have to have 'the talk' again?"

"Is that the talk where you say you love my idea?"

"*Love* is such a strong word—and wildly inaccurate."

"Hey, I'm trying to be chivalrous here."

"Chivalrous—chauvinist, potayto—potahto. I appreciate the offer, but I got this."

I chuckle as I watch her lips shiver. "Your call. You're the lead."

"Thank you, dear." Niki gave a slight curtsy. "And tell Rick to order me another dark roast, as long as you're buying."

Honestly, I was happy to go to HCMC, and not just because it was face-splitting cold outside, but because that's the only part of Jenni's life that held shadows. If she uncovered something dark enough to bring about her murder, I'd find it at the hospital where she worked. It's the only thing that made any sense.

The enormous, sprawling arms of HCMC serve as the first, and sometimes last, refuge of the injured and the broken in Minneapolis. It was where Jenni worked, and its parking ramp was where she died. I entered the ER and found the attending physician, who told me that Dennis Orton was in pretty bad shape when they brought him in. He had been wearing a winter coat made of a flammable material, the doctor thought maybe polypropylene, which caught fire and melted into his skin.

"Second- and third-degree burns on his chest and neck and face," the doctor said. "The third-degree burns kill the nerves. It's the second-degrees that hurt. We stabilized him and moved him to the Burn Unit."

"Where are his clothes and possessions?"

"We bagged 'em. They're in a locker on the Burn Unit."

"I'll be getting a search warrant to take possession of those, so don't let him leave."

"Leave?" the doctor looked surprised. "He's not going anywhere. Not for a while. We have him intubated right now. I don't expect him to be awake any time soon."

"Intubated? So he's not able to talk?"

"If a person breathes in too much fire, it can swell the airway shut. It's a precaution."

I pursed my lips and started to rearrange my day in my head. "How long until that changes?"

"We can do a fiber-optic exam later to see how it's going. If it looks good, we could pull the tube out this afternoon. No promises."

I thanked the doctor and headed out of the ER. The Burn Unit was nearby, but I had a stop to make before I went to visit Orton.

Just outside of the ER was a small collection of offices that I knew well—one of them used to be Jenni's. The hospital keeps a social worker on duty at the ER around the clock to deal with emergency-room patients who need additional services. The battered wife, the abused child, the homeless, these were the people whom Jenni helped. I hadn't been back to her office since she died, and I didn't know what to expect. I just knew that Jenni's office was where my digging had to start. What was she doing on the day she died? Who were her patients? What did she know that she wasn't supposed to know?

I peeked into the Social Services Office, relieved to see a familiar face. I breathed a sigh and knocked. "Karen?"

"Max?" Karen stood up behind her desk, her jaw slack with surprise.

"I see they got you working on a holiday."

She smiled. "Someone has to be here—and I'm not much of a college football fan. God, it's been a long time."

"Four and a half years," I said. And with those words, a stampede of painful memories came crashing into the room. That hadn't been my intention. "You look well," I said, hoping to sidestep our shared history.

She pointed to a chair, and we both sat down. "I'm doing my best," she said. "But, I got to tell you, this middle-age crap is a bitch. I tore my rotator cuff last year just raking the yard."

"I hope you learned a lesson about the dangers of raking." I smiled. "I steer clear of it myself."

She smiled back, not because of my wit but because I believe she was remembering Jenni. They had been close, not best friends, but allies and office confidants. On those days when Jenni came home with a pebble in her shoe because of hospital politics, it had always been Karen who stood shoulder to shoulder with her.

"What brings you to these quiet halls on a day like today?" Karen asked.

I stepped into my pitch. "I want to talk about Jenni's death."

Karen stopped smiling.

"I need to tell you something, and I need you to keep it between us. Okay?"

"Sure, Max." Karen, who had already been sitting rigid in her chair, lowered her hands to her lap.

"Jenni's case was closed as a hit-and-run. They never found the driver."

Karen nodded.

"But things have changed, Karen. I can't tell you how I know, but what if I told you that it wasn't an accident? What if I said that Jenni was killed on purpose?"

Karen gave a slight gasp. "Who would do . . .? Why would anyone . . . ?"

"That's what I'm trying to figure out. That's why I'm here. I believe that she was murdered because of something she was doing here at work. I think she knew something that she wasn't supposed to know."

"Are you sure?"

"Karen, I need to know what she was working on when she died."

"Oh, no, Max. I can't . . ." Karen brought a nervous hand up to her lips. "We have HIPAA rules."

"I wouldn't be here if this weren't important. I don't have any other way to re-create what Jenni was doing back then. I have no other option, Karen. There's got to be something you can do. Can't you look at her calendar from back then? There might be something there. Please. Anything you can give me, no matter how small. I just need a place to start."

"I'm not even sure . . ." Karen began clicking on her keyboard and shuttling her mouse around. "Our calendars are . . ." She trailed off distracted by something on the screen. "Hmm. It's still there."

"What's there?"

"Jenni's day planner. I would have thought . . . I guess they don't delete that kind of thing when you . . ." Karen's face turned pink. "Well, when someone . . . leaves."

"Can you tell me what she was doing the day she died?"

"July 29th right? That's the day she . . ."

"Yes, July 29th, but anything around that time might be helpful."

"There's not much here. Just names of patients she met with. I'd get in big trouble if I gave you any of those, of course."

"Please, Karen. There's got to be something you can tell me."

"She had a meeting with some insurance reps that day, and an office powwow. Nothing unusual. Just looks like a normal—" Karen squinted into the computer screen. "Well, I'm not sure . . . this may be . . ." She opened a drawer and pulled out a book, running a finger down a list of names, then she looked back at the screen as if confirming a match. She wrote a name and phone number on a piece of paper, sliding it across the desk to me. "She's not a patient, so I'm okay to share this. Her name was on Jenni's day planner on the day she died. I don't know if it means anything."

I read the name. "Farrah McKinney?"

"She's an interpreter—Russian, and I think a couple other languages too. I've met her a few times. She's really smart."

"I appreciate this, Karen," I said. "You were always one of Jenni's favorite people. I wish I'd gotten to know you better when she was alive."

"Me too, Max." Karen's apprehension gave way to a warm smile. "Jenni was one of my favorite people as well. And, Max," Karen folded her hands together as though she were going to pray. "I hope you find what you're looking for and that it brings you peace."

I was taken aback by both her words and her knowing tone. I could do little more than nod my thanks and leave. I was pretty sure that when I found what I was looking for, peace would be the last thing on my mind. I was hunting wolves. Did she understand that? Did she see that in my face? No, I was reading too much into it.

I left the Social Services Office and made my way to the Burn Unit, showing my badge to get buzzed through the locked doors. Just inside the unit, I found a young, uniformed officer leaning against the counter at the nurse's station, chatting up a pretty young woman in scrubs. I'd seen the patrolman around before, but I couldn't remember if I'd ever known his name. He straightened up when he saw me coming.

"He's sleeping," the officer said as I got within earshot. He pointed at a door just a few feet ahead of me. I walked into that room and saw a man, bandages covering most of his torso and face, an intubation tube taped across his lips. He had an IV in his left forearm, the only part of his body without gauze wrapped around it, and a pulse oximeter on his index finger. I could tell that he was Caucasian, and, according to the light hair on his arm, probably a blond. Beyond that, he could have been just about anybody. I was about to leave when I saw a small tattoo on the back of his wrist, a circle with the points of a compass around it.

When I left the room, the young officer was standing in the hall, almost at attention. The name bar on his uniform read Fuller. I nodded for him to follow me, and we walked to the end of the corridor. "Did he say anything when they brought him in?"

"No, sir. He—"

"Max."

"What?"

"Max. That's my name. Not a big fan of 'sir.' Wasn't a fan of it back when I was in uniform, so I don't see why I should go by anything other than Max now."

"Okay . . . Max." Fuller seemed to relax. "He was in pretty bad shape. All he did was howl and moan."

"I'm going to get a search warrant for his clothing and his phone. I'll need you to sit tight until I get back with that. Once we have his stuff, you can head out. I don't expect him to try and make a break for it, but if he does, you place him under arrest."

"Arrest? What for?"

"Didn't Martinez tell you what was in the van?"

"No. He just said to get down here and make sure the guy doesn't leave. He said to stay here until I hear otherwise."

"If he tries to leave, tell him to go back to bed or you'll place him under arrest for setting a fire without a permit."

CHAPTER 6

The corridors of City Hall seemed eerily quiet as I walked toward the Homicide Unit, almost as if the structure itself were holding its breath, a spectator waiting for a fight to start. The sound of grit crunching under my shoes filled the hallway and pinged off the granite walls around me. I unlocked the door and stepped inside, taking a moment to absorb the emptiness of the room, the closeness of the silence pressing against my skin. I was glad to be alone that day. I had a warrant to write up, yes, but I had other business to tend to, business best performed in secret.

No more half measures.

First, I contacted Dispatch to see where I could find the on-call judge and was told that a Judge Krehbiel had called in to let them know that she was in her chambers, working on an order that she needed to get out the next day. If any warrants needed to be signed, she would be in the Government Center, which meant I could walk across the street to get a signature instead of having to drive to her home.

I pulled Farrah McKinney's phone number from my pocket. I'd never heard of her, or, if Jenni ever mentioned her name, it had gone right past me. I dialed the number.

"Hello?"

"Ms. McKinney?"

"Yes."

"My name is Max Rupert. I am a homicide detective in Minneapolis. Do you have a moment?"

A slight hesitation, then, "Um . . . sure. What's this about?"

"I'm sorry to disturb you on a holiday like this, but I'm looking into a cold case. Your name came up and I was hoping I might be able to meet with you to ask a few questions."

"On New Year's Day?"

"If I could have just a minute of your time. The victim was a social worker attached to the emergency room at HCMC. She was killed in a hit-and-run about four and a half years ago. The case has been reopened and—"

"Yeah, I remember. Her name was Jenni, right?"

A spark of excitement flickered inside me. "Yes, that's right. Your name was in her day planner. I was wondering—"

"That was terrible, what happened to her."

"Yes, it was. Can I ask how you knew her?"

"I didn't know her. I mean, I didn't know her personally. I worked with her on a case. I'm an interpreter. Russian and Baltic languages."

"Were you working on a case with her on the day she died?"

"Yes. That's the first time I met her—that day."

"Ms. McKinney, could we meet? I'd like to ask you a few more questions. Just some routine, follow-up stuff."

"That was a long time ago."

"I promise, I won't take up to much of your time."

"I guess. Sure, when?"

"Today, if that's possible. If not—"

"Today? Um . . . sure. We can meet today. What did you say your name was again?"

"Detective Max Rupert."

"Rupert? Wasn't that . . ."

"Yes, that was Jenni's last name. She was my wife."

"I'm sorry. She seemed really nice. If I can help in any way—"

"I appreciate that. Would you like me to come to your house?"

"No, I need to make a trip downtown anyway. You know where the Hen House Eatery is?"

"I know it well. Noon?"

"That works. I'll be wearing a bright yellow coat."

"I'll be the guy with a badge," I said.

Silence.

"And a smile," I added.

I hung up and began slapping the search warrant together, typing what facts I knew into the probable-cause statement. As search warrants go, this one was easy. The items to be searched? The clothing, cell phone, and other possessions of the man found next to a burning van which housed a dead body.

I finished the warrant application, stood, and looked around the room, even though I knew that I was alone. Then I sat back down and logged into the Computer Assisted Police Resource System, what we call Cappers, and typed the name Raymond Kroll. Cappers lit up with dozens of entries for Mr. Kroll. I scrolled down until I found the first-degree assault case matching the file Boady brought to me.

Kroll hit a man with a patio brick in a bar fight. I held my breath as I opened the link to see if Kroll had given any statement to the arresting officer—a squad video or body-cam capture—anything that might have his voice. I only needed a few words from him and I would know if he was one of the men plotting my wife's death. My heart sank when I saw no recordings in the file. I didn't expect to find anything. Had there been a recording, it should have been in the attorney's file that I had at home. But it was worth a shot.

Next, I logged into the Minnesota Court Information System to see what had happened to the case. The file was short. The case hadn't made it as far as the omnibus hearing before Kroll turned up dead in St. Paul. I had read all about his untimely demise when I was doing my Internet research last night. Kroll's body was found on the bank of the Mississippi River with a bullet in his brain. They never found the shooter. I sent the court record to the printer so I could add it to my collection.

I went back to Cappers and scrolled through other cases involving Mr. Kroll, hoping to find one with audio. Case after case, Raymond Kroll faced his accusers with ruddy silence, a well-trained dog. I was down to the petty misdemeanor speeding cases when the rattling of the outer door interrupted my reading. I walked to the printer and stacked my reports together, folding them in half. A moment later, Niki stepped through the second door and into the office, her nose and ears red from the cold. I leaned awkwardly against the copier, aware that my posture looked far from natural.

"What's with the bat-cave bit," she said as she turned on the lights. With the low morning sun rolling through the windows, I hadn't noticed that I left the lights off. I slipped the reports into my pocket as Niki made her way over to the cubicle that we shared.

"I'm just getting ready to take a search warrant over to the Government Center," I said. "Fireball's still unconscious, so I couldn't get a statement."

"Who's Raymond Kroll?" Niki had an eye on my computer screen as she laid her coat over the back of her chair.

"Ray Kroll? He's . . . um . . . he's a guy."

Niki looked at me with the narrowed eyes of a parent trying to discern a child's shenanigans. "You printing something?" she asked.

"The search warrant."

"This search warrant?" she said, holding up the already completed application I had laid on my desk.

I walked to my computer, blocking her view as I closed the screen with Ray Kroll's reports on it. I typed the name Dennis Orton into an Internet search.

"Are you okay, Max? You seem a bit—"

"I'm fine. Just . . . there was a lot of noise in the neighborhood last night. Fireworks and stuff. I didn't get much sleep. What did you find out at the scene?"

"Well, the ME says that the woman in the back seat of the van is dead."

"Impressive. I was on the fence about that one."

"Preliminary exam suggests strangulation. Her hyoid bone and larynx both appeared disfigured. Autopsy will be back after lunch."

"Was she dead before the fire?"

"Probably. The ME saw no signs of burning in the throat." Niki pulled up a DL photo of Pippa Stafford. She was pretty, blond, blue eyes, thirty-one, with a big smile and dimples. Niki compared the DL photo to a shot she took at the scene. "Could be her," she said. "Is Fireball who we think he is?"

I found a picture of Dennis Orton with a young, pretty blond on his arm—Pippa Stafford. They were at some political function, and Orton had his sleeve rolled up enough to expose the compass tattoo. I turned the screen toward Niki. "Here's our boy." I pointed at his wrist. "I saw that tattoo on Fireball."

"And that's probably our victim standing by her man?"

"Happier times, I guess. Did Crime Scene find anything of value?"

"Not yet. They hauled the van to the impound warehouse. It was too damned cold to do much at the scene. Did you run a history on Orton?"

"I was just about to."

"What about Ms. Stafford?"

"Been busy."

She glanced at my thin warrant application, a document that could have been typed in ten minutes. "Looking up Ray Kroll?"

I stood up. "I have to get this search warrant signed before the judge leaves." The look on Niki's face told me that she saw through my bullshit. She always could.

"Max, what's going on? Why are you acting so—"

"I gotta run."

I didn't wait for a response. Rushing out of the office, I was happy to get a door between us. She saw past my subterfuge—my ink, as she would say. It was one of her favorite expressions. It referred to the cuttlefish and how it could spray a cloud of ink into the water to distract and confuse a predator.

I left Homicide, disappearing behind my cloud of ink, but she knew I was up to something. It was like working with a psychic. I would need to come up with a plan to keep her out of my way, at least where it concerned Jenni's case.

CHAPTER 7

Up North

I get about halfway across the frozen lake, retracing my steps back to the cabin where the chase began, when I pause to catch my breath. My lungs feel heavy, thick. I can hear my breath wheeze as I exhale. I am less than a quarter mile away from the man. I can no longer see or hear him, but I assume he's still yelling his head off, hoping that his cry finds some wandering hiker. I'd be yelling if I were in his place.

I start walking again, letting my mind float through the rough outline of my plan. It's not really a plan, I suppose, more of an idea with a firm beginning, a fuzzy middle, and no clear ending. My drifting thoughts stay away from what that ending might be. I don't want to go there. Instead, I swat at pesky criticisms and chew on uncooked details. I recall a quote by Sun Tzu about the folly of entering a war without a plan for how to end it, something like: tactics without strategy is the noise before defeat. I shoo those thoughts away, but I feel like a man who has just jumped into a river, the current pulling me toward a bend. Around that bend there could be a tranquil pool or a plunging waterfall. I don't want to know. I don't care. It's out of my control—at least that's what I tell myself.

Trudging through knee-deep snow seems to alter the planet's gravitational pull. It's like walking with a cinder block strapped to each thigh. I remember a day when I was a kid and I was walking in deep snow like this. My little brother, Alexander, was following behind me. He was small enough that the only way he could move at all was to step in my tracks. I began taking bigger and bigger steps until his little legs couldn't reach and he fell in the snow, crying. I thought it was funny until I saw Nancy watching me from the house, a look of disapproval on her face. Then I felt bad.

You're going to kill him . . .

I stop.

It's Nancy's voice again—faint, struggling to find a foothold among the rest of my muddled thoughts. I can't quite tell if she's asking me a question or making a statement. Either way, I know she will not approve of what I'm doing. I resume my march.

My mother died when Alexander was born. I don't remember her; I was too young. But I remember her pictures watching me in almost every room of the house. Even after my dad started dating again, the pictures remained on the walls.

I was five the day I first laid eyes on Nancy Rosin. My grandma—Dad's mother—had been babysitting Alexander and me the night before, which meant that we played in our rooms while she watched television. The next morning, Alexander woke me up because he wanted to go downstairs. He was only three years old, and the steps in that old house were terribly steep. He needed someone to go down ahead of him to catch him if he fell, which he never did.

As I descended the stairs, I could smell something warm and delicious coming from below. That was, in itself, unusual because my dad switched between instant oatmeal and dry cereal for our breakfasts. This was definitely neither of those.

At the bottom of the stairs, I stopped and waited to catch Alexander, who came down on his butt, plopping from one step to the next. As I waited, I peeked around the corner and saw a woman in the kitchen with her back to me, humming quietly as she poured pancake batter onto a griddle. I had never seen this woman before. I looked around for my dad or Grandma or someone to explain why this stranger was in my kitchen.

Alexander was getting closer to the bottom of the stairs, and he had added sound effects to his plopping, saying "wump, wump, wump" as he hit each step.

I put my finger to my lips to shush him, and instead of shushing, he said, "What?"

I exaggerated my movement, hitting my finger to my lips in the hopes that his child's mind could understand my obvious signal. He again said "What?" This time he said it loud enough to be heard in the kitchen. I peeked back around the corner, and the woman was looking over her shoulder at me. She smiled and went back to humming and making pancakes.

When Alexander saw her, he froze behind me, holding onto the shirttail of my pajamas. We proceeded forward in a slow shuffle and were almost to the mouth of the kitchen when the woman turned around to look at us. She had a kind smile and soft eyes that made me want to like her.

"You must be Max," she said pointing at me. Then she bent down to make herself smaller for Alexander's benefit and said, "And you must be the famous Alexander. I've heard so much about you two."

Right then, our dad came out of his bedroom and walked into the kitchen. He was smiling, which set me off balance almost as much as finding a stranger in our kitchen. He walked up to the woman and kissed her on the cheek and said, "I see you've met Nancy."

He sat down at the head of the table to await his breakfast, without another word of explanation. It took me years to gain enough understanding about adult relationships to piece together that they had been dating for a while and keeping it a secret from us boys. Then Dad figured the time had come for Nancy to move in and brought her home for a trial run.

Those memories give me warmth as I trek across the frozen lake, the smell of her cookies and roasted chicken, the way she used to sway and hum when she played her old blues albums, the gentle glances she would give my dad when she thought he was treating Alexander or me too harshly. The last time I saw her was the day after Alexander graduated from high school—the day she left.

As I enter the woods, those memories give way to the work ahead. The first hill, just off the lake is the steepest. During the chase, we both slid down its slope more than we ran. The climb back up is a slippery affair. I try to walk in the foot holes we made earlier, but they're too far apart. I pull myself up, grabbing onto tree branches and scrub. Beyond that hill is a valley thick with woods. I can see the portage path cutting through the forest like a scar in a hairline. I follow our tracks back across the valley and to the top of the second hill.

It's been less than an hour since I left the man lying on what I am now sure is Canadian soil, but it seems like I've been walking for an entire morning.

I crest the second hill, stumbling through the snow, and see the snowmobile. The man had turned a corner too fast and one of the skis caught a sprig of aspen, tossing him off the sled. I can see where he landed in the snow and rolled, and I can see his footprints coming back, tromping around the ski that had caught the tree. I bend down to brush away the snow. The ski is not broken, but it's jammed tightly between two shoots of the tree. He must have briefly tried to dislodge it before taking off on his run north.

I look around the sled and don't see any obvious damage. I pop the hood. The engine is untouched. It's a new machine in pristine condition, other than being stuck.

I climb up the crux of the aspen and lower myself between the two shoots. With one foot on the thicker of the two branches and my back pressed against the other, I push. The tree bends. I place my second foot against the tree and push with all I have until I hear a crack. The smaller shoot gives way, freeing the ski.

A thin blanket of snow has covered the snowmobile. I brush it away from the dashboard, find the choke and the starter, and give it a go. After a few wheezes, it starts. I let it warm up as I turn it around on the narrow trail, lifting the ass end a few inches at a time until it faces in the direction of the cabin.

As I make my way back down the path, now with the power of one hundred and fifty horses under my butt, my thoughts again turn to Nancy and the day she could have left us but didn't.

I was in sixth grade and by that time knew enough about relationships to know that my dad's and Nancy's was falling apart. I would hear them having heated conversations, their angry words smudged by the thin walls that separated their bedroom from the living room. I knew they were fighting; I think Alexander knew, too. And when they emerged, they barely spoke, and what few words they exchanged were as fragile as eggshells. Yet Nancy never stopped talking to us boys, her words light and cheery, her smile genuine. It was her way of plastering over the fissure that was splitting our little family apart, probably hoping that my brother and I might not notice what was happening.

But we noticed.

I never let it show, especially to Alexander, but the thought of her leaving filled me with a dread more powerful than any emotion I had ever known. Alexander couldn't remember a time before Nancy. He was so young when she appeared that it seemed to him as though she had always been there. But I remembered. I remembered feeling alone in our house even though my father sat in the next room, drinking his after-work beers. I remembered the hole in my life, a sense of missing something. Although as a five-year-old I had no way of understanding that feeling, I remembered what it was like before Nancy came to us, and the thought of losing her scared me.

Then, one day, when I was in sixth grade, we came home from school and everything had changed.

Our house had three bedrooms upstairs, so Alexander and I each had our own room. The third we used for storage. That day, Alexander and I came home from school to discover that Nancy had cleaned out the storage room and had moved upstairs with us. She never again shared a bed with my dad.

At the time, she told us that she had moved upstairs because my dad snored too much. We accepted that explanation without question. But, over the years, as I watched my dad sink deeper into his own solitude, I came to understand something much more profound. Nancy had left my father. To use the vernacular of my teen years, she broke up with him. They had dated for six years, and then she ended their relationship. But she didn't end her relationship with me or with my brother. Nancy moved upstairs to be with us, to raise us. She had no obligation to do that. She and my dad had never married. She hadn't adopted us. She chose to stay because she knew that we needed her. That was all there was to it.

When I pull up to the cabin where the chase began, I figure it's close to midmorning, the dim glow of the sun barely breaking though the low cloud cover. In the west, I can see a sliver of blue where the edge of the clouds gives way to an open sky. I can expect a drop in temperature once the sky clears. Hopefully by then I'll be finished with what I have to do.

I stop the snowmobile near a shed about fifty feet from the cabin. I remember peeking in there earlier and seeing implements and tools, the standard fair that you might find at a cabin in the middle of a forest. None of those implements meant a thing to me at the time. I had only cared that the shed was empty of any human threat. But as I sat in the snow, trying to decide what to do with the man at my mercy, I had remembered the shed and the tools and the ice auger that was hung on a nail.

Just inside the door, I find a length of nylon rope, about forty feet long, and the tarpaulin cover for the snowmobile. I roll the tarp into a small bundle and wrap the rope around it, tossing the package onto the seat of the snowmobile. Then I return to the shed, where I locate the centerpiece of my plan, an old-fashioned ice auger, a steel rod with a hand crank on one end and a small shovel—six inches wide—on the other. I look at the auger and imagine boring down through at least three feet of ice, punching through to the lake. I examine the blade and wonder, how many holes will I have to drill in the ice to create a mouth big enough to swallow a man?

CHAPTER 8

Minneapolis—Two Days Ago

I arrived back at Hennepin County Medical Center just before 11:00 a.m. to find Officer Fuller still diligently working on the pretty woman in scrubs at the nurse's station. He again stood at attention as I approached.

"Did our guy escape yet?" I asked.

"Um . . . no, Detective. He's still unconscious, I think."

I handed a copy of the signed search warrant to the nurse. "This is a court order saying that I can take possession of the personal items of the man they brought in this morning. Would you be so kind as to go and get those for me?" I smiled my politest smile.

"I'd be happy to," she said.

"And could you give that copy of the warrant to him when he wakes up?"

She glanced at the warrant, nodded and left.

"Is Orton still intubated?" I asked Fuller.

"Yes, sir . . . I mean, Max."

The nurse returned with a large paper bag, folded shut at the top, and handed it to me. I asked her for a pair of latex gloves, which I snapped on before opening the bag and pouring the contents onto the countertop. Fireball's pants had large patches where they had burned through. His shirt and coat were mere remnants of their former state. Only his socks, shoes, and tighty-whities came through the ordeal in one piece. I didn't need to get my nose close to smell the scent of gasoline coming off the clothes.

Folded into his pants, I found the cell phone that he used to call 911. I laid the phone to the side and emptied the pockets of the pants: a set of keys to a BMW, not the minivan, and a wallet. I opened the wallet: a debit card, a driver's license, fifty-eight bucks, unused tickets to a Toby Keith concert, and a convenience-store receipt time-stamped earlier that morning.

"He can't be that stupid," I said half to myself.

"What?" Fuller asked.

I showed him the receipt. "He kept a receipt showing that he bought gas at the Holiday station on Sixth Avenue. They have cameras all over that place. Unless I miss my guess, we'll have video of Mr. Orton driving the van that he set on fire." I shook my head.

A sharp smile crossed the nurse's face and she said, "Your man doesn't sound like much of a mastermind."

That made me grin because Judge Krehbiel had the same reaction when I went to get the search warrant signed. The judge, working on her day off, didn't seem particularly cheerful when I first entered her chambers. But I watched her eyes brighten as she read down the probable-cause statement. Soon she stopped reading and looked at me.

"Let me get this straight," she said. "Your guy kills a woman, puts her in the back seat of a minivan, drives the van out to a secluded area to destroy the evidence . . ." She paused to connect the remainder of the dots. "Then, he sets fire to the van, catching himself on fire in the process . . . and calls the police."

"That's our working theory," I said.

"A real criminal mastermind you have here," she said as she signed the warrant.

I called Niki as I put Orton's clothing back into the paper bag.

"Did you know that Toby Keith was playing at Mystic Lake Casino last night?" I ask.

"I didn't know you were a fan," Niki said.

"Huge fan. Fireball had two tickets and didn't go."

"Got sidetracked I guess."

"I also found a receipt in his wallet. Looks like he bought some gas this morning—at 6:28. It's from the Holiday on Sixth Avenue North."

"Not far from the funeral pyre," she said.

"Close in both time and place. Can you call Holiday and have them preserve the security footage for me?"

"Seems like Orton did just about everything he could to get caught."

"All our cases should be this easy."

"While you were over getting the warrant, I did some cyber stalking. Orton and Pippa Stafford were an item, at least according to Orton's Facebook."

"Didn't have time to change his status after he killed her?"

"Apparently it slipped his mind. She's a loan officer at US Bank. No criminal record. Not even a ticket. As white-bread as they come."

"Lover's spat?"

"It's as good a theory as anything else right now. Is Fireball able to talk yet?"

"Still sedated. I have his phone. I'll have forensics dig through it, maybe get some text messages to give us a motive. Who knows."

"I'll order up the surveillance footage from Holiday. Want to meet for lunch and compare notes?"

"I . . . uh . . . I have an errand to run. I'll have to catch up with you later."

"Is that errand named Farrah?"

"What?"

"She called back on your office phone. Wanted to tell you that she was running a few minutes late. So, you got something you want to tell me?"

"Fine . . . I admit it . . . I'm really not a Toby Keith fan."

"I'm not kidding, Max. What's going on?"

"Nothing, I just have some things I need to take care of."

"Things that have nothing to do with Fireball?"

"Believe it or not, I have interests outside of my job."

"And as I recall, the last time you got caught up in those interests . . ." Niki paused as if weighing her words carefully. "Things didn't turn out so great. You almost lost your job, and I almost lost a partner. I just want to make sure that doesn't happen."

"I don't need a mother." I responded a little angrier than I had intended. "I have everything under control."

"You may not need a mother, but you do need a friend."

I could think of nothing to say that would not hurt Niki, so the phone connection filled with silence. Then I said, "I got to go. The doctor's here. I'll catch you after lunch." I hung up before she could respond. I needed time to come up with a lie, something plausible enough that Niki would pretend to believe it. I needed to keep her clear of this avalanche.

I put my phone in my pocket and turned to Fuller. "You don't have to stay here any longer," I said.

"What if he wakes up and tries to leave?"

"If he leaves, he'll probably die of an infection. I don't think even *he's* that stupid."

I looked at my watch and saw that noon was approaching, and I wanted to be at the Hen House early. I wanted time to think about things before Ms. McKinney arrived. McKinney was an interpreter. How did that fit into my wife's death? Maybe it didn't. But, then again, this was all about looking at things with fresh eyes. Jenni didn't die because of someone I had arrested. She died because of something she knew. Somewhere out in the farthest outskirts of my mind, the notion of an interpreter being involved made sense, but I still felt as though I was looking though a lens smeared with Vaseline.

CHAPTER 9

The Hen House was a street-level restaurant that offered more ways to eat an egg than there were colors in a big box of crayons, the kind of place that preferred the clatter of plates and cups over the soothing tones of violin music. I took a seat at the lunch counter where I could keep an eye on the door, and ordered a coffee. The waitress brought it with a smile that seemed to be working hard to hide a hangover. The restaurant was starting to fill up, so I asked the hostess to hold a table open for when my companion arrived.

My phone buzzed in my pocket, and I pulled it out to see a text from Niki. *We need to talk*, was all it read.

I was about to call back when a woman with a bright-yellow ski parka walked into the Hen House, stopping at the door to scan the room. I put my phone away and walked toward her. When she saw me, she smiled broadly and waved. I hadn't shown her my badge or gun, but she seemed to recognize me. She slipped the hood of her parka down, revealing light-brown hair, curly and highlighted; it had a bounce to it as she walked. Despite the cold, she wore ripped jeans tucked into brown leather boots with buckles around the ankles.

"Farrah?" I held out my hand to her and she shook it. "I'm Max Rupert."

"I know," she said. And there it was—that look of condolence that flashes across the faces of people when they remember that I am a widower. The hostess brought us to a table near the window where we could watch the brittle winter swirl by. Nothing moved outside except the occasional newspaper page or plastic bag skidding down the street. Inner-city tumbleweeds.

"It's supposed to be warming up," she said.

"Really? I hadn't heard," I said.

"Yeah, a heat wave. May even get up as high as ten above."

"Time to break out the T-shirts," I said. My lame attempt at humor received an obligatory smile from Farrah. I picked up my menu to have something to do with my hands. I had so many things I wanted to say, to ask, but I still hadn't organized my thoughts. The awkwardness at our table hung thick in the air. Finally, I asked the question that seemed to be blocking all others.

"Have we met?" I said. "When you walked in, you acted like you knew me already."

"No, we haven't met, but I've seen you before." She paused as if her next statement were giving up a secret, then said, "I was at Jenni's funeral."

"You were? I don't recall."

"You had . . . other things on your mind."

"Were you and Jenni friends?"

"No, I'd only met her once—the day she died."

The waitress came to take our orders, jotting down everything on a green pad of paper: "How do you like your eggs? Pancakes or toast? Sausage or bacon? Hash browns or breakfast potatoes? Juice? Milk?" I wanted to scream at her to leave, but I smiled instead and answered her questions politely. When the waitress was finally satisfied that every possible detail had been settled, she left.

"You were saying that you saw Jenni the day she died?"

"I got a call to go to the emergency room at HCMC that morning. I'm fluent in five languages, but I specialize in Russian and Baltic languages. Your wife had a patient who couldn't speak English."

"Do you remember the patient? A name? Anything?"

"I'm not sure it's appropriate to talk about a patient."

"It might be very important. I need to find out what happened to Jenni."

"I thought she was killed in a car accident—a hit-and-run in the parking garage."

I hesitated before saying any more. The fewer people who knew the inner workings of my clock, the better. At the same time, I needed to hear what she had to say about Jenni's last day on Earth. I decided that I had little choice but to trust her with a couple of my bread crumbs. "Jenni's death wasn't random. It wasn't an accident."

Farrah's eyes narrowed as if searching for something in the past.

"I need to know what was going on in Jenni's life that day. You're the only one who can help me."

Farrah looked out through the frozen window, biting her lower lip as she considered my request. Then she turned back to me and leaned into the table.

"There was this girl. She was young, maybe sixteen or seventeen. I think she was a . . . I think she was a prostitute. She had all this makeup on. It didn't look right, because she seemed so young."

"Do you remember her name?"

"I think it was Zoya. I'll have her name in my old files, but I believe it was Zoya."

"Why was she at the hospital?"

"That's why I remember this case so well. Your wife told me that a patrol officer found her stumbling down the street, all cut up. She had been thrown through a window at a motel—a second-story window. They found the room, but no one was there. Whoever did that to her also beat her up. Her face was swollen. She had cuts and bruises all over her body. The doctors said that two of her fingers were broken, she was bleeding from her ears, and . . . well . . . your wife thought maybe she'd been raped."

"Was there an investigator there with you?"

"Yes, but . . ."

"But?"

"Not at first. When I first got there that morning, it was just me and your wife. We talked to Zoya, and she told us that she was scared. She didn't want to tell us what happened. Your wife asked her if she had been raped. Zoya started crying. And then the investigator walked in and Zoya clammed up."

"Which investigator?"

"I don't remember his name. All I remember was that when he

walked in, Zoya's eyes grew big and she stopped talking. She wouldn't say another word."

"Did the cop say anything to Zoya to make her do that?"

"No. He was polite. Very professional. Your wife said that sometimes victims of rape react that way to men, so she took him out of the room and suggested that he listen from the hallway. But it didn't work. Just the sight of a man put Zoya into like . . . shock. She just stared at the wall and cried."

"She was Russian?"

"Belarusian. It's a country between Russia and Poland."

"What else did she say?"

"Nothing really. I only spoke to her for a few minutes before she shut down. After about half an hour of trying to get her to talk again, your wife told that cop and me to leave. We'd try it again after Zoya settled down."

"And did you try it again?"

"Well—"

The waitress stepped up to the table with a tray full of plates. That kind of fast turnaround was one of the things I appreciated most about breakfast restaurants, but the interruption, as polite as it was, annoyed me. She skillfully placed the meals in front of us, getting everything correct. I had been hungry when I ordered my food, but now my stomach felt twisted and queasy. Farrah waited for the waitress to leave before she continued.

"That's the disturbing part of all this. Later that day, probably around lunchtime, Jenni called me back. I didn't answer—I can't remember why—but she left a message. She said that Zoya was talking again. Your wife was recording it all in a notebook—writing it all down phonetically, but she had no idea what the girl was saying. She wanted me to come back in and try to get her statement. When I got the message, I called Jenni back and she asked me if I could be there at 3:30. I said sure."

"You had a meeting for 3:30 on the day Jenni died."

"Yes."

Farrah had been picking at her food as she spoke, but now she put her fork down and turned her full attention to me, her eyes soft with sympathy. "When I got to the hospital, the parking garage on Eighth Street was shut down. I didn't know what was going on. I went to your wife's office and was there for about ten minutes before someone told me that she got hit by a car in the ramp. I'm so sorry for your loss."

"I appreciate that. I also appreciate that you came to her funeral even though it sounds like you didn't know her all that well. That was nice of you."

"I could tell that she wanted to help that girl. Your wife really seemed dedicated to her clients. And I admired her for that . . . but . . ."

Farrah poked at a piece of bacon and again bit at her lower lip, her eyes averting away from mine.

"But what?"

"But . . . that's not why I went to the funeral—I mean, that's part of it, but there's more."

I could tell that she was struggling to say something, so I let the conversation go silent and waited for her to fill the void.

"You're going to think I'm strange." She folded her hands together on her lap, her eyes slowly rising to meet mine. "I went to the funeral to see you."

"To see me?"

"To give you something." Farrah seemed to be pulling hard on an old memory that made her sad. "When I got home, I felt so depressed and shocked. I'd never had someone die like that—just before we were supposed to meet. It unnerved me, I guess. I went to clear my answering machine of voice mail, and I heard her voice. I put my finger on the delete button, but stopped. It occurred to me that I had what was probably the last recording of your wife's voice. I couldn't bring myself to erase it. So, I downloaded it onto a thumb drive. I was going to give it to you at the funeral. I thought you might like to have it."

I could feel a lump growing in my throat. I swallowed it back and took a sip of lukewarm coffee to wash it down. "But you didn't give it to me."

"No. You were so broken up. I didn't have the nerve." She went back to moving her eggs around with a fork.

"I was in pretty bad shape," I said.

"I should have given it to you."

"It was a nice thought at least."

She looked up from her plate. "I think I may still have it. I'm not sure, but I could check if you'd like."

I turned my gaze to the frozen street, almost too afraid to hope. I'd watched every home movie Jenni and I had ever made—hundreds of times. I memorized her words and replayed them in my head. The sound of her voice gave her memory a presence in my world. Now, something as simple as an old voice-mail message, words that were never meant to be preserved, filled me with a surge of emotions. "I'd like that very much," I said.

"I'll look when I get home. I have your number."

"Let me give you my cell," I said, writing my number on a napkin and handing it to her. "So, I take it you didn't go speak with Zoya again?"

"No. In fact, after I'd heard about what happened to your wife, well . . . it was kind of confusing. The whole ER was flipping out. People were crying and hugging each other. I thought I might be of some help, maybe explain to Zoya what had happened, so I went to her room. When I got there, she was gone. No one knew where she went. I think she just walked out in the middle of the confusion."

"Anything else you can think of that might identify her—in case she was using a false name?"

"Well, like I said, she looked young, dark hair, five foot five, maybe. Pretty under the bruising and makeup, I think. And, oh yeah, she had a tattoo, right about here." Farrah touched a spot of skin behind her left ear with two fingers. "Do you know what a ruble is?"

"Russian money."

"She had the symbol for the ruble tattooed behind her ear." Farrah reached into her purse and pulled out a pen. On a napkin she drew the ruble symbol, a capital *P* with a crossbar just below the loop of the *P*. She slid the napkin with the ₽ on it across the table to me.

An old memory creaked open somewhere in the wayback of my brain. I stared at the symbol on the napkin, my mind digging deep, searching. I'd seen that tattoo before. But where? When? Then it came to me. Jane Doe. I had seen the ruble symbol tattooed on the neck of a young woman found dead four years ago. I remember because hers was the first case I worked after my bereavement leave—a leave Commander Walker forced me to take. The case was never solved. What were the odds that two women would bear that same tattoo on the same part of their body?

The waitress came with our check, and I handed her a debit card.

"Does that help?" Farrah asked.

"I'm not sure. Maybe. Whether it helps or not, I want to thank you for meeting with me. It means a lot to know that Jenni was trying to help someone the day she died."

"I'd take it a step further," Farrah said. "Your wife believed that Zoya was being trafficked, sexually. Jenni was hoping to get her out of that life. As I saw it, your wife was trying to save that girl's life."

My phone buzzed in my pocket again. I pulled it out to see another text from Niki. *I really need to talk to you, Max.*

"It's my partner," I said. "I need to get back to the office." I texted back. *On my way.*

My phone then buzzed again. *Don't come in. I'll meet you out front. Text when you're here.*

CHAPTER 10

Up North

I ride the snowmobile back to what has to be the border of the Boundary Waters Canoe Area—a buffer zone between Canada and Minnesota where motorized vehicles are not allowed. From here I walk. I only take a couple steps before a thought occurs to me. Later, on my trip back, I may be too exhausted to turn the snowmobile around. I go back to the sled and pick up the ass end, heaving it in a semicircle until the machine faces back toward the cabin. Then I head north.

About the time I start my third trek across the lake, something that the man said comes back to me. "Who are you?" he'd asked. At the time, it pissed me off. The gall of that man—to look me in the eye and pretend he doesn't know exactly who I am. I didn't answer him, and now I begin to wonder that maybe he took my silence as some kind agreement that he had no reason to know me.

Is that the game he wants to play? Does he really think that if he denies everything, he'll put me to some burden of proof? If that's the case, he's made a grievous miscalculation. The man has a noose around his neck and he thinks we're playing tug-o-war. He doesn't realize that denial is more dangerous to him right now than any wolf or subzero night could ever be. His denials feed me. They put steel in my bones and warmth in my muscles. *Go ahead. Pretend you're innocent. Let's see where that gets you.*

I stop walking when I get to a spot that seems to be the middle of the lake. I separate the rope from the tarp and shove the tarp into the snow so that a gust of wind can't blow it away. I also drop the auger, which disappears beneath snow. Then I tuck the rope under my arm and start walking again.

As I near the northern shore, I stop to listen. If he were still yelling for help, I'd be able to hear that by now. He must have given up. Maybe that thump on the head has him floating in and out of consciousness—or maybe he's dead. I step over the rocks and head up the hill. I can see his shoulders sticking out on either side of the tree, and I can see the belt that holds his neck against the trunk. Branches scrape against my coat as I make my way up toward his position. He hears me and starts to yell.

"Help? Is someone there? Help me! Please, help me! Please—" His voice is raspy, worn down by his yelling and the cold and the squeeze of the belt around his throat.

When he sees me, his hollering stops and he turns plaintive. "Why are you doing this to me? I don't understand."

Still breathing hard from my march across the lake, I squat down beside him, close enough that my knee is touching his left shoulder. I look at him for a few seconds while I catch my breath. At first he's looking directly into my eyes, but then he averts his gaze away from me. He knows me all right.

"What's my name?" I ask him. I already know he'll lie, but I want to see how good of a liar he is.

"I don't know you, mister. What the hell's going on? Why are you doing this to me?"

"You don't know me? Are you sure? Look closely." I lean in and take off my stocking cap.

"No. I don't know you. Who are you?"

He's good. His eyes stop pulling away and he locks his focus on me, even managing to put on a mask of fear and befuddlement as he talks. He wants to play. So let's play.

"I'm Detective Max Rupert," I say. "Ring a bell?"

"Detective? You're a cop?"

I don't answer.

"Let me go. You can't do this to me. I didn't do anything wrong. You have no right."

"Shut up!" I say through gritted teeth. "I have every right."

"Whatever you think I did, you're wrong. I didn't do anything. You have to believe me."

"I have to do nothing of the sort." I lean back and sit in the snow.

"If you're a cop, show me your badge."

I say nothing.

He digs his heels in and pushes back against the tree, sliding his neck and the belt a couple inches up the trunk to give his throat a finger-width of slack. "You know that we're in Canada," he says. "If you're really a cop, you have no jurisdiction here. You can't arrest me. I didn't do anything, but if I did, you can't arrest me. We're not in America anymore."

He's right about that, but this stopped being about cops and jurisdiction and courts a long time ago. I lift the rope from under my arm, tie a small loop into one end, and pull a length of rope through that loop to make a slipknot.

"What . . . What are you going to do with that?"

"You're coming with me."

"The hell I am," he says.

His tone is getting bolder as he reassesses his circumstances. He must think I'm going to take him back to America and place him under arrest. I stand up, walk around the tree, and tug the belt tight to unbuckle it. He gags and coughs for effect as I take the belt off his throat, roll it into a coil, and put it in my coat pocket.

"I'm not going with you!" he yells. "You're a man of the law. You can't do this. You're insane if you think I'm going to go with you. Cut me loose now and maybe I won't sue you for breaking my arm."

I wrap the rope around his neck and pull it tight.

"What the—?"

With the rope in one hand and the ax handle in the other, I begin to drag him down the hill toward the lake. I can hear him choking and making gurgling sounds, but no words can escape past the rope around his throat. It takes me only a minute to get him to the edge of the lake. He's not heavy, but his shoulders plow up a pile of snow as we go. I know I won't be able to pull him very far before I fall over from exhaustion. But then again, how long will he be able to go without breathing?

Before stepping onto the ice, I stop and put some slack into the rope. His airway opens and he starts to cough and sputter and gasp for air. When he can take a full breath, he grits his teeth and lets loose a wail. His eyes are still pinched shut as he yells, "You broke my arm, you fucking lunatic."

He is trussed up, helpless, and in a great deal of pain. I think I have a pretty good starting point for negotiations, so I again squat down next to him.

"Like I said, you are coming with me. That is not up for discussion. You can come with me voluntarily or I can drag you. It doesn't make me a bit of difference. You decide."

"You think there's no payback for this?" he says, spitting the words out of his mouth. "I'll have your badge. I'll sue your department and you personally. If you don't let me go right now, I promise you, I'll make you pay for this."

"Okay," I say. "Dragging it is."

I stand back up and shrug.

"No! No. I'll walk."

I start to tug on the rope.

"I said I'll walk!" And then in words that barely leaked past the slipknot, "For Christ's sake, stop!"

He's lying on his back and I plop down onto his knees to separate his boots so he can walk. I keep the rope around his neck and lift him to his feet.

"March," I order.

He seems a bit shaky at first—it's probably hard to walk through deep snow with your arms bound. Or it could be the crack I put in his skull that's making him wobbly. He's not talking, but he gives an occasional grunt to let me know that he's struggling.

As we trek across the frozen lake, I start to feel a bit shaky myself, and it occurs to me that I haven't eaten in over twelve hours, nor slept in twenty-four. I should have grabbed a bite when I went back to the cabin to get the rope and auger, but I was concentrating so hard on the task that I overlooked the long game. The physical exertion of tromping back and forth through the snow was already starting to take a toll, and we're just beginning this crucible.

As we near the middle of the lake, I keep an eye out for where I had stashed the tarp. When we come to that spot, I give a short yank on the rope and like a well-trained horse, the man comes to a stop. I drop the ax handle and throw my shoulder into his back, sending him toppling face-first into the snow. He curses and screams as I use the rope to tie his feet together. When I am satisfied with the strength of the binding, I roll him over onto his back.

"Have you completely lost your mind?" he yells. "I swear to God, if you don't let me go right now, I'll spend the rest of my life making sure that you pay for this!"

"You'll make me pay for this?" I stand up and use my legs like a snow plow, creating an opening down to the lake's surface as I talk. "And what will that price be? What could you possibly do to me to make us even? I'd really like to know what you think is fair?"

"What are you doing?" he asks.

I ignore him and keep clearing snow until I have a nest about the size of a tractor tire. Then I find the auger. When I pick it up, I see a spark of recognition in his eyes; and, behind that, I see what I'm hoping to see—fear.

CHAPTER 11

Minneapolis—Two Days Ago

On the drive back to City Hall, I was lost in thought, immersed and weightless in a deep pool of illumination brought to me by Farrah McKinney. On the day she died, Jenni was trying to help a girl named Zoya, a girl of maybe sixteen or seventeen, a girl being trafficked for sex, or so they thought. Jenni was trying to save her life. As I floated in this new information, my squad-car stereo played softly in the background. The whispers of a song broke through to my consciousness and I was pulled out of my trance. The song was "Runaway Train," by Soul Asylum. I stopped thinking and turned up the volume, letting the lyrics perforate walls I'd built up over a lifetime of being a cop.

With its lines about being in too deep, with no one to help and no way out, the song melded with my thoughts about a young girl I'd never met, a girl thrown from a motel window, a girl beaten and raped, who needed help. She was here, in my city, alone and scared, and I didn't protect her—we didn't protect her. But Jenni tried. Was that why they killed her?

I parked beside City Hall and cranked the volume up, my head sinking back into my headrest, my eyes closed to the tears that tried to escape. I let the song rip into me, but I felt no absolution. When the song was over, I turned the stereo off and gave myself a moment to ease back into my cop face before texting Niki that I had arrived.

Niki came out through the front door of City Hall, jogged to the end of the block where I parked, and jumped into the passenger side of my car. I drove away, meandering through the empty streets of downtown.

"What's with the cloak-and-dagger?" I said.

"Lieutenant Briggs is in the office. He's been hovering around my desk for the past half hour."

"Maybe he's finally worked up the courage to ask you out."

"I've got a gun, Max."

"I mean you're a young, desirable woman—"

"I will shoot you."

"Sure he's a bit doughy, but, who knows, maybe the third marriage will be the charm."

"You're an asshole, you know that?"

"I've heard rumors."

"I think he was trying to listen in on my phone calls. He actually came into the cubicle and asked me what I was up to. He leaned against your desk and wanted to chat like we were old friends."

"He doesn't work a holiday unless he's trying to impress someone."

"Or he thinks there's an advantage to his game. Think about it, Max."

"Orton?"

"Deputy chief of staff to the mayor."

I took a moment to wade into thoughts that I normally ignored—politics—a world where Briggs spent most of his energy.

Niki said, "Remember a few weeks back, the mayor was pissed off at Chief Murphy? There were all those rumors that the mayor was looking to replace the chief? What if those weren't just rumors. What if there's a shake-up in the works? Having close ties with the deputy chief of staff might come in handy."

"I have no doubt that Briggs is here to play his game. We need to keep him out of the loop. I don't like the idea of our investigation being used as a political football."

I stopped my aimless weaving through downtown and turned around to head back toward City Hall.

"There's something else we need to talk about," Niki said with an air of seriousness that made me uneasy.

"What would that be?"

"Your lunch date. Was she helpful?"

"Helpful? Oh, she's just an old friend."

"How long are you going to keep feeding me crap, Max?"

"How long are you going to keep asking questions that you know I'm not going to answer?" I focused on the road, hoping the subject might fall away but knowing it wouldn't.

"Dammit, Max. What's going on?"

"Nothing."

"Who is Farrah McKinney?"

"No one." I started to formulate a plausible lie, as the heat of Niki's anger and hurt burned against my cheek. I hated lying to her.

"And by no one, do you mean Farrah McKinney is a figment of your imagination, or she's no one you should be talking to?"

I don't answer.

"Because when she called to tell you she was running late, I asked her what this was in reference to. Do you know what she told me?"

Crap.

"She told me that you had contacted her about the death of your wife."

I stopped at a red light and looked out my window so that Niki couldn't see my face.

"And Ray Kroll, the guy you had on your computer earlier. I'm betting he has nothing to do with this Fireball investigation. I'm betting he's a name from the past that you shouldn't be digging up. Tell me I'm wrong."

I turned to face Niki, but I couldn't look her in the eye. "You don't want to know what I'm up to," I said. "We have the Fireball case to work. Anything beyond that is best left alone. I'm not putting you in the crosshairs. Please—"

"Crosshairs?" Now she was really angry. "What are you talking about?"

The light changed and I turned onto Third Avenue, pulled up to the curb next to City Hall and parked. "You know what I'm talking about, Niki. Let's assume I'm doing what you think I'm doing. If I get caught, Briggs will make sure I'm out the door. I'm not taking you down with me. That's all there is to it."

"You're such an idiot," she said, her indignation flushing red on her face. "For a smart detective, you're a bastard and an idiot and you're as blind as a . . . as a . . . you can be such an asshole."

I sat in stunned silence, each word stinging like a slap to my face.

"I'm already on the hook with you," she said. "I know what you're doing. I'm not stupid. And because I'm not telling anyone, that puts me on the hook. You're not protecting me by keeping me out of the loop."

"You have plausible deniability. You can—"

"I don't want plausible deniability. I want to help you. I want to find your wife's killer. I want you . . . I want you to trust me."

"I do trust you. I—"

"No you don't. Not really. To you, we're partners, that's all—a business relationship. At the end of the day, you don't give me another thought. You have this wall you've built, and you won't let me past."

"What are you saying?"

"I'm saying . . . I'm saying that I feel like a replacement still. We've been together three years, and you still don't trust me—not the way I do you. You say you're protecting me, but that's bullshit. You either trust me—all the way—or you don't. That's all there is to it."

While my brain lined up a counterargument, another voice inside of me whispered that she was right. She knew what I was working on. If she helped to cover it up, she'd be in trouble. And for what? Was it fair that I trusted her to keep silent about my investigation, but not to be part of it? I had put her in jeopardy yet kept her in the dark as to why she was making that sacrifice.

"This investigation can never go on the books," I said.

"I figured as much."

"I'm serious, this crosses a line. I'm beyond just getting fired. There could be real consequences."

"Max." Niki leaned forward so that I could see the seriousness in her soft, dark eyes. "I want to get the prick who murdered your wife. I am in this all the way—neck-deep if that's where it leads. Let me help."

I leaned back in my seat, hoping to come up with one last way out. Nothing came. "Okay," I said. "I'll tell you." I closed my eyes and spoke in a low whisper. "It goes back to the day I killed Ben Pruitt. Boady Sanden and Pruitt were in Sanden's office. I was standing just outside, separated from them by a pair of French doors, glass doors, so I could see into Boady's office. Pruitt had a gun in his hand. I thought Pruitt was going to kill him."

"I know," Niki said. "I read the report."

"But there is something I left out of the report. I busted into Boady's office with the idea that I would either arrest Pruitt or shoot him. I had him in my sights, and I was yelling for him to drop his gun. But Pruitt didn't drop the gun, and he didn't point it at me, either. Instead, he brought it up to his own head. He pointed the gun at his temple and pressed his finger against the trigger. I could see the white in his knuckle. He was serious."

I turned to look at Niki so that I could see her reaction to what I told her next. I said, "That's when Pruitt told me that he knew who killed Jenni."

Niki's eyes tightened as she realigned the chain of events to see it from a new perspective. "But how'd Pruitt know?"

"That's where Raymond Kroll comes in."

"The guy you were looking up this morning."

"Yeah. Boady Sanden showed up on my doorstep yesterday and handed me a file on Kroll. He was Pruitt's client. When we were in Boady's office, and Pruitt wanted to bargain with me, he said that if I let him go, he'd tell me who killed Jenni. He said if I didn't agree, he'd kill himself and I'd never find my wife's murderer."

"But you shot him."

"I didn't believe him. I didn't think he'd go through with it, so I told him that he was going to prison. I'd let him think about that bargain from his prison cell. I figured he'd give up Jenni's killer in exchange for better conditions or maybe a reduction of his sentence. People talk big when they're bluffing."

Niki shook her head slowly. "He wasn't bluffing."

"No. But he didn't shoot himself, either. He shot at me. He was standing right in front of me and he shot wide. I couldn't stop myself. I killed him before I realized what had happened."

"Suicide by cop."

I nodded. I could see the cogs turning behind Niki's brow, trying to connect the death of Ben Pruitt to my new investigation. "After Pruitt's death, Boady Sanden became the executor of Pruitt's law practice. He was responsible for shutting it down, returning retainer money, closing files, that kind of thing. When he was going through Pruitt's cases, he came across Ray Kroll's file. When Boady opened the file, he saw Jenni's name written inside the cover."

"Kroll was Pruitt's source," Niki said. "That's how Pruitt knew about Jenni's death."

I nodded again. "I think Kroll might have been blackmailing someone. That's the only reason I can think of why Kroll kept the evidence all these years—as proof of the crime. There was a CD in the file. It was a recording of a telephone conversation. Two men. They were talking about Jenni's murder. They were planning it."

Niki sat back and mouthed, "Holy shit."

"I suspect that one of the men on the CD is Kroll. He probably recorded the conversation as insurance. Making sure he didn't become the fall guy in Jenni's murder. Or, maybe he saw this as a way to make some money. I don't know."

"Where's Kroll now?"

"He got into a bar fight not long after Jenni's death. Charged with first-degree assault. That's the case Pruitt represented him on. He spent some time in jail before bailing out. The assault case never went to trial because someone put a bullet in Kroll's head. They found his body on the bank of the river in St. Paul."

"Maybe he used the recording to raise the bail money."

"That'd be my guess. Kroll was a thug who needed one hundred grand in bail money. A guy like that isn't rolling cash. How else could he afford that kind of bail and a high-priced lawyer like Pruitt?"

"You said you think Kroll is one of the voices on the CD."

"Yes."

"Is the voice on the CD distinctive? I mean, could you identify him if you heard it again, even if it was only a word or two?"

"I think so."

"If Kroll gave a statement as part of his assault case, we'll have his voice."

"I'm way ahead of you," I said. "There's no statement—not in any of his cases."

Niki leaned back in her seat. "Let me think on that. There has to be a way to find his voice. YouTube? Internet?"

"I checked."

"Does Kroll's file give you any motive? I mean, why would he kill Jenni? What's the connection?"

"In that phone conversation, one of the guys says that they're killing a cop's wife because she knows something she's not supposed to know. The fact that she was a cop's wife was secondary. All this time, I've been operating under the assumption that Jenni died because of me—because of someone I busted or pissed off. But that wasn't it."

"What do you think she knew?"

I shook my head. "I don't know. I'm trying to re-create Jenni's life from back then—trying to understand what she was doing."

"Farrah McKinney?"

"That's my starting point." I told Niki what I'd learned about Zoya and that day in the hospital. "My best theory so far is that Zoya was being trafficked and Jenni got in the middle of it somehow."

"Does Zoya have any connection to Kroll?"

"Not yet, but something else came from our talk. There's this Jane Doe case I worked before your time. She had a tattoo." I tapped behind my ear. "Here, on her neck." I reached into my pocket and pulled out Farrah's drawing. "Ms. McKinney gave this to me. It's a drawing of a tattoo Zoya had on her neck. I think my Jane Doe had the same tattoo. It might be an odd coincidence, but then again . . ."

Niki nodded her understanding "We should take a look at Jane Doe," she said.

"There might be a connection."

"What do we do about Briggs?" she asked.

I gave that question a couple seconds of thought, and then said, "Briggs is still in the dark about most of Fireball's case. I say we keep him there until we figure out his angle. Let him hover but don't give him any details—not yet. We let him maneuver, but do our best to keep him outside the circle."

CHAPTER 12

I *am* an asshole—Niki was right. I am a bastard and an idiot. I knew these things to be true, and her words echoed in my head as we made our way back to the Homicide Unit. Against my better judgment, I made her an accomplice to my professional suicide. The smile on her face and glint in her eye told me she was all in. If I allowed it, she would see this through to the end, no matter the cost.

I'm an asshole because I let her think that we were a team. Butch and Sundance charging forward against all odds. She didn't know that I lied to her. I had to. This wasn't a noble charge, it was a freefall. We were plunging toward Earth and only one of us knew it—the one without a parachute. I knew then, that when the time came, I would have to pull the cord on her chute and leave her behind. She would never forgive me, but I would never forgive myself if I took her down with me.

We got to the door of the Homicide Unit and she paused and nodded as if to say, "Here we go." Then we went in.

Niki and I no sooner sat down at our desks when the door to Lieutenant Briggs's office swung open. I looked at Niki and she rolled her eyes. He sauntered up to the opening of our shared cubicle like some bored coworker hoping to shoot the breeze. Briggs never just wanted to shoot the breeze.

"I hear you two have a hot one going."

I saw the joke—hot one—burned minivan. I didn't play along. "Actually, it was about twenty below zero this morning." I looked at Niki and she nodded as if this were a serious discussion of the weather.

"Even colder than that, if you count the wind chill," she said.

"Yeah," I said, "but luckily, there wasn't that much wind."

"There was a little bit of a breeze. I could feel it on my face."

Briggs interrupted our shtick. "I hear that some guy ended up in the hospital with burns? Is he your suspect?"

"We're looking for surveillance footage from the area," I said, ignoring his question. I heard Niki pick up her phone and dial.

"Got an ID on the guy yet?" Briggs asked.

I was pretty sure that Briggs knew full well who we had in the hospital. "We're working on a few things," I said. Not an answer, but true nonetheless. "What brings you in on a holiday?" I asked, trying to turn the table.

"Just catching up on some stuff," he said, not answering my question either.

"Has he said anything?" Briggs asked. "You take a statement?"

"Not yet, but that reminds me. I need to call the hospital to see if he's conscious." I picked up my phone and dialed the number for my own landline phone at home.

"What's his—"

"Yes, could I speak to Doctor Patel? Tell him this is Detective Rupert calling." My voice-mail greeting yapped in my ear as I pretended to call the Burn Unit. "Yes, Doctor Patel, it's Detective Rupert. I'm just calling to check in . . . Yes. Is he still intubated? Tell me what we're looking at."

Behind me I could hear Niki pretend to contact companies in the area where the van burned, searching for surveillance cameras. We both kept up our ruse until Briggs huffed and walked back to his office.

Once he'd gone, we laid our receivers down on our desks, keeping the lines lit up so Briggs would think we were still on the phone.

"See what I mean?" Niki said.

"Yeah, he's up to something."

From his office Briggs had no clear line of sight to our desks. I quietly got up and walked to a filing cabinet at the opposite end of the Unit—our cold-case drawer—and brought back the Jane Doe file.

"A Salvation Army employee found her in a dumpster behind their facility on North Fourth Avenue. The worker was tossing a bag into the trash when he saw a shoe that looked nicer than what he expected to see in the garbage. He reached in to retrieve the shoe and discovered that it remained attached to a human foot."

I handed Niki a crime-scene photo. Jane Doe had black hair tangled around fair skin, her face showing a hint of freckles under her makeup. Her eyeliner and lipstick were both badly smeared and had been applied in thick, dark shades, the work of someone wanting to look older—or sexier—than her years allowed. She wore a black dress, skimpy, with no bra and no panties.

"Given her attire, we're pretty sure she was killed indoors and moved to the dumpster postmortem."

"Rape?"

"The autopsy couldn't determine if there had been sexual penetration at or near the time of death, although the evidence suggested that the she'd undergone significant sexual abuse in the days and weeks preceding her death."

"She looks young."

"Mid to late teens, we figured. We could never fully determine her age because we never figured out who she was."

"Cause of death?"

"Drowning."

"Drowning?"

"She had bruises on both cheeks and around her neck, as if someone had held her by the throat and smacked her around. She also had bruises up and down her torso, and finger marks on both arms. She had been handled roughly in the hours before she died. My first thought was that she was beaten and then strangled, but the medical examiner's report came back with drowning."

"She's not dressed for the swimming pool, so . . ."

"The water in her lungs didn't have enough chlorine to be pool water, nor was it lake or river water."

"Bathtub?"

"That was my conclusion, but this was no accidental fall. She wouldn't step into a tub with a full complement of makeup, nor the black dress. A young girl, drowned, dumped, and left to be disposed of like trash. That was all we knew about Jane Doe—except for the tattoo."

Niki spread the file across my desk, fanning out the autopsy and crime-scene photos. "You think this is Zoya?" Niki whispered.

I picked up one of the autopsy photos. With her face scrubbed clean of makeup, Jane Doe looked childlike, freckles, thin eye lashes, thin lips. "She matches Farrah's description: five-five, dark hair. And there's the tattoo behind the left ear." I laid Farrah's napkin drawing next to a close-up photograph of the ruble symbol on Jane Doe's neck.

"You know," Niki said, "I think I remember meeting a girl . . . when I was in Vice. She had . . . I swear it was the same tattoo."

"You met Jane Doe?"

"No. It wasn't her; at least I'm pretty sure it wasn't her. We were doing a sting at one of the hotels downtown." Niki paused as if struggling with her memory. "I had agreed to meet one of the guys in the hotel bar. While I was waiting, I struck up a conversation with another working girl who was also there to meet a client. She had an accent."

"Russian?"

"I believe so."

"But you don't think it was Jane Doe."

"No. The girl I met looked nothing like these pictures. Part of the job back then was to build up a network of informants. Try and gain their trust. It's the only way to learn who the inside players are. I remember this girl fidgeting with her hair, and I saw a tattoo behind her ear. I think it was like this one." Niki pointed at the ruble on Jane Doe's neck.

"Identical tattoos on two different girls?" I said.

"Branding," Niki said.

I closed my eyes, and to myself I whispered, *of course*.

"If it's a brand," Niki continued, "it's pretty low-key. Most pimps put their marks where it's more visible. Back in the day, I saw tats that covered the girl's entire chest. The name of their pimp plastered forever for the world to see. I mean, that was the point. Brand the girl so other pimps stay away."

"So why the small ruble? Hidden behind the ear? Doesn't that cut against the rationale?"

Niki leaned back in her chair to ponder. On this subject, she was the teacher, having spent five years in Vice. "My guess? When you work for a really bad man, you don't need the billboard on the chest. All you need is enough proof of ownership that the other gorillas know to leave her the hell alone."

"And you only saw the one ruble tattoo during your time in Vice?"

"As far as I remember. That suggests that the pimp is careful. Probably does referral clients only. You have to be vetted to get into the club. I'll check the database of known tattoo brands, see if that ruble's on the list." Niki turned to her computer and started typing.

For my part, I began looking for the reports tied to Zoya's visit to HCMC. I searched Cappers for anything written on the same day as my wife's death. If Farrah had her facts straight, then an officer found Zoya wandering the streets. She was taken to HCMC, which suggests that she was found in Minneapolis. Also, an investigator showed up at the hospital. That investigator would have made a report even if no information had been gained at the hospital.

The Homicide Unit took on the solemnity of a library as Niki and I clicked away on our keyboards. The wind had picked up outside, but it was still too cold for snow. A furnace kicked on somewhere in the bowels of City Hall and added a low hum to the room, a base note beneath our keyboard castanets. Neither of us spoke for a long time.

Then Niki said, "Do you think there's a connection?"

I had been so deep in my concentration that I didn't understand what she was asking. "Connection?"

"Between this Zoya girl and Jenni's death."

"I honestly don't know. This could be important, or it could just be a coincidence."

"Don't worry, Max. We'll get 'em."

There is no we. I wanted to say. This was a mistake. I should have never let her get involved. I was about to say something, although I had no idea what words were going to come out of my mouth, when an incident report popped onto my screen with the name Zoya on it.

"Here it is," I said. "I think I found it." I read down the page. "It's a report from the same day Jenni died. A patrolman with the Second Precinct found a girl walking down Broadway. She was bleeding and dazed. The report lists her as Zoya. She couldn't speak English, and the officer thought she might be speaking Russian. He couldn't understand if she gave a last name or not. He took her to HCMC."

"Are there any pictures in the file?"

The directory for the case had a file marked *Photos*. I held my breath and clicked it. Nothing but an empty page.

"God dammit!" I muttered through gritted teeth. "It's empty. There's a file for photos, but there's nothing in it. Just when you think you're catching a break."

"Empty?"

"The officer created a file for the photos but forgot to—or just didn't bother to download 'em."

Tendrils of lost possibilities twisted around my fingers, knotting my hands into fists. No last name. No address. No path to known associates, occupation, enemies. If we had a picture, we could have gotten a search warrant for Zoya's hospital records. That might have opened a thousand doors. Without those records, all we had was speculation.

"Does the incident report give us anything to go on?" Niki asked.

I read through it again. "It's pretty thin. The girl had glass in her hair, so they did a search of the area to see if they could find any broken windows. Found a motel five blocks away with a broken front window. Room rented for cash."

"Yeah, that sounds like the life of a sex worker."

As I stared at the screen, at the scant report by the patrol officer, something caught my attention—not something I saw in the report, but something missing from it. "That's strange," I said. "There's no supplemental."

"What do you mean?"

"Ms. McKinney said that an investigator showed up at the hospital that morning. She said that Zoya freaked out when the investigator walked into the room. But there's no supplemental. No mention of an investigator at HCMC."

"Maybe it got logged in under a different incident number," Niki said. "Let's come at this thing another way."

Niki pulled up Cappers on her computer and typed Jennifer Rupert into the search box. The screen lit up with rows of reports listing Jenni as a witness.

"Holy crap," Niki said.

"Yeah, Jenni was a mandated reporter. She dealt with this kind of thing all the time—girlfriends and wives getting assaulted, sex workers being abused, children molested. Her name will be listed as a witness on hundreds of reports."

"But, Max, look at this." Niki pointed to the screen. "The day she died, there's a report of the hit-and-run, but there is no report of an investigator meeting with Jenni at HCMC."

"That doesn't make sense."

"Maybe Ms. McKinney got it wrong. It's been over four years. Maybe the guy that walked in was a doctor or . . ."

Briggs's door creaked open again. I folded the Jane Doe file closed and Niki and I returned to our fake phone calls. When Briggs stepped past our cubicle, Niki was pretending to convince a convenience store manager to check his security system, and I was pretending to learn the healing time for third-degree burns. Briggs stood at the opening of our cubicle for less than thirty seconds before giving up. This time he went back to his office, grabbed his coat, and left the Homicide Unit, waving at us without actually looking our way.

Niki and I hung up our phones and looked at each other.

"So where does that leave us?" she asked.

"About the same place we started," I said. "We know that Farrah McKinney was right about Zoya. Brought to HCMC after getting beat up. Probably a working girl. Has a tattoo of a ruble behind her ear that may or may not be a pimp's brand. What do you see?"

Niki gave pause, then said, "I see a witness who is spot-on, but also said there was an investigator at HCMC—yet we have no supplemental—nothing to verify that the man in the room was a cop at all. There's a file for photos, but no photos. Something's not adding up."

"Welcome to my world," I said.

"Where do we go next?"

"Home." I looked up at the clock on the wall. Almost three o'clock. "Let's finish up what we need to do on Fireball and call it a day."

"I got ahold of the Holiday station this morning," Niki said. "They should have a copy of the surveillance footage ready for pickup anytime now."

"I need to stop by the Burn Unit to see if Orton is able to talk yet. I want to question him before he has too much time to think."

"I'll swing by and pick up the surveillance footage," Niki said. "It's on my way home."

"It's the opposite of your way home, but thanks."

"What are partners for?"

"Look, Niki, about that—"

"No you don't. I will kick your ass if you take back anything you said today."

"But the thing is—"

"Fuck you. We had a beautiful moment. Don't ruin it."

"But—"

"I mean it. Not another word. You get out of here. Go interview Fireball. I'll shut the computers down and lock up."

I stood but hesitated.

"Go!" She pointed at the door, her face scrunched up into her best tough-matriarch look.

I picked up my coat and shuffled out the door.

CHAPTER 13

Up North

I put the tip of the auger on the ice and turn it. The spoon-shaped bit doesn't bore at first, so I push down on the cap of the auger. With that, the bit starts to dig. The growl of metal against ice breaks a silence that holds little more than my own heavy breathing. I expect the man to start talking again, but instead he just sits there, watching me. He's probably trying to figure out his next move, studying me to size up the strength of my backbone. His silence is fine by me.

I drill down an inch or so, enough to see the full circumference of the shovel—a first impression for my template. I move the auger to start another hole, this one a quarter of an inch away from the first. When that is marked, I start a third and a fourth. I keep a thin partition of ice between the starter holes so that the blade won't catch on an edge and jam up as I drill down to the lake.

When I finish my fifth starter hole, I step into the middle of my pattern and look down to see if it's wide enough to accommodate a man's chest. I'm a little bigger than he is, and if I can fit through the hole, he will fit. The six-inch-wide shovel on the business end of the auger is duller than I'd expected. It forces me to push down on the tool, exerting energy that I'd hope to save. I mark three more notches, completing the oval—eight starter holes in all—big enough to slip a man through. I step back and give the project one last look before taking on the arduous task of drilling through three feet of ice with that dull-bladed auger.

Satisfied that I have the dimensions right, I go back to my first hole and begin cranking.

"I don't think you'll do it," he says.

My better judgment tells me to ignore him, but I don't. "Do what?" I ask.

"I see what you have going there. You want me to think you're going to cut a hole through the ice so you can drop me through. Am I right?"

I turn the auger and don't answer.

"My guess is that this is all some ill-conceived plan to get to me to . . . I don't know what your goal is here, but I'm sure you'll tell me at some point, probably when you get close to finishing your little project there."

"You and I are going to have a talk," I say. "There's no question about that. We can do it now or we can do it later. That's up to you, but we will have a talk."

"I have nothing to say to you—except that you're a fucking psychopath. You're not going to get to me with your little game of . . . what did they call it in those old black-and-white movies . . . the third-degree? That's right. You're giving me the third-degree here. But we both know it's all pretend, so you may as well give up, because I'm not buying it."

"That would be a mistake," I say.

I keep the auger turning at a steady pace. I don't want him to know how slowly it's cutting through the ice. But this is his auger, taken from his cabin. He's surely used it before. He has to know how dull the blade is and what an effort it takes to cut through the ice. He has me at a disadvantage on that score.

But on all other accounts, I have the upper hand because he doesn't understand how much I know. If I were to lay it all out for him—cut to the chase, so to speak—it would hit him like a baseball bat to the chest. I could do that, and I briefly consider it, just to see the look of astonishment on his face. But I can't do that. That's not why I came here. That's not what this is about. I will not accept remorse from a man who has no other choice. What good is a confession if the sinner has to be dragged kicking and screaming down the church aisle?

Time and pressure. Stick with the plan.

"Want to know how I know that this is all bullshit?" he says. "Do you? You fucked up. You tipped your hand. Think it through. There's a flaw in your logic, and you don't see it."

I lean onto the auger, using my weight to give the blade more bite. I can still see the top of the shovel above the ice shavings, which means that I've only drilled down about six inches. How long has it been? Ten minutes, maybe? *Christ.* I stop drilling and scoop the ice shavings out of the hole. As I scoop, I inspect the sides of the blade hoping to see that one side is sharper than the other, looking for a slight glint where a file may have turned rusted steel into fresh metal. No such luck.

"Don't you want to know your flaw?" the man asks.

"I'm sure you're going to tell me," I say, as I go back to drilling.

"If you had the balls to kill me, you would have done it by now. You had me out cold. I was completely defenseless. You could have killed me and left me out here for the wolves to clean up, but you didn't. You see the problem? How are you going to convince me that you're going to kill me now if you didn't do it before?"

I turn the auger and do not answer.

"For fuck's sake, quit wasting my time with this charade. You said you're a cop. A cop isn't going to kill a man in cold blood. You and I both know that. You're not a killer."

I want to tell him how wrong he is, but when I had the ax handle poised above my head, ready to crush his skull, I didn't bring it down. I remember the struggle that froze my arms. Am I not a killer? That can't be right, because I've killed before. Three times. All in the line of duty. I didn't have a choice—not with any of them. I had no time to deliberate over whether my actions were justified. I followed my training and my instinct. Action and reaction—that was it. I almost pause my drilling as the memories of those faces come flooding back to me, their lifeless eyes staring up at me.

They made me see a psychologist after each of the three killings, a nice woman with a voice that reminded me of a purring cat. She would ask me if I'd been losing sleep or if I had difficulty eating or felt anxious.

I lied to her and said no. I didn't see that it was any of her business. Yes, I've had a great many sleepless nights, but those nights had nothing to do with the three people I killed. Their eyes weren't the eyes that visited my dreams; it wasn't their voices whispering to me in the dark hollows of my bedroom as I tossed and turned. It was Jenni's.

I shake my head to clear away those thoughts. My hole is now two feet deep. A slight pain pinches deep in my bicep as I turn the crank. Nothing to worry about yet, but I know it's the harbinger of a much worse pain to come. I take a moment to examine the hole and rest my arm.

I glance at the man lying on his backside, watching me as though he doesn't have a care in the world. His death will be different than the others; I know this. I will look him in the eye as I end his life. There will be no heat of battle. I can't ignore the deliberate nature of what I plan to do. I can't pretend that this is anything short of vengeance. I tell myself that I have the mettle to finish the job despite the second thoughts that poke at my resolve.

I force my thoughts back to Jenni. I think about my visit to the parking ramp where she died. They had tried to clean her blood away, but I could still see where it had collected in the tiny fissures and cracks. I bent down and ran a finger along the seam of an expansion joint, lifting a thin line of red. Jenni's blood. I spread it on the palm of my hand, closing my fist to hold her there.

I had promised to protect her. I had failed.

I think about what this bastard took from me, and I start to get mad. I want to get mad. I want to feel the burn of my rage again, have it course through me as it did when I chased him into Canada. I find that rage and turn the auger with renewed vigor, cranking nonstop until I finish the first hole. A guttural bark escapes my throat as the auger blade breaks through to the lake. Cold water comes gushing up through the cut like an overflowing toilet, spreading across my little nest, soaking beneath the snow at the outer edges.

I put the auger in the next starter hole and turn.

"Jesus Christ," the man says. "Would you just stop?"

My back is already starting to ache, but I keep turning the auger.

"What do you want from me? I don't know what you want. For fuck's sake man, stop drilling holes."

On the western horizon, the thin line of blue sky is pushing the clouds to the southeast. Colder weather is on its way. When it gets here, it'll drop the temperature below zero and wind will feel like sandpaper against my cheeks. I have a lot of work yet to do.

One down, seven to go.

CHAPTER 14

Minneapolis—Two Days Ago

I brought a small recorder into the Burn Unit on my second visit. Orton had bandages wrapped around his entire head, with holes for his mouth and eyes, but his eyes had cotton balls taped over them. The room was small and clean, and it smelled of antiseptic cream. The breathing tube had been removed from his mouth, and peeling skin made his lips look badly chapped. I sat in a chair next to his bed and watched him breathe for a while, labored breaths. In . . . out, pause. In . . . out, pause. I don't think he heard me come in, or maybe he was asleep. I turned my digital recorder on and placed it on a table beside him.

"Dennis?"

He stirred, turning his head only slightly in my direction. He was awake.

"Can you hear me?"

"Yes," he whispered.

"Dennis, my name is Detective Max Rupert. I need to ask you a few questions."

He swallowed hard and ran a dry tongue gently across the inside of his lips.

"Would you like a drink of water, Dennis?"

"Yeah."

Someone had placed a cup of water with a bendy straw on his bed stand. I held the straw to his lips, and he took a sip.

"I need to talk to you about what happened."

"I couldn't stop them," he said. "I tried to stop them. I couldn't."

His voice was rough, his words passing over the early scabs from having inhaled fire.

"Stop who, Dennis?"

"The men who killed Pippa. They killed her, and I couldn't do anything."

"Okay, let's slow down a bit here. What men are you talking about?"

"Three black guys. They tried to steal her car. I told her to let them have it. We were going to let them have the van. But then they started . . ." Orton stopped talking and put his lips together and carefully licked them again. "They started grabbing her. I wanted to help her, but they held me back."

"Were you in the car? Was this all happening in the car, Dennis?"

"Yes. I was in the driver's seat and they pulled her into the back."

"Wait, Dennis. Let's start at the beginning. Where were you and Pippa before this thing with the black men happened?"

"We were home. I mean . . . earlier, we were at home. We decided to go out for a bite."

"What time would that have been?"

"I'm not sure, maybe around six in the morning. We were going out for breakfast."

"Just getting up, or out all night?"

"What?"

"Well, are you an early riser? Six a.m. is pretty early on a day most people sleep in."

"We were . . . um, we had pulled an all-nighter."

"Did you go out for New Year's Eve?"

"Does that matter?" Although still a bit raspy, his speech seemed to clear up as we went along—as he forgot his act.

"Just trying to get a full picture, Dennis. Filling in the blanks."

"We went out for a couple drinks, sure."

"Where?"

"I don't . . . it was just a bar; I think it was on Marshall. I'd never been there before. I don't remember the name. That has nothing to do with this."

"Okay, so you and Ms. Stafford went out, had a few drinks, came home. You live together, right?"

"Right and we—"

"Did you meet anybody for drinks?"

"What?"

"When you were out at that bar, did you see anybody you knew?"

"That's not relevant. We didn't get jumped at the damn bar."

"Alright, Dennis, don't get upset. So you and Ms. Stafford went out for breakfast. What happened?"

"Okay. We're driving along and—"

"Who was driving?"

"I was driving. I told you that already."

"That's right."

"I'm driving down, I think it was Second Street, I'm not sure, and I stop at this stop sign. There's a car in front of me and one pulls up behind me. I didn't think much of it."

"What restaurant were you going to?"

"What?"

"You were going out for breakfast. What restaurant? That might help us narrow down where the attack took place."

"Um . . . I, uh . . . The Eatery."

"I didn't know they served breakfast."

"They don't. I didn't know that. It was Pippa's idea. She thought they were open for New Year's Day. She wanted to check, so we went there and they were closed."

"So then, where were you going?"

"We were just driving around. We didn't have a plan B, so we were talking about where to go, you know? Just roaming through the streets, trying to think of who might be serving breakfast."

"And that's when you pulled up to that stop sign?"

"Yeah. A car in front and one in back. And these three black guys get out. I think they were gang members, because they were wearing bandanas."

"Did you happen to see what color the bandanas were?"

"Red. Yes, red."

"And you said three of them got out?"

"Yeah, two out of the front car and one out of the back. And before I knew what was going on, they pulled guns."

"All three had guns?"

"Yeah, I think. The guy who came to my door had a gun. I know that. He pointed it at my face and yelled at me to get out of the car. The other two came around the passenger side. They opened the doors and one got in the back seat; the other shoved Pippa. They pulled her into the back."

"The guy on your side, he had a gun, you said? Do you know what kind? Was it a revolver? Automatic?"

"I don't know; automatic, I think."

"And he ordered you out?"

"Yeah."

"Did you get out when he ordered you to?"

"He had a gun in my face; of course I got out."

"But, you said that they held you in the driver's seat when they pulled Pippa into the back."

"He . . . yeah, he grabbed my collar . . . and my arm. He grabbed me through the window so I couldn't help Pippa. Then he pulled me out."

"Your window was open? It was twenty below."

"Wait . . . I . . . I rolled it down when he was walking back toward me. I thought they might be having car trouble."

"And he pulled you out through the window?"

"He pulled me out through the door. He opened the door and yanked me out."

"By the collar and the arm?"

"Yeah. I realized that we were in trouble, so I started fighting with him. I tried to break away. I wanted to help Pippa. He was bigger than me and—"

"Where was the gun?"

"The gun?"

"He had one hand on your collar and one on your arm. Where was the gun?"

"He must have . . . I don't know. It all happened so fast. It was dark. Maybe he had the gun in one of his hands when he grabbed me. I just remember getting yanked out of the car. Pippa was screaming. That's when he hit me in the head."

"He hit you?"

"Yeah. I don't remember anything after that. Not until the fire. I woke up in pitch black. I didn't know where I was at first, but I could smell gas."

My phone buzzed once in my pocket. I pulled it out and saw a text from Niki. *Got Holiday footage. Very interesting. You still in town?*

I typed back, *Yes. Want to meet up?*

Rusty's?

Give me half hour.

I switched back to my interview with Orton, trying to remember the last thing he said. Oh, yeah, he smelled gas. "Where were you when you smelled the gas?"

"I was in the van—in the front passenger side. I could smell the gas and everything was black. Then I saw a flame, like a lighter, then a bigger flame. One of the black guys was on the driver's side. The back window was open and one of them lit something on fire and tossed it through the window. I got my door opened just as the whole van blew up."

"You were in the front passenger side?"

"Yeah. I don't know how I got out. The blast must have thrown me."

"And then you called 911?"

"I was on fire . . . rolling in the snow. I couldn't see, but I managed to dial 911."

"When did you shut the door?"

"What door?"

"The van door. When I arrived at the scene this morning, the front passenger door was closed."

"I don't know. It must have blown open and then . . . you know . . . it bounced back shut."

"That's probably what happened," I said. "Now, you said that it was dark when you woke up. You said that it was pitch black and you didn't see anything until someone lit a match?"

"That's right."

"So you didn't see any headlights? Running lights? Nothing?"

"Lights?"

"I'm assuming those three guys didn't walk back to town. It makes sense they'd have a car follow them—to give 'em a ride back to the city."

"I suppose."

"And if they drove a car out there to use as a getaway car, well, if it was me, and it was twenty below, I'd leave the car running. I'm just wondering why you didn't see any running lights in the darkness."

"I don't know. I wasn't worrying about running lights at the time. I didn't give a rat's ass whether they had a getaway car. I was just trying to survive. Why are you being a dick? They strangled my girlfriend. They tried to kill me and all you can do is focus on why I didn't see running lights?"

"They *strangled* your girlfriend?"

Orton's lips closed, squeezing together, trembling. His left hand, the one free of bandages, balled up into a fist. He'd fucked up.

When his lips relaxed, he said, "Detective, I need some rest. I'm in a great deal of pain. I need you to leave now."

I stood. "That's fine," I said. "I have a few more questions, but they can wait."

CHAPTER 15

Rusty's Bar had been a neighborhood fixture since before the neighborhood had electricity. It had burned down three times—only one of those times had arson been proven—and it had changed its name at least eight times over the near century and a half of its existence. What hadn't changed was the clientele. Rusty's never tried to be more that it was. Trends came and went: flappers, zoot suits, rebels, hippies, yuppies, and now Gen Xers and millennials. Through it all, Rusty's served cold beer and poured its drinks with honest measure—except, of course, during Prohibition. In those years, root beer topped the menu unless you had the clout to go down to the basement where they served Canadian whiskey.

Rusty's was one of those long, narrow saloons with tin ceilings and pock-marked hardwood floors. The plumbing and duct work crisscrossed in the open spaces above the lights, and no seat in the house sported a cushion of any kind. Nothing fancy, with its long row of taps lining the cherry-wood bar, Rusty's could feel a bit sticky on the elbows at times, but again, it never pretended to be anything else.

I found Niki in one of only three booths. The old Hamm's clock on the wall had just ticked on five o'clock, and already Rusty's was half full. She had a bottle of Grain Belt waiting for me. I tapped the neck of my bottle against the neck of hers and took a long pull.

"Did Fireball confess?" she asked.

"No. He did the blame-it-on-the-gangs thing," I said. "His explanation is all over the place. Tried to make it out as a car-jacking gone bad, as if that POS minivan was a hot commodity at the chop shops."

"You gave him a day to come up with a story, and that's the best he could do?"

"I know. I am deeply disappointed in our deputy chief of staff."

"You want to see something that'll make you even more disappointed in him?"

Niki lifted a laptop from the bench beside her and placed it on the table between us. She had the surveillance footage from the Holiday station cued up and ready to go. She hit the mouse pad and turned the screen toward me.

The camera angle was downward facing, framing a bay between two sets of gas pumps. The bay was empty for a few seconds before a white minivan pulled up to one of the pumps. I could see the front of the vehicle, and there was no one in the passenger seat. Already Fireball's story was wrong.

Orton got out and walked around to the passenger side, slid a credit card through the slot, plugged the nozzle into the gas tank, and started pumping. Then he went back to the driver's side, got in, and waited.

"So where's Pippa?" I asked.

"Wait for it."

After a few minutes, I saw a window get lowered—back seat passenger side. Orton exited the minivan and walked back around to the pump. He looked over the hood of the car toward the store and the clerk. Then he pulled the nozzle from the gas tank and stuck it through the open window. I could not see into the back seat, but I had no doubt that Pippa Stafford lay dead beneath the spray of gasoline.

"Jesus Christ," I whispered, shaking my head. "He doused her with gas right there at the station."

"Can you imagine the drive from there to the turnaround on First Street—in a car filled with gasoline? He had to be choking the whole way."

"And the whole way, his clothes were absorbing the gas fumes. How did he not see the problem?"

Orton held the nozzle through the window for about thirty seconds, his arm jerking as if spraying as much of the interior as he could reach, before returning the nozzle to the pump. Then he pushed a couple buttons on the pump, waited, and pulled his receipt, slipping it into his wallet as he walked back to the driver's seat.

"I don't see any gang members, do you?" I said.

"Not in this angle."

Niki popped open the tray and handed me the CD.

I rotated the disc in my hand, the lights sparkling off the readable surface. "I can't wait to talk to Fireball about this," I said. "See if he can explain where the black gangbangers disappeared to."

"Do we tell Briggs? He's going to be pestering us again tomorrow. We can't dodge him forever."

"I want to have a chat with Orton in the morning. That should button this case up. Get the confession so there're no loose ends. Then we can hand it to Briggs all tied in a ribbon. He won't be able to do much with it after that."

"Have you figured out his interest in this case yet?"

"Not yet. I was thinking of talking to Commander Walker about it tomorrow."

"Is that wise?"

"Walker and I go way back. He trained me when I first came to Homicide. He's not like Briggs. In fact, the only reason that Briggs made lieutenant is because Chief Murphy pushed it. If Walker had his druthers, Briggs would never have become his second-in-command."

"Who would have? You?"

I smiled and shrugged, remembering the conversation Commander Walker and I had when he tried to ease my disappointment for not getting a job that I didn't want in the first place. "Let's hold off telling Briggs anything until I either get a confession from Orton or I talk to Walker."

"Not a problem. What's one more day on the dark side?"

I tipped my beer in her direction and took another pull.

Over Niki's shoulder, a young couple at a stand-up table caught my attention. They looked to be in their midtwenties. He wore a Vikings cap over a closely shaved head, and his coat fit snug across his broad shoulders. What drew my attention was the anger in his face when he talked to—or rather talked at—his female companion. I could not hear his words over the din, but he pointed his finger in her face when he spoke, his other hand resting on the table in a tight fist.

For her part, she didn't look up until after his outburst ended.

When she talked back, she'd only get a few words out before he would interrupt her again. They each had a beer and a shot in front of them. He downed his shot and pointed at the shot in front of the girl. She shook her head no, and he went back to berating her.

"Max?"

Niki had been talking, but I lost track of the conversation. "I'm sorry, what were you saying?"

"I was saying that I'm going to start wearing pinwheels in my hair, so maybe I can keep your attention for more than a few seconds at a time."

"That'd be a good look for you. I'm in favor."

"You really can zone out sometimes, you know that?"

"I was going for aloof and mysterious?"

"Keep practicing—but you have obsessed down pat."

"Ouch."

"Don't get me wrong. I'm not saying it's a bad thing. That word can be so loaded, but in your case, it fits."

"How so?"

"Your thoughts are dominated by one thing. They have been ever since I came on board here. Sure, it ebbs and flows. Some days are better than others. But your wife's death is always there, just below the surface. It makes sense that you live, eat, and breathe that obsession now that there's been a break."

The man at the table behind Niki pounded his fist to make some point. The girl curled into herself, her hair falling to hide her face.

"Max, when it comes to solving a murder, you are the most observant man I've ever met. But you live in a tunnel. You have your job and you have your memories. Beyond that, there's no room."

Rusty's had filled up pretty good. I looked at the door. No bouncer. Behind the bar, one female bartender on the far end served up beer as fast as she could. On the near side, an older guy, maybe early sixties, stood behind the bar chatting with another old-timer. Not much for backup.

"And no one can build a wall like you, Max Rupert," Niki continued. "But sometimes I wonder what it would be like if we were friends, you know, off the job. It sounds weird when I say it out loud, so—"

The man grabbed the girl by the face, digging his fingers into her cheeks to raise her head up. He spit some more words at her and when she pulled away, he slapped her.

I jumped up from my booth and lunged at the man. I was on him in two steps. He wore a down coat, unzipped in the front. I turned him toward me and in a single motion, punched him as hard as I could in the stomach and yanked the collar of his coat over his head. I grabbed the back of his belt with one hand and the back of his coat with the other.

Now doubled-over, he faced the door. I gave him a shove to get him moving in the right direction and ran him toward the exit. Just before we got there, he started swinging. He was blind with his coat over his head, but he managed to land a pretty hard punch to my side. The crowd parted, clearing a path to the door, and I used the man's head to open it.

He fell to the sidewalk and immediately started to get up. Both his hands were balled into fists. I lifted my coat to show him the badge on my hip. "I'm a cop, asshole! Just walk away!"

I could see that he was contemplating doing something stupid. We stood there for a few seconds before his girlfriend came bounding out the door, with Niki right behind her. The girlfriend looked at my badge, then at her boyfriend.

"Come on, Dave," she said. "Let's go."

Dave wadded his face into a scowl and said a final "Fuck you" to me. Then he turned and walked away, his girlfriend following a few steps behind. This would not be the end of it for them—for her. I wondered if I had only made things worse.

"You want to tell me what the hell that was all about?" Niki said.

I unclipped my badge from my belt and walked back into Rusty's, my badge held up so that the old-guy bartender could see it. He was on the phone, probably to 911. When he saw my badge, he hung up.

"He slapped his girlfriend," I said to Niki. "It kind of pissed me off."

"You want to give me a heads-up, next time?"

We sat back down in our booth and both took a drink from our beers. "You were saying something about my living in a tunnel?" I said with a grin.

"Really? I open up to you, and you're going to give me shit?"

"I'm sorry," I said. "I know I get fixated on Jenni. I can't help it. Sometimes I feel like that part of my life just froze. I don't know how to explain it, exactly."

"You can't move on until you resolve it. I understand."

"There's more to it than that." I took another drink of my beer and then drained it, holding the empty bottle in both my hands in the middle of the table. I didn't look at her as I put the words together. When I was ready, I said, "Jenni was pregnant when she was killed."

I squeezed my eyes shut to try and block out the images that I knew were coming: Jenni lying naked in the guest room, the bracelet on her wrist, the Christmas trees with room for so many more presents, the blood on the floor of the parking garage.

At first Niki didn't say a word. She just sat there looking shocked, then sad. Then she said, "I'm so sorry. I had no idea."

"Neither did I. I mean, I didn't know until I learned about it from Dr. Hightower, after the autopsy."

"So Jenni . . . she didn't know?"

"No. I mean . . . I don't think so. She didn't say anything. She wasn't acting any different than normal. No morning sickness. Nothing like that. The day she died was ordinary. I not only lost my wife that day, but I lost a child. . . . They took everything from me. They killed my family. I can't let this go."

"Nor should you," Niki said. "I meant what I said today, Max. I'm in for the full ride."

"I know you are, Niki. But . . ."

"But the wall is still there."

"Nobody knows what I've just told you. You're the only person I trust right now. But there are places I need to go and you can't follow. I can't tell you any more than that."

I expected Niki to look hurt, but she didn't. Instead, she looked melancholy. She dropped her eyes and nodded her understanding. "Will you come back from . . . where you need to go?" she asked.

I picked at the label of my empty beer bottle and said, "If I can."

CHAPTER 16

Up North

The second hole in the ice goes slightly faster, as my technique has improved. I begin to count the turns of the auger, switching hands every twenty rotations. I also keep a cadence in my head, counting to a waltz rhythm like I'd seen dance teachers do in movies: one, two, three; two, two, three . . . The counting keeps me moving at a steady pace and, more important, it fills my head with noise, which helps to block out the voice of the man as he continues to try to get under my skin.

Despite my improved technique, the auger shaves its way down at a snail's pace, and soon other thoughts—memories—find their way in. I think about a morning when Jenni and I were lying in bed, listening to rain fall against the bedroom window in an easy patter, like fingertips tapping against leather. We had just made love and neither of us had a reason to get out of bed, so we didn't. That had been a month or two before she died—before he killed her. And as I think of that morning, I wonder if that was the day that we conceived our child.

We had wanted a baby for so long. Early in our marriage, it seemed a game. Behind every flirtation pranced the lure of having sex with a woman whom I loved more than anything else in the world. But those flirtations also carried the possibility of starting a family—the prize at the bottom of the Cracker Jack box.

After she made up her mind—that day she seduced me in the guest room—we became serious, tackling the endeavor with books and research, even indulging in a few old wives' tales. From there came the doctor visits and the minefield of conversations that we would eventually learn to avoid, simple conversations about things like parks or toys or the room that was to become a nursery. Those conversations now touched bruises that never seemed to heal. Officially we were still trying; neither of us had given up. Yet there were times when I could see in her eyes a loneliness that I knew I would never be able to end on my own.

I'm just beyond the halfway point on the second hole when I stop to catch my breath. It is then that I hear a ruffling sound behind me. At first I ignore it and start pulling slush from the hole. When I hear the ruffling sound again, it seems a little bit quieter, more distant. I turn and look at the man. He has managed to push his body about thirty feet away from my circle. His feet are still tied together, but he is able to bend his knees, dig his heels in and push his torso through the snow. I'm not sure how far he expects to get; it has to be a quarter mile to the nearest shore—and then what?

When he sees me looking at him, the man stops his effort and says, "Fuck you."

I walk over and reach for the rope tied around his calves. When I do, he rears back and punches his bound heels at me. It is a futile attack, and I swat his legs to the side. I take off my gloves, grab the tail of the rope and start to drag him back to the circle. As I do, he screams like a wounded animal. I assume that the act of dragging him puts new pressure on his broken arm, because he's twisting to lift that elbow off the ground. When I drop his legs onto the ice, he bares his teeth like a dog and yells, "God damn you!" It's the first time he's unleashed the rage that I know he has under the surface.

"No," I say politely. "God damn *you*."

I walk back to get my gloves and when I turn around, he's pushing himself through the snow again. He's found a new game, a stall tactic to slow down my progress.

I walk to his feet again and reach for the rope, but I'm careless. I get too close and I'm bent over. He rears back and shoves both his heels into the side of my head. I stumble back as a jolt of pain shoots through my skull. For a moment I can't hear out of my right ear.

"God dammit!" I shout through gritted teeth.

He's trying to squirm his way over to kick me again. I spy the ax handle at the edge of the nest, go pick it up, and step toward the man. His legs are cocked and ready. I swing the ax handle at his knee, but at the last second I alter the trajectory. If I hit his knee, I'll break it and that injury will be the focus of his attention. That won't do. Instead, I hit the side on his calf and he yelps and turns over onto his side. He's in pain, but that pain will pass.

He curses me in great detail, as I ponder on how to stop him from pushing away again. I could tie his ankles to his thighs or ball him up like a roped calf, but then he'd be too crooked to fit through the hole. I need to lock his knees straight somehow. I look at the ax handle in my hand. I don't need it as a weapon anymore. An idea forms in my mind.

The man is writhing in pain as I bend down and grab his good arm, turning him the rest of the way onto his stomach. When I do this, he shrieks and bucks. His face is buried in snow, which muffles his ranting a bit. I pull the fillet knife out of my boot and cut a slit in the hip of his expensive snow pants. Then I quickly slide the ax handle down the leg before he can think to bend his knee. The handle hits up against the man's boot.

I keep my body on his legs to hold them down as he kicks and twists. I pull his belt from my coat pocket and wrap it around his thigh twice, buckling it to hold the wood in place, creating a splint against his knee that locks his leg straight. He won't be able to push away now, and more important, he won't be able to bend his knees to stop me from sliding him through the hole in the ice when the time comes.

When I'm done, I turn him back over, his face full of snow and anger.

"I'm going to kill you!" he screams. "You think you're coming out of this alive?"

Now we're getting somewhere. I stay on my knees, next to him, and brush some of the snow off his face, giving him a moment to ponder his impotency. The muscles in his face harden, but he controls the outburst that seethes just below the surface.

"You think you're tough?" he says. "You're not tough. You don't know tough. Untie me and I'll kick your ass, even with a broken arm. You could never beat me in a fair fight, and you know it."

"A fair fight? Like the one we had over there?" I nod in the direction of the Canadian shore.

"Why are you doing this?" he asks, his voice now shaking with emotion. He's switching his tack. "There's no point to your cruelty. At least tell me what it is that you think I did."

"You know what you did."

"No. You're wrong. I've done nothing to you. I'm innocent. You have the wrong—"

I can't help myself. I slap him in the side of the head as hard as I can. "Don't you dare tell me you're innocent! Don't you fucking dare!"

He answers back through clenched teeth. "What do you want from me? Just tell me, for Christ's sake. You can beat me all you want, but what good is it if I don't understand?"

I stand up and go back to the auger, taking a cleansing breath before I start drilling again. There is pain in the center of my palms. At the top of the auger I push down on a metal cap with a sizable hex nut fixing that cap to the top of the shaft. As I crank the auger, the cap remains motionless in my hand, but the nut turns, grinding its way through my glove and into my skin. In a matter of drilling two holes, that nut has chewed up my gloves pretty good. I'll have to do something about that.

"Talk to me, dammit! Give me a chance to defend myself."

I break through the ice and water floods up through the second hole.

"This ain't right. Why won't you tell me what I've done? I'll prove you're wrong, but you have to tell me what I did."

"We both know what you did. You can play games all you want," I say. "But we both know, and that's all that matters."

"*I'm* playing games? You break my arm, club me in the head. You tie me up and start drilling holes though the ice—and you think I'm playing games? Well, fuck you. I'll play your game. I'll wait you out, because this is all for show. You don't scare me."

"I didn't bring you here to scare you," I say. "I brought you here to kill you."

CHAPTER 17

Minneapolis—Yesterday

The tide of a man's mind isn't always governed by those conspicuous forces whose gravitational pull is so massive as to be able to bend light. Sometimes a guy can fall into a mood over a single misplaced word or an almost-imperceptible scent that summons the reek of an old, gangrenous memory. I wasn't aware of the source, but on the second day of the New Year, I awoke in just such a temperament. I had never been this close to the truth about my wife's death. I had Fireball just about wrapped up. I should have been happy, but I wasn't. I couldn't seem to escape the cloud of melancholy that swirled around my head.

The reason for my skewed disposition came to me in the shower, my eyes closed, the steaming hot water cascading down my face. It was then that I remembered the dream—only a vague outline at first, then more. It was a little girl, four or maybe five years old. I tried to talk to her, and she kept turning away from me as if she hadn't heard me, her face hidden behind a fine veil of red hair. When nothing seemed to work, I sat down on a stone wall and sang "My Girl," a song I used to sing to Jenni when she felt sick or sad.

At the sound of my shaky tune, the little girl turned around to face me, lifting her chin and letting the light catch her eyes. I had seen those eyes before, and that hair and smile, in a picture that sat on the shelf in my bedroom. It was Jenni when she was a child—but at the same time it wasn't Jenni. This little girl was different, a likeness but not a reflection. She reached her hand out to me, and I took it in mine and held it the way a father would hold onto a daughter's hand.

Despite the hot water raking my skin, a chill ran up my back. *It was a dream*, I told myself. Nothing more.

I arrived at the HCMC Burn Unit at 8:00 a.m., anxious to see Orton's face—or what was left of it—as I fed him the rope for his execution. He would try to explain away the bits and pieces of what he thought I knew. They all did. But in the end, his bullshit story about gang members would shatter and fall to the floor. I was betting that I would have a confession in less than half an hour.

I buzzed the nurse's station and flashed my badge, walking to the ICU section where Orton was being kept. Orton hadn't changed since the day before, except that they had removed the bandages covering his eyes. He was awake and looked up at me when I entered the room, his eyes showing no hint of recognition.

"Good morning, Dennis," I said.

With those words, Orton's eyes grew large and he took in a sharp breath. "I don't want to talk to you," he said. "I don't have to talk to you."

"Dennis, I'm Detective Rupert. We spoke yesterday, remember?"

"I know who you are. You took advantage of me. I want you to leave."

"I don't understand," I said. "We—"

"You can't talk to me if I say I want an attorney. I want an attorney. You have to leave."

"What's going on?"

Orton fixed his gaze on the ceiling, his eyes dancing as though trying to remember a script he'd memorized. "I'm not saying anything else. I've invoked my right to remain silent. I want you to go now."

I nodded as though I understood, but I did not. The man on the bed in front of me was a vastly different man than the backtracking fool I'd left the previous evening. Someone must have gotten to him, convinced him to button up.

I stepped out of his room and went to the nurse's station, where a young man in blue scrubs was typing on a keyboard. I showed him my badge in case he hadn't seen it when I walked in. "I was wondering, do you keep a sign-in sheet of visitors on this unit?"

"No, we don't. We have the locked door over there." He pointed to the unit doors. "If you're a family member, we'll let you in."

"But I'm not a family member."

"I suspect the badge gets you in a lot of doors that most folks can't get in."

"Did anyone come to visit Mr. Orton recently?"

"There was someone in his room when I came on shift an hour ago."

"Do you know who that might have been?"

"Honestly, I didn't pay much attention. I think it was a man, but I can't even be certain about that. If you want to get a picture, though . . ." The nurse pointed at a bubble on the ceiling where a security camera hid behind tinted glass.

"Thanks," I said. "Can you aim me in the direction of the Security Office?"

The nurse pulled out a map of the sprawling hospital and circled a small box on the second floor.

On my way to the Security Office, my phone buzzed in my pocket. I pulled it out expecting to see Niki's number. Instead, I saw a number that I didn't recognize at first. Then it came to me. Farrah McKinney.

"Max Rupert here."

"Detective Rupert, this is Farrah McKinney . . . from yesterday."

"Yes, Ms. McKinney, how are you?"

"You said that if I could find that recording, the one with your wife's voice on it . . ."

"You found it?"

"I did. And I am downtown interpreting at the courthouse this morning. We should be done by around ten, if you want to meet."

"I do. If you're at the Government Center, there's a cafeteria in the basement. You ever been there?"

"I know where it's at. That works fine. I'll be there around ten."

"See you then."

I hung up and walked into the Security Office, where a man in a blue uniform sat behind a bank of monitors, scribbling on a pad of paper. I showed him my badge. "I have a suspect in the Burn Unit," I said. "I was wondering if I could look to see who he's had as visitors."

The man, a rotund fellow with an overgrown mustache and a clip-on tie hanging from his shirt pocket looked at my badge, his eyes squinting as if badge inspections were a specialty of his. A name tag on his shirt read Clark, and I was unsure if that was his first name or last, so I didn't use it.

"You want what again?" he asked.

"I'd like to see if any visitors have been on the Burn Unit this morning. I have a murder suspect in there, and I think one of his visitors may be a person of interest. Can you pull the surveillance footage up for me?"

"Nope," he said, with a slight air of smugness. "I run security. I'm not an IT guy. That's something for the computer geeks to handle." Clark made no move to pick up a phone or page a computer tech. I paused for a couple beats, waiting for him to act, and he just stared at me.

"Is there by chance a computer guy around that could rewind the footage for me?"

"You don't just rewind it. This is high-tech stuff. It's not like we're some Podunk gas station with a VCR in the back room. We're talking state-of-the-art."

I leaned my elbows onto the countertop between us, lacing my fingers and giving them a good squeeze to try and pull the stress away from my face. "Someone in this hospital has the ability to pull up footage of visitors to the Burn Unit, am I right?"

"Well . . . yeah," Clark said. "Of course."

"And you have enough tech savvy to pick up a phone and summon that person here, don't you?"

Clark shifted in his seat and glared at me without answering.

"So would you be so kind as to make that call?"

Clark shot me a fake smile. "Tech folk are a busy bunch, you know. Maybe you should just leave me your card and I'll get back to you."

He struck me as a man who carried a sizable chip on his shoulder when it came to cops, and I wondered if he'd been kicked out of a police department in his past, told to resign or get fired, a mark that would ensure he'd never wear a badge again—even a security badge.

I made a point of holding Clark's gaze in mine and said, "I'll tell you what . . . Clark. You see what you can do while I go upstairs to visit my old friend Doctor John. Maybe he can grease the skids a bit."

I had met the CEO of HCMC at a conference once, a symposium on dealing with mentally ill clientele. We were by no means close friends; in fact, I don't think I would have even recognized him had he walked into that Security Office right then. But I knew his name—not the name on the letterhead, but the name he preferred to be called by those under his watch. Doctor John. To Clark, that name was as good as knowing the secret password.

He tried not to show his concern, but the man had an easy tell. He brushed his thumb across his lips, and his nostrils flared as his breathing shifted into a slightly higher gear. I took out a card, laid it on the counter, and smiled, hoping to calm Clark's pulse. "It's important," I said.

"Sure," he said, the weight of the chip now gone from his shoulder.

I left the Security Office and checked my phone as I headed to my squad car. I had missed a call from Niki, so I called her back.

"Did you come back to the office last night before meeting me at Rusty's?" she asked.

"No. Why?"

"Both of our computers were on when I came in this morning. I know I shut them off before I left."

"Briggs?"

"Has to be."

"Dammit," I whispered. "He's digging through our investigation."

"His door's been shut all morning, and Commander Walker's out sick."

"Again? What's that been? Ten days out in the last month?"

"You think something might be seriously wrong with Walker?"

"I think Briggs knows something we don't," I said. "I don't like this one bit. I'm on my way back now so we—"

"No, don't come back here. I have a bunch of stuff to show you, but we should meet outside the office."

"Meet me at Eddie's. I'll buy."

"I'm heading out now. See you there."

I cut off the call and paused at the revolving door before leaving the hospital, looking out at the steam rising from the taxis picking up and dropping off patients. I thought about Commander Walker and his many recent absences. Had he been losing weight? Or was that my imagination? We hadn't always seen eye to eye, but if you brushed away the mud of office politics, I always trusted him to deal straight with me.

I pulled up his personal cell number and hit send.

CHAPTER 18

Commander Walker answered his phone as he always did—with a single word. "Walker."

"Commander, it's Max Rupert. I'm sorry to bother you at home, but . . . I have a question that I think only you can answer."

A pause. Then, "Go ahead."

His voice came through the phone flat and tired, and I regretted the call. I felt like a school kid tattling to a teacher. "It's nothing too urgent," I said. "It's about Lieutenant Briggs. I thought you might be able to fill in a blank or two."

"What's Briggs doing now?"

"Niki and I are looking into the death of a woman on New Year's Day. They found her burned up in a minivan. Everything points toward her boyfriend." Now it was my turn to pause as I tried to put my suspicions into words.

"Okay," Walker said. "What's that got to do with Briggs?"

"Lieutenant Briggs has been . . . well, I'd call it hovering. He's pressing Niki and me for information, and we believe he's been digging through our computers and spying on our investigation. I'm just trying to figure out what his interest is."

"You think he's got a political angle?"

"I do," I said. "The woman's boyfriend is Dennis Orton, the deputy chief of staff to the mayor."

"I see."

I thought about saying more, but realized that I had no more to say. All I had was hovering and a couple computers that turned on overnight. A wave of embarrassment passed over me, and I was trying to figure out a way to get out of the conversation when Commander Walker cleared his throat and spoke.

"Max, what I'm about to tell you is confidential. Do I have your word on that?"

"I'll need to tell Niki," I said.

"That's fine. She's good people. You got lucky with that one."

"Best partner a guy could ask for," I said.

"Here's the thing, Max. I have cancer—colon. They diagnosed it just before Christmas. They say I have a good shot at beating it, but I'm taking a leave of absence. I've been talking to Chief Murphy about the timing, and we were thinking about an announcement before the end of the month."

My heart dropped into my stomach, and I wished that I hadn't called.

"I'll need surgery and probably some follow-up chemo."

"I'm sorry to hear it, Matt. How's Lydia handling it?"

"Like a good wife. She's all smiles when she's near me, but I can see in her eyes that she's scared."

"If there's anything I can do . . ."

"I know, Max."

"So Briggs knows about this?"

"He does. Murphy brought him into the loop because Briggs will become the interim head of Homicide while I'm gone."

A groan escaped my lips.

"And, Max . . . I can't promise that I'm coming back. In fact, Lydia's been pushing me to retire."

"And Lieutenant Briggs will become Commander Briggs."

"That's not my choice, Max. You know that. Hell, if I had my way there would be no Lieutenant Briggs—there'd be a Lieutenant Rupert. But I don't call that shot, Murphy does."

"I'm not the management type, Matt. You know that. The one who should be moving up is Niki. She's the brightest in the department—hands down. She'd make one hell of a commander."

"I know that, Max, but more important, Briggs knows that. You have to be careful with him. He's a climber. While you and Niki are out solving crimes, he's scheming his way into my chair. That's where

Dennis Orton comes in. I don't know the connection, but it was Orton who lobbied Chief Murphy to make Briggs a lieutenant. If Briggs gets his way, he'll be the youngest commander in department history."

"And the most unqualified," I said.

That brought a snicker out of Walker. "Your words, not mine."

"Fucking politics. I wish I could just do my job and be rid of the rest."

I could hear the smile in Walker's voice as he said, "Being in government and ignoring politics is kind of like being in the middle of the ocean and ignoring water."

"I suppose you're right about that," I said.

"You and Niki should watch your backs when it comes to Briggs. That man is good at his game, and his specialty is to get dirt on his rivals. Take them down in a preemptive strike if he can. He was behind that reprimand you got last year."

I found myself, in my mind, back in Walker's office, getting chewed out for taking Jenni's file out of archives. I remember Briggs standing in the corner, watching my castigation with an air of self-satisfaction and a smug grin that just screamed "punch me."

"If it were up to me, I'd have dressed you down and called it a day. But Briggs went over my head to Chief Murphy. I had no choice but to issue the reprimand."

I shook my head in disgust. "And he's going to be the new head of Homicide."

"Maybe . . . well, probably. But watch your back—you and Niki both. He sees you as threats. He may pull some stunt to shore up his front-runner status between now and my official retirement. Don't put anything past him."

I thought about our computers. What was on them? What could he find? Niki did a Cappers search for Jenni's name. Briggs will follow the bread crumbs and know that I'm back on Jenni's case. He'll also know that Niki is helping me. I shake my head again and whisper, "Fucking politics."

CHAPTER 19

Up North

My palms are sore and it's only the third hole; I have five more after this. With every turn of the handle, that hex nut on top of the auger has been eating through my gloves and digging into my skin. I can feel blisters starting to form. I pause about one foot down into the hole to consider this problem. I'm wearing a stocking cap and my coat has a hood, so I take off my cap and draw the hood up over my head. I'll use the cap as a buffer between the hex nut and my hands.

I'm not wearing a watch, but I'm sure that we're into the afternoon. The sun is barely visible through the low-hanging clouds, and to the west, the line of blue sky advancing ahead of the cold front is growing wider. I know that I'll have to finish this project in the dark. I'm fine with that. In fact, it seems fitting.

"I have to ask you something," the man says. He tries to sit up in the snow, taking on as much alpha as a bound man can muster. "You say you brought me out here to kill me. And you're cutting holes through the ice to make me believe that you'll drop me into the lake when it's all said and done. Fine. Let's say I buy it. Okay? I concede. You have the balls to do it. That make you happy?"

I ignore him.

"But you won't talk to me, because you don't want to know that you're wrong. You have doubts. I get it. It's best to keep those doubts to yourself—keep 'em secret. You're here to get your payback, and you can't let those doubts get in the way."

I scoop ice chips out of the hole. Christ, that man can prattle on.

"You need your vengeance—your compensation. I understand that. You're a man who feels cheated. You don't want to walk away from here empty-handed."

I now see where he's going with this.

"I don't know what I supposedly did to you, but whatever it is, I'm sure we can come to an understanding."

I don't stop drilling, but I look over my shoulder and say. "Understanding? What understanding?"

He gives me a smarmy grin. "Well, all that stuff I said before—that I was going to sue you, get you fired. I don't see any reason that we have to go there. I can tell that you're operating under some terrible misunderstanding. You seem to have considerable conviction, even though it's based on a mistake. I can't hold that against you. I admire a guy who can act on his convictions. I mean, under other circumstances, I could see you and me being friends, so I can't fault you for doing what you think is right. You made a mistake. It happens. You let me go now, and I'll make it worth your while. You know what I mean?"

"You'd do that for me?" I say.

"Come on. Stop cutting that hole and talk to me."

I don't stop drilling.

"I'm a rich man. You ever hold a hundred thousand dollars in your hands? Two hundred. I can get you two hundred grand. I can have it to you by sundown."

I keep turning the auger. "Two hundred thousand dollars?" I say.

"Yeah. Cash. Maybe more. What do you say? You strike me as the kind of guy who could take that seed money and become a millionaire in no time."

I contemplate what I would do with two hundred thousand dollars. What's the thing I would most want to buy? The answer comes rushing into my head. If I had that kind of money, I would give it all up for just one more day with Jenni. I would give everything. I would offer up my life to have her back, to have our child born.

My hands start to shake with anger. I pull the auger out of the hole and lunge at the man, jamming the shovel up against his throat. "You're offering me money?" I scream. "Money! You kill my wife and my child and you want to give me money?"

"Whoa! Whoa!" His eyes are bulging out with fear. "I never did! I . . . I didn't kill your wife. I've never killed a child in my life. I don't know what you're talking about."

"Don't lie!" I push the auger blade into his neck as he stretches to pull away. "Don't fucking lie to me!"

Tears well in my eyes, and the blade against the man's neck becomes a blur. I fear that I may cut his throat by accident. I don't want that. I'm not ready for that. I pull the auger back and step away to see what looks like fear or maybe confusion in the man's face.

"Jesus Christ," he whispers. "You think I killed your wife? Your child? No. You're wrong. I never . . . Christ, I—"

"Her name was Jenni Rupert."

"I've never even heard of your wife before. I don't know that name. I swear."

"I could understand how a man with your résumé might forget the names of some of his victims." I put the auger back into the hole. "How many people does a man have to kill before it's okay to forget a name or two?"

"I don't know your wife. And I sure as hell didn't kill her. I swear to God, I'm innocent. You've got to believe me."

I go back to turning the auger. "You know, I've always wondered why people say stupid shit like that. You tell me I've got to believe you—like it's proof that you're not lying. Well, excuse the hell out of me, but I don't have to believe a God-damned thing you say, seeing that I'm the one with the auger and you're the one tied up."

I punch through to the lake and water comes rushing out of the third hole.

I set the auger blade into the fourth starter hole and rest my arm across the top. "You've been lying to me ever since you started talking. If you want to start telling me the truth, I'll listen. But if you're going to keep going on with this 'I'm innocent' crap . . . well, I got holes to drill."

CHAPTER 20

Minneapolis—Yesterday

In the three years since Niki and I became partners, we've shared many a cup of coffee at Eddie's Soup and Sandwich, a notch in the side of the downtown skyway, a couple blocks from City Hall. Eddie's had great coffee, and we could walk there in bone-brittle weather without ever having to step foot outside.

I found Niki seated at a corner table with two cups of coffee in front of her. A thirtysomething man in a charcoal suit and rubber covers on his shoes—my guess an attorney on his way back from court, grabbing a cup of joe on his client's dime—waited at the counter for his order, his back turned to the register, his eyes brushing up and down Niki's body, tiny, fit, a lock of her hair suspended in front of her eyes, dark and twisty like a jungle vine. No doubt he was judging her, knowing her only with his eyes, appraising her worth by the physical qualities that pressed against the cotton of her blouse and filled the curve of her jeans.

If she noticed the gawker, she didn't show it. "I saved you a seat," she said, moving my chair out with her foot.

"You're so kind."

The guy in the suit swiveled back to pay for his coffee, apparently yanked out of his daydreams by my presence.

"What took you so long?" she asked, sliding one of the coffees to me.

"Got tied up with a phone call," I said.

"Good news, I hope?"

"Just the opposite."

I sipped my coffee and replayed my conversation with Commander Walker. I watched her eyes grow damp as I told her about his cancer. I saw her face sag in despair when I explained how Lieutenant Briggs would be Walker's likely replacement. I didn't cushion the blow. She needed to see how grim her future might be, especially if she continued helping me dig into Jenni's death.

"Briggs? Head of Homicide? That empty-suited, pencil pusher? He doesn't know the first thing about investigations."

"He's been put on this earth for bigger things, Niki. He's a great man suffering the indignity of having to build his own pedestal. Have a little compassion."

"He's a worm who thinks he's a caterpillar, that's what he is."

"Regardless, there's no denying he's a wiz at climbing ladders," I said. "While you and I have our brains soaking in the muck of criminal cases, he's playing a whole different game. Fuck all that crime-solving crap. It's a distraction."

"Screw him," she said, rolling her eyes.

"You need to take this seriously, Niki. If Walker's right, Briggs will come after you. You're a threat to his plan."

"*I'm* a threat? How do you figure?"

"You're smart, well-liked, and would make a great commander. Briggs sees that."

"I don't have the seniority to be a commander."

"Walker thinks you'd give Briggs a run for his money, even with Briggs having his nose smashed up against Chief Murphy's prostate. He needs to take you out of the running. He's going to be looking for a reason to muddy your record."

"Let him come after me. See what happens."

"Niki, if he was digging through the computer, he saw the Cappers search you did on Jenni. He'll know I'm back on the case and that you're helping me. Briggs is an asshole, but he's not stupid. If he's looking for a hook to take you out, he may have already found it."

"I don't care," Niki said. "If that's what it's going to be like to work under Briggs, then I'd rather he fire me."

"He can't fire you if you aren't doing anything wrong." I hesitated before I spoke again, bracing myself for the pushback I knew would come. "I want you to quit working on Jenni's case," I said. "If Briggs asks, you tell him that you were looking stuff up for me, but I didn't tell you why."

Niki didn't speak; I waited. She just stared at me.

"Niki, this is my problem, not yours. I can't have—"

"And if this were my problem, would you turn your back?" She spoke in a whisper, but yelled nonetheless. "If I told you to stay out of it, would you?" She raised a finger to my face. "Hell no, you wouldn't. You'd be right there at my side. God dammit, Max, sometimes you make me so mad I want to . . ."

Her hand went rigid, her index finger curling back to complete a fist. For a second there, I thought she might actually hit me. Then she turned in her chair to face away, crossing one leg over the other. She stayed turned away while she calmed down. I'd never seen her that angry, and I had been the cause of it.

When she turned back to the table, she smiled. "You're not the boss of me," she said raising a defiant eyebrow. "I can be just as ornery as you when I want to be, and . . . well, I want to be. So go ahead and give your little orders, say what you got to say, but I'm going to keep working on this case, and there's nothing you can do to stop me. You don't like it? Take it up with my boss. His name is Lieutenant Emil Briggs." She cocked her head as if to say—your move.

I had no move, other than to squirm in my seat. "Fine," I said. "And by *fine* I mean it's not fine at all, but I don't have much of a choice."

"I thought you'd see it my way."

"With one caveat," I said. "Promise me that if Briggs comes after you for this, you tell him that I was keeping you in the dark. You tell him you didn't know what I was up to."

"I'll tell that blowhard that he can go—"

I reached across the table and grabbed Niki's hands and squeezed them. "No!" I said. My interjection punched the air with a sharpness that brought our conversation to a halt. Then quietly, I whispered, "No.

I don't want you stepping into Briggs's trap. He wants you to be insubordinate. He needs you to be insubordinate. It's one of his favorite weapons. You have to promise me: if he confronts you—you tell him that you didn't know." I squeezed her hands a little harder. "Please, promise me."

She hesitated, looking into my eyes as if searching for a crack in my resolve. She found none. I wasn't about to let her skip merrily along at my side as I charged down the dark path unfurling before me. She didn't know about the wolves. She didn't know the lengths that I would go to hunt them down. She had no idea how deep my rage and hatred ran. There would be carnage at the end of this; I felt it in my bones. I would protect her from that at all costs.

"Okay," she whispered. "I promise."

"You're looking into things because I asked you to. Understand? I told you that it was part of the Jane Doe cold case. That's all."

"I got it, Max."

"Good." I loosened my grip on her hands.

"But this *is* about the Jane Doe case. That's not a lie."

"What do you mean?"

She reached into a briefcase beside her and withdrew a file. From the file, she pulled out two photographs, laying them on the table in front of me. One, I recognized as the autopsy photo of Jane Doe. The second picture was of the same girl, only she was alive, badly beaten and bruised, but alive. My confusion could not have been more obvious.

"Meet Zoya, the girl they brought into HCMC the day your wife died."

"Where did you get this?"

"It bothered me that Cappers had a folder for the pictures but no pictures. Why would the officer take the time to create the folder and not transfer the photos? So I went down to the Tech Unit this morning. There's a lady there that I knew from back when I worked Vice. She's a wiz at metadata and computer forensics. She used to track IP addresses for our child-solicitation cases. This morning, she ran a forensic examination using the metadata for the picture folder and found the deleted photos still in the system. They were deleted the same day they were uploaded."

"Deleted? Why? How?"

"Could have been an accident, or it could have been intentional. The data doesn't say. All we know is that the photos were there and then gone."

I looked at the pictures again. There's no mistake. These girls were one and the same.

"I also did some research on the tattoo. Vice keeps records of tats that are linked to prostitution. I looked in the database, but no ruble."

"Is every known pimp brand in the database?"

"There's always scuttlebutt in Vice, tats that we believed were brands but couldn't prove."

"So someone in Vice . . . say, the guy who runs the unit—"

"Don't even go there."

"He might have some information. We should at least call."

"Who's this 'we' you're talking about?"

"Whitton likes you. He'll talk to you if you call."

"That man is a pig, and I'm not talking to him."

"I'm not so sure he'll speak to me," I said. "He hasn't said a word to me since I stole you away from him three years ago."

"You didn't steal me away. I wanted the transfer. I couldn't stand to be around that bastard."

"It's good to let it out. You should call him. It'll be therapeutic."

"Did I ever tell you that he once told me to take my top off during a sting? We were doing hotel busts and a couple of the tricks wouldn't talk money unless I showed them my tits. Commander Whitton told me to go ahead and strip down. 'Take one for the team,' he said. 'Women walk around topless all the time in Europe.' I think he just wanted to get my breasts on surveillance footage for his private collection."

"Well, he was plenty pissed when I convinced Chief Murphy that you should be in Homicide. Called me all kinds of names. Like it or not, he may be able to help."

"We may never know," she said. "If you want to call him, more power to you. But I haven't spoken a word to that jackass for three years and I'm not about to break that streak."

"Fine, I'll call him about the ruble tattoo—and by *fine*, I mean you win again."

"Do send him my love, would you, darling?"

"I'll do that. You have a number?"

"In my desk, I'm sure. I'll text it to you when I get back to the office. Then I'm heading over to the Government Center."

"Warrant?"

"No, doing you a favor," she said. "I have an idea where we might get a copy of Kroll's voice."

"The Government Center?"

"I checked the court records. He made his first appearance without an attorney. Most courts use electronic court reporters—basically it's a fancy digital recorder. Kroll would have had to answer a couple questions at that first appearance: name, address, does he understand the charges, that kind of stuff. They may still have that recording somewhere in the courthouse."

I grinned, then chuckled. "You're brilliant, you know that? You were made for this job."

She gave a humble shrug of her shoulders. "I don't know if a recording exists," she said. "But keep your fingers crossed. We might get lucky yet."

CHAPTER 21

Arriving early for my meeting with Farrah McKinney, I bought a cup of coffee and found a table in the back of the cafeteria where someone had left a newspaper. I might have paid no mind to the news of the day had a headline not jumped up and caught my eye:

BODY FOUND IN BURNED VEHICLE

"Aw, shit," I muttered.

I read the story, which gave very little insight beyond the basic facts of the fire and the presence of a body. I assumed that the source for the story had been one of the patrol officers, or maybe a firefighter. I held that thought until I read the second paragraph. There, the story referenced what the reporter called "suspicions" of the investigators. The story quoted an anonymous source as saying authorities believed the incident to be "gang-related."

"What the . . ." That's no firefighter saying that.

I leaned back in my seat, pressed a thumb and finger against opposite temples and rubbed. I had hoped to put Fireball aside for my meeting with Farrah. I didn't need that blight of a human being stealing brain cells as I listened to Jenni's last recorded words.

I had just started whittling away at possible sources for the story, a short list with an ending that I was pretty sure I already knew, when my phone buzzed in my pocket. I pulled it out to see a text from Niki: the name Whitton and a phone number. I called the number.

"Whitton here."

"Commander Whitton, this is Detective Max Rupert. You have a minute? I'd like to get your help on a case."

Silence met my request, and in that silence, the memory of our last exchange came flooding back to me, a confrontation we had after Whitton lost his argument to keep Niki in Vice. Niki knew about most of that fight, but there was one part she didn't know.

I'd gotten Niki as a partner on a temporary assignment to handle a spate of murders three years ago. When things calmed down, Whitton requested that Niki be transitioned back to Vice. She was attractive and Asian, and Whitton saw little beyond those assets. I fought to have her remain in Homicide. I won that battle, which ended with Whitton storming out of Chief Murphy's office.

The second part of the fight, the part I'd never mentioned to Niki, happened on the steps of City Hall. I was leaving that day and found Whitton waiting for me. Although he pretended that our meeting was the product of mere chance, I knew better.

"Congratulations," he said. "You got yourself quite the little geisha there."

I tried to ignore him and walk away, but he stepped in front of me.

"Don't think I don't know why you want her for your partner, Rupert. I know exactly what you're up to. Got yourself a case of yellow fever. Think you're going to bang her between calls. Well, think again. She's a frigid bitch."

My eyelids sank to half mast, which is something I've noticed that they do just before I lash out. It probably makes me look more sleepy than dangerous. I started to ball up my fists, and the thought of striking a higher-ranking officer played out in my mind.

"She struts around like she's the queen of the fucking Mekong Delta, but in the end, she's a tease. She'll use you the same way she used me. I'm just another stepping-stone, and so are you, Rupert. You can have the bitch—get her the fuck out of my hair. I'm done with her."

With that, he turned in a sharp twist and walked away. He'd said what he needed to say, and that was the last time that I'd spoken to Commander Reece Whitton.

Whitton ended our silence by clearing his throat and saying, "Yes, Detective. What can I help you with?"

Good, he was going to keep it professional. "I'm looking into a tattoo.

I believe it may be a pimp brand. We've found it on two different females. I was hoping you might have some background on it."

"Maybe," he said, with an air of being an authority on the subject. "We're seeing more and more of that going on lately. What's the tattoo look like?"

"It's a ruble—you know, the symbol for Russian currency. It looks like a capital P with a—"

"I know what a ruble looks like, Rupert. I'm not an idiot."

So much for professionalism. "Have you seen any of these around town?"

"Where did you find this tattoo? On what part of the body?"

Does that matter? I thought. "They had the tattoo on their necks, just behind the ear."

"And you say you've seen more than one?"

"Have you seen any tats like that? Can you give me a name?"

"When was it that you came across any of these ruble tats?"

"It's a cold case that we're taking a fresh look at. If you have any names we could check out . . ."

"No." He drew out his words as if giving my query due consideration. "I can't say that I've seen a tattoo like that on any of the girls we've picked up. Nope, doesn't ring a bell."

What a waste of time. "Well, I appreciate the input anyway," I said. "If you come across anything like that, let me know. Okay?"

"Certainly, Rupert." He gave emphasis to my last name as if it were an insult.

I hung up the phone and stewed in my remembrance of why I hated that prick. I didn't expect Whitton to be helpful, but it was a bridge that needed to be crossed.

Farrah McKinney walked into the cafeteria at exactly ten o'clock, looking like a model from some businesswoman's catalogue: black suit, white blouse—both stiffly pressed, a leather coat over one arm and a computer bag under the other. A far different look than what she wore to the Hen House. I stood as she took her seat.

"How was court?" I asked as a way of breaking the ice.

"Slow. Court is the worst part about being an interpreter. I have to translate legal documents, and my God it can be boring. Lawyers use ten words when one will do. But, it pays the bills."

Farrah lifted the computer bag onto the table and pulled a tiny black thumb drive out of one of the pockets, sliding it toward me. "After the funeral," she said, "I wasn't sure what to do with this, so I tossed it into a drawer—just in case I ever got the inclination to send it to you. I honestly forgot about it until you called."

"I can't tell you what it means to me . . ." I picked up the drive and held it like a present that I wasn't allowed to open.

Farrah must have guessed my thoughts and asked, "Would you like to listen to it? I could play it on my computer."

"I'd really appreciate it," I said.

She slid her laptop out of its case and flipped it open. I handed the thumb drive back to Farrah, and we sat there in an uncomfortable silence as she waited for her computer to wake up. Then she plugged the drive into the port.

"It's not much. She only spoke for a minute or so."

Farrah looked up from the computer screen, I suppose to see if I was ready to listen. Then she hit play, and I heard the voice of my dead wife fill the air. "Ms. McKinney, this is Jenni Rupert, from HCMC. We met earlier today . . . with Zoya. I came by her room just now, and she's awake and talking. I'm writing down what it sounds like she's saying, but I can't make anything out."

Jenni must have turned the phone toward Zoya because the girl's unintelligible rambling became clearer. Then it faded again, and Jenni resumed talking. "I've set up a meeting for three thirty today . . . if you can make it, that is. If you can't, let me know, and I'll reschedule. She still seems frantic, almost terrified. I don't know what to make of it. Give me a call."

I couldn't speak past the knot in my throat, so I just sat there, staring at Farrah's computer, letting Jenni's voice soak in. Yet, mixed with my wife's voice, were the words of a young girl, frightened words uttered in a language that tangled in my ears. I didn't understand what she said, but I could hear the desperation in her voice.

I found my voice. "The girl in the background . . . that was Zoya, right?"

"I assume so."

"Can you make out what she's saying?"

Farrah played the recording again. At the part where Zoya's voice gets louder, Farrah said, "She's talking about wanting to go home."

"What about the rest?"

"I've never really listened that closely before."

Farrah played the recording a third time, her eyes squinting as she strained to hear the voice behind Jenni's. "I think she's saying . . . 'Don't call him. Please don't call him.'"

I put my hand on Farrah's arm to signal for her to pause. "Does she say who not to call? Does she say a name?"

Farrah backed it up and listened again. "I can't make it out. I don't—wait." Farrah hit pause, reached into her bag, and pulled out a set of earbuds. She plugged them in and played it again, translating as she listened. "'Don't call him. Please don't call him.' Then she says, 'I just want to go home. I want to go back to . . ." Farrah backed up and played a small portion again. "'I want to go back to' . . . it sounds like she's saying 'Lida.'"

"Lida? Does that ring a bell?"

"No, but it sounds like it may be her hometown."

I brought out my phone and typed in a search for Lida. Right at the top was a *Wikipedia* page, and I began to read. "'A city in western Belarus . . .'"

"That would make sense," Farrah said. "The girl is speaking Belarussian, and I can hear the Polish influences in her accent."

"So, if I want to track down Zoya, I should be looking for a Belarussian from the city of Lida."

"It's hard to make it out, but that's what it sounds like to me."

"Okay, go on."

Farrah put the earbuds back in her ears and played some more. "She repeats that she wants to go home . . . 'I miss my mama.' Then she says, 'Don't call him. Mikhail will know and—'" Farrah sat up straight in her seat, her eyes staring at her computer as though it had become something to be feared.

"What is it?"

She listened again and said, "I never heard this part before. I never listened that carefully."

"What did she say?"

"It sounds like she says, 'Mikhail will kill me.'"

CHAPTER 22

Up North

As I dig my fourth hole, I can feel roots of fatigue spreading through my shoulders and down my arms. I have a long way to go, and I start to question my plan. What good would all this effort be if I don't have the strength to complete the opening? I hear those whispers of doubt, and I remind myself that this is about much more than simply opening a hole in the Earth to feed him through. If my plan works—if he follows me to where I'm leading him—he'll understand why he needs to die. He won't accept it, but he'll understand.

It's just a matter of time and pressure.

I adjust my technique again, putting my forearm on the top of the auger at times to give my hands a rest. This lets me use more body weight to push the blade into the ice. I also start switching arms every ten turns of the crank, instead of twenty.

The temperature has dropped a few more degrees, and the breeze has picked up slightly, turning crisp against my cheeks and nose. It will be dark in a few hours. And with the darkness, the drop in temperature will be deadly.

My fingers are freezing and I wad them up into fists inside of my gloves when I can. My size 11 feet are worse. I've always had trouble keeping my toes warm, ever since I can remember. I've never experienced frostbite, although I've come close a few times, causing the tip of one of my pinky toes to go numb and stay that way for years. Hell, now that I think about it, that toe might still be numb; I've probably just gotten used to it. I consider shuffling my feet or rocking up on my toes to get blood flowing, but I don't want him to know that the temperature is getting to me.

It's all about the mind game with this one. He's lying in the snow, out of the wind, so the cold doesn't hit him. He's watching me, with his head propped up like he's in bed watching television.

I covet his snowsuit. I'm not much bigger than him, but there's enough difference that I'm sure the suit won't fit me. I can tell it's expensive, though. The pants and coat match, and have pads on the knees and elbows. Probably cost him close to a grand. His boots are way better than mine too, expensive, like they were made for an Artic expedition. I think about taking his boots, but I can see that they are at least a size too small.

My clothes, on the other hand, don't match at all. The most expensive piece of my ensemble is the imitation Carhartt coat that I found on a clearance rack at Gander Mountain. My boots are old and green, and there's a slight gap in the left toe where some of the stitching has ripped open. Jenni bought the snow pants for me, gray, nothing fancy.

The last time I wore these snow pants, I took Jenni sledding in Como Park. It was five years ago—our last New Year's Day together. On our first run down the hill, we tumbled sideways and she ended up on top of me. We laughed and she kissed the snow from my face.

That memory gives me the strength to turn the auger a little faster. I go back to counting, to keep my pace steady: *eight, two, three; nine, two, three; ten, two, three.* I switch hands and start again: *one, two, three . . .*

I focus on my breathing, remembering that I should inhale through my nose to warm the air before it gets to my lungs, but my nostrils feel like they have been scraped raw with a blade and the air has taken on a metallic scent. I watch him as I crank. If he tries to slide off again, or wriggle out of his bindings, I'll see it. He's looking hard at the hazy tree line on the Canadian shore, his face placid except for a slight smile, the look of a man holding aces.

I stop cranking and examine the hills to the north, seeing nothing of interest. But then I hear it, the howl of a wolf rising up from somewhere deep in the woods, a mournful, throaty wail slithering around the trees, echoing off the bluffs, and curling past our little nest on the lake. As if in answer, a second wolf, standing watch on a hill just east of the first, lets loose a howl, the two voices mixing in a discordant braid that fills the sky and breaks like a wave against the Minnesota shore. I hadn't heard them over the grating of my auger. I pause to listen for a moment and to let my burning arms rest.

"Are you afraid of wolves?" the man asks.

"Wolves don't bother me," I say.

"You know, some Native Americans believe that if you kill a wolf, the others in the pack will hunt you down. Did you know that?"

"I think you're full of shit."

"Wolves are incredible creatures," he says. "Smart. Almost human in some ways. You see, I think wolves understand emotions like revenge. They're pack animals. They have leaders and they obey those leaders. They love their alphas. Most people think the alpha stays on top out of intimidation, and that's partly true. But once he's the alpha, all the others fall in line and they'll fight to the death to protect him from outsiders."

I want to continue listening to the howls, but the sun is working its way toward the edge of the world, and hunger is starting to leach from my stomach up my arms and down to my fingers. I am ten times weaker than I was a mere hour ago, and I still have a lot of work to do. I must keep on task. I start the auger again.

"You know what I think?" he says. "I think that if an alpha wolf goes missing—say he doesn't join the pack when he's expected—I think the other wolves will come looking for him. That's what I think."

I lift my eyes to the northern shore again. I know what he's doing. He's still trying to get inside my head—and I'm letting him in. His wolf story has me scanning the horizon for boogey men. It's a ridiculous notion, I know. He sees me looking and it pisses me off.

"I think you should just let me go," he says. "We can let bygones be bygones. You still have time."

"If you think a veiled threat is enough to bring this to a halt, you have misjudged the current," I say. "You have friends? I'll be more than happy to entertain them if they show up. But I'm thinking you might not be as popular as you think."

"Friends? What are you talking about?" he says. "I was making a comment about wolves. You're not making sense, Detective."

"How about you shut the hell up," I say. "I'm getting sick of your yammering."

"And I'm getting sick of this bullshit," he shoots back, his words dripping with challenge. "What are you going to do to me if I don't shut up? You going to kill me twice? You think you have what it takes to kill me? Bring it. Otherwise, fuck you, Detective. And fuck your wife, too—what's her name again? Jenni?"

"I said shut up!"

"Yeah, fuck Jenni. Fuck her."

I dive at the man and punch him in the face. Grabbing his throat with my left hand, I punch twice more, and when I raise my fist for a fourth blow, I hold off.

I expect to see fear, or maybe a grimace of pain. Instead, he's looking at me with calculating eyes. He knows he's gotten to me. I relax my grip, and a slight smirk crosses his face. There is blood trickling from his nostril, and his left eye has already begun to puff up.

I stand, walk back to the auger, and start to turn it again.

He spits out some blood and says, "You think I'm a monster, but what are you? I'm wounded. I'm tied up. I can't defend myself, and you jump on me and beat me? You must be so proud. Your wife must be so proud of you too."

I grunt and turn the crank harder, hoping to drown out his voice.

"You tell yourself that you're doing what you have to—stomping out evil in the world—but which of us is the monster here? I'm willing to put my cards on the table. You think you know something, well, give me your proof. I dare you. Show me what you got, because I'm betting you have nothing. I'm betting you won't say a word because you're afraid I'll prove you wrong. Kill me without a trial? You're the monster here."

I stop turning the auger and look at him, my face devoid of all expression, and say, "You may be right about that, but that doesn't bode very well for you, now does it?"

I'm getting closer to the bottom of my fourth hole, so I get down on one knee and drill from that position. He can see my exhaustion, but I don't care.

"Talk to me, dammit. What did I do? How did I kill your wife? Give me a chance."

The noise of the blade isn't enough to drown out his voice, and I can hear reverberations of panic and desperation in his words. He's scared. He's trying to get to me, but I'm getting to him. He knows I'll do it.

Time and pressure.

I'm almost through to the lake, and I double my effort.

"This isn't justice. This isn't right. You can't do this to me."

I break through to the lake with my fourth hole.

"For Christ's sake!" He's pleading now as a ripple of lake water washes up to touch his heels. "Give me a chance to defend myself! Give me a chance to prove that I didn't kill your wife. I'm begging you. I didn't do it. I swear to God, I didn't do it."

I look at the fifth starter hole. My palms are raw from pressing down on the cap of the auger. There's no way I'll have all eight holes drilled before it gets dark, and I still haven't gathered my stones. That's a task I cannot do in the dark.

"Talk to me," he says.

I walk over and pick up the snowmobile cover, the pouch to hold the stones that will carry him to the bottom of the lake.

"What are you doing with that?"

I take the auger with me so I can drop it far enough away that he can't reach it. No sense leaving a blade—even one that dull—lying around to tempt him with thoughts of escape. As I'm walking away, I look over my shoulder and say, "I'll be right back."

CHAPTER 23

Minneapolis—Yesterday

I had planned to be back at the office by noon, but that wasn't going to happen. Just as I finished my meeting with Farrah McKinney, I got a call from Mr. Clark, the security officer from HCMC, letting me know that he'd found the Burn Unit footage from that morning. Clark, whose first name I learned was Dan, seemed a different man on my second visit: polite, helpful. I'd even go so far as to say friendly. He led me to a little breakroom adjacent to his office, where he had set up a laptop.

"I have it loaded on there." He pointed at the computer. I can have someone from tech burn you a disc when they get here."

"I appreciate this very much, Dan," I said.

He lined the cursor up on a play button and clicked it. "Enjoy," he said. Then he closed the door, leaving me alone.

I watched for several minutes as men and women in scrubs moved from room to room at a casual pace, chatting and typing on computers at the nurse's station. Nothing remarkable. Then, about seven minutes into the footage, a man entered the frame, wearing a suit jacket, dress pants, and a baseball cap pulled low over his eyes, the bill of the cap casting a shadow over his face. The man spoke to a nurse, who pointed at Orton's door. The man then walked into Orton's room, not removing his cap until it was too late for a camera to catch his face. There was something in his gait, in his avocado-shaped midsection, that looked familiar. He could be any one of a million men, but I believed him to be one particular man.

Every few seconds, his shadow would brush across the floor outside Orton's door. The man must be pacing in the room. He was anxious. Then, eighteen minutes into the footage, the shadow appeared at the door again and stayed there for a few seconds. I waited.

He walked out of Orton's room, his hand fiddling with the bill of his cap until he fixed it over his eyes again. I hit pause and walked it back frame by frame. Click. Click. Click. The man lifted his cap. Click. Click. The bill of the cap cleared his forehead enough to show his face. I zoomed in and smiled.

I got you, you bastard.

I borrowed Dan Clark's laptop and walked to my car to retrieve the footage of Orton pouring gas on his girlfriend. Then I returned to the Burn Unit and with the flash of my badge, I strolled into Dennis Orton's room.

"You're not supposed to be here," he said. "I asked for an attorney. They said you can't talk to me."

"Relax, Dennis, I'm not here to question you."

I opened the laptop and popped the Holiday-store CD into the tray. My refusal to leave apparently took Orton off guard because I could see a hint of desperation pull at the corners of his eyes. "I'm not talking to you," he said. "I'm not saying a word."

"Then might I suggest that you shut the hell up?" I said. "Let's get something straight, Dennis. I don't want you to talk. Understand? Anything you say will get kicked out of court anyway. I want you to sit there and be quiet. I'm just going to play you a little movie. You'll like it." I cued up the footage of Orton pulling into the gas station. Then I gently placed the laptop on his stomach, adjusting the screen so he could see it.

"You see, Dennis, I don't want you to talk because I don't need a confession. I have everything I need right here. That minivan there?" I pointed to the screen and checked to see that he was watching the video. "That's Pippa Stafford's minivan. And that's you getting out of the driver's side. I guess you needed some gas, huh."

Orton's eyes began to grow large, and his bottom lip took on a slight quiver. We watched as he pumped gas into the gas tank of the minivan.

"Dennis," I said in a soft voice. "You know what happens next. Pippa is dead in the back seat. You choked her to death. You crushed her larynx. Did you know that? It takes a bit of force to crush a larynx—the kind of force that comes with rage."

Tears welled up in his eyes, soaking into the gauze bandages covering his face.

Interviewing technique 101: First, make the suspect believe you know everything.

"And there you go," I said sitting up and pointing at the screen again. "You're pouring gasoline directly into the back seat. You're dousing your dead girlfriend's body. You probably thought it was a perfect plan, but you're really bad at this. You're a complete dunce when it comes to committing murder. You couldn't have made it easier for us if you tried."

Orton watched the video and saw himself return the nozzle to the pump, get into the driver's seat, and drive away.

"You see, Dennis, gasoline is a . . . well it's a gas. A fume. When you got back into that vehicle, you were dousing yourself with gasoline too. You just didn't know it. You were done-for the second you lit that lighter."

Second, make the suspect believe you sympathize—that you are on his side.

"And that's why I know you're not an evil man, Dennis. You were just reacting. You didn't plan all of this, I can see that. I don't know what happened between you and Pippa—and I don't want to know. Things get out of hand sometimes. We all do stuff we don't mean to do. I get that. All we can do is try and do the right thing going forward."

He was in a full-blown cry now, the flush of tears filling his eyes and spilling over in rivulets, spit collecting in the corners of his lips, and snot seeping from his nose.

"You want to see it again?" I asked.

"No. Please, don't."

"Like I said, Dennis, I'm not here to get a confession. I don't need one. Hell, we have video."

I pulled the digital recorder from my pocket, turned it on, and placed it on the edge of the bed. Then I lifted the laptop from his stomach and click on the Burn Unit footage.

"But, Dennis, I do have a problem you might be able to help me with. Has nothing to do with Pippa, but I could really use your help."

"Help with what?"

"Yesterday, you and I had a little chat about what happened to Pippa. That's when you told me that cock-and-bull story about the gangs. Now, I don't want to rehash all that. I don't want you to say a word about that. Am I clear?"

He nodded.

"We're agreed about that, Dennis?"

"Yes."

"Well, this morning I came back to chat some more and all of a sudden you wanted a lawyer. And that's just fine. You're entitled to have one. But what concerns me is why you changed your mind. Who told you to get a lawyer?"

With that, Orton's eyes sharpened and he stopped crying.

"You see, I know who it was." *That was true.* "And I know what he said." *That was not true.*

I put the laptop back onto Orton's stomach, being careful not to irritate his injured skin. I showed him the man on the screen. "I just want to understand why Lieutenant Emil Briggs would come all the way over here to tell you to lawyer up."

Orton looked at the face on the screen, the picture zoomed in to its clearest resolution. There was no mistaking Briggs. Orton's eyes danced back and forth between the screen and my face.

"And, Dennis, I need the truth about this. You already know you're a terrible liar. So tell me—what is your connection to Briggs?"

Orton looked at the ceiling and didn't answer.

"Dennis, I said a bit ago that I don't think you're an evil man. I meant it. But this . . . this thing with Briggs . . ."

"I know I'm going to prison," he said, somewhat out of the blue. I let that statement hang in the air while Orton gathered his thoughts. "And when they take these bandages off of me, I'll see the scars of what I did. My face will be the face of a murderer. Every day, when I look in the mirror, I'll see the reminder of what I did, what I am. I've had to live with guilt before, Detective, and I know that I'm no good at it. I can't live with this."

"What's that got to do with Briggs?"

Orton closed his eyes, as if pulling up a memory before he spoke. Then in a low whisper, he said, "Emil Briggs and I met in college. We were in the same fraternity. I was a couple years ahead of him, so we didn't hang out all that much. To be honest, I thought he was a bit of a douche."

Orton smiled, and I wanted to tell him how accurate his assessment had been, but I held my tongue.

"After I graduated, I didn't give him much thought. Never figured on seeing him again. Then, about six years ago, right after I got the job as the deputy chief of staff to the mayor, Briggs shows up at my door. Wants to grab a beer. I thought, what the hell. We'd do a little catching up, tell some stories about the good ol' days. I figured that would be that."

"I take it that *wasn't* that?"

"No, it wasn't. As the evening wore on, he got weirdly serious and asked me where I saw myself in ten years. I told him that I would like to be on the city council down the road, and, who knows, maybe even run for mayor one day. Then he tells me about how he wants to move up through the ranks and become the chief of police. This is a guy still wearing a patrol uniform and talking about becoming the chief of police. I think, well, it's okay to dream, right?"

"But this isn't just some idle dream for Briggs, is it?"

"No. It's not. He had this whole plan worked out. You see, getting elected to the city council is a shoo-in if you have the chief of police on your side. He said that if he was the chief, he'd back me up. In turn, I needed to use my influence with the mayor to move him up the ladder."

"That's quite ambitious," I said. "Lots of variables. Lots of things could go wrong."

"But it was working. Briggs may be a douche, but he knows how to maneuver. I've never seen anything like it." Orton gave a half smile and turned to look at me. "He was particularly worried about you, Detective. He said that if you ever wanted to challenge him, he'd have trouble."

"He worried for nothing," I said.

"That was Briggs, though. Always thinking six moves ahead."

"And this morning, what exactly did he say to you?"

"He told me not to talk to you until he figured out how bad it was. He wanted to help me. He told me to sit tight and not give you any more rope. You see, Briggs owed me a favor—a big one. He came here to pay off that debt."

"What kind of debt are we talking about?"

Orton looked away from me again, as if ashamed by what he was about to tell me. "You see, five years ago he invited me to go to WE Fest with him—his dime."

"The country music deal up in Detroit Lakes?"

"Yeah. I thought, like me, he was a fan of country music, but that wasn't the case. He just wanted to get away from his wife for a weekend. Chase some tail, you know? I hated that about him—he used me to cover for his infidelity. He didn't even ask. He just assumed I'd be okay with that. What a dick."

Orton looked at me, maybe seeking a sign that I agreed with him, which I did, so I nodded.

"And then, on the second night of the festival, he meets this woman, better-looking than what you'd expect from Emil. And, of course, he gives her a fake name, calls himself Joe Something-or-other. They spend the day making out and drinking, and then Emil tells me he and . . . I can't even remember her name anymore. Anyway, they decided to drive out to the country to find some privacy. About half an hour later, I get a call. There's been an accident. He needs me to come get him. So I go and I find him standing beside the wreck of a black car. It's down an embankment far enough that you can't see it from the road. The woman is unconscious—in pretty bad shape. The car's upside down, and she's lying on the ceiling."

"Who was driving?"

Orton gives me a look. "Who do you think was driving? He lied at first, but when I started calling 911, he stopped me. He said he'd been behind the wheel when they crashed. He wanted to leave her there. If the cops came and saw him all banged up, they'd do a deeper investigation with DNA and stuff. They'd know he was the driver. But if they found her alone, they'd assume she was driving and close the books."

"You went along with it?"

"Worst mistake of my life . . . well, until . . . you know."

"Briggs was drunk?"

"Drunk enough to make it a felony."

"Criminal vehicular injury."

"That's what he said. Before I got there, he had adjusted the seat and steering wheel and mirrors to fit the woman's height. He cleaned her makeup off the passenger airbag and . . . and Briggs even smeared her face against the driver's airbag. I can't believe I ever went along with it."

I could see a tug of emotion pulling at the corners of Orton's mouth.

I asked, "Did the woman die?"

"No. I drove him about a mile away, sent him into the woods to wait while I called the ambulance. She was in pretty bad shape, but nothing permanent. The cops figured I was just a Good Samaritan passing by. When the dust all settled, the woman couldn't remember much about the accident. She got convicted of a DWI even though she swore that some guy named Joe was driving the car."

"And Briggs gets off scot-free," I said.

"He cleaned the scene up pretty good, except . . ."

"Except?"

"I've never really trusted Briggs. As you probably know, he can be a real snake."

"You have something?"

"When he called me from the accident scene, I didn't hear my phone over the music, so I didn't pull it out of my pocket fast enough. He left a message. It's short, but it's enough. He gives his location. It's his voice. He admits to being in an accident."

"And you still have that recording?"

"I saved it on my computer at home—just in case."

"Mr. Orton, do I have your permission to go to your home and secure your hard drive?"

"Yeah. My computer is under my rolltop desk. You have my permission."

"Dennis, if you don't mind my asking, why are you telling me all this?"

"Truth is, Detective, I don't like Emil Briggs. For five years, I've had to live with what we did. That poor woman didn't deserve what she got. He shouldn't have put me in that position. And it never seemed to bother him. Not in the least. I should have cut the cord a long time ago, but I thought I might need him if I ever ran for city council. I let on that we were friends, but, deep down, I wish I'd never met the man."

"The fact that you have a conscience about all this is a good sign, Dennis. I'm not going to soft-pedal it. You're going to have a tough go from here on out."

"I really did love Pippa," he said. "I would have walked through fire for her."

I looked at his burns and bandages and wondered if he was trying to be ironic.

I stopped the interview. I had gotten what I needed on Briggs, although I violated Orton's *Miranda* rights to get it. Everything he said to me would be kept out of any trial, but this wasn't about a trial. I wasn't there to gather evidence against Orton. His guilt was a foregone conclusion. My sole purpose for talking to Dennis Orton was to get the ammunition I needed to protect Niki. What I was doing might have been against the rules, but, in my view, it was a long way from being wrong.

I shut off the recorder and was packing up Dan Clark's laptop when Orton asked, "You see me as a monster, don't you?"

"That's not my call, Dennis. I just put the cases together."

"Doesn't matter. I am a monster. I killed the woman I love. You ever love someone so much that the very thought of living without her makes you stop breathing? Have you ever loved someone that much, Detective?"

I didn't answer.

"I had this great evening planned," he said. "Flowers, dinner, a concert. Then, out of the blue, she tells me that it's over. She's been seeing someone else behind my back. I was blind-sided, didn't see it coming. She said she loved him—not me."

Orton turned his head away from me and stared at the gray sky outside of his hospital window. When he spoke again, his voice barely rose above a whisper, and I had to lean in to hear him.

"I was so angry. I . . . I grabbed her by the throat. I wanted to stop her from saying those things. I wanted her to stop loving this other man. I squeezed and squeezed. I just wanted to stop the pain. And when I stopped squeezing, Pippa was dead. I watched her life drain away. I wasn't out of control. I could have stopped, but I didn't. I killed her to satisfy my own selfish needs. I can't live with that."

"You can live with it, Dennis," I said. "You'd be amazed what a man can live with."

"I suppose that's true," he whispered. "But why would anyone want to live with that on their conscience?"

CHAPTER 24

Thanks to Dennis Orton, I now held a grenade to use in my approaching knife fight with Briggs—not forgetting, however, that a knife could kill no matter how many grenades I held. The time had come to get comfortable in that mud pit where Briggs spent his days. Like Orton said, Briggs always thought six moves ahead. I need to do the same.

Some years ago, Boady Sanden gave me a book, a small treatise on ancient Chinese battle tactics called *The Art of War*, by Sun Tzu. I never turn down a gift, but for the life of me I couldn't figure out why Boady thought I'd have the least bit of interest in battle tactics used before the invention of gun powder. After I read it, I understood. The ideas in that book reached far beyond the battlefields. I summoned my memories of Sun Tzu as I drove back to City Hall.

Six moves ahead.

When I got back to Homicide, I went to the evidence room and pulled a computer hard drive from a closed case that hadn't yet been sent to the archive room. I peeled the evidence stickers off of the drive and slipped it into the side pocket of my jacket. Then I went to my cubicle and plugged my digital recorder into my computer to copy my interview with Dennis Orton. You can never have enough backups of something that explosive. I was just finishing with the copy when Niki walked in the office.

"Any luck finding Kroll's voice?" I asked.

"It took a while but..." She pulled a CD from her purse and twirled it in her fingers.

"He talks? You can hear him?"

"Loud and clear. He doesn't say a lot, but it's good-quality." She handed me the CD.

"How'd your meeting with Farrah McKinney go?" Niki asked.

I opened the CD tray and laid Niki's CD inside. "Zoya was terrified that she would be killed by a man named Mikhail. Farrah found a recording of Zoya saying that she wants to go home to Lida. Mikhail might be from there. Who knows, maybe he's Russian mafia or something."

"Lida?"

"A town in Belarus." I click to start the CD from the court proceeding. We listen as the case is called by the clerk.

"The next case is State of Minnesota versus Raymond Alan Kroll, file number—"

A boom echoed through the office as Lieutenant Briggs slammed open his door. "Rupert! Vang! In my office now!"

He was standing in his doorway, his hands on his hips and legs squared up as if he were doing his level best to fill the space, his face already approaching pomegranate red. I clicked off the CD and turned to Niki, who was giving me a look that said: *Here it comes*.

She started to stand up, but I put my hand on her shoulder and shook my head no.

"Coming, Lieutenant!" I hollered back. And then to Niki I whispered, "Do you trust me?"

"Of course I do, but—"

"Stay here."

"What?"

"I'm going to have a chat with Briggs. Can I borrow your recorder?"

"Don't you have one?"

"Yeah, but I need two: one to play and one to record."

She pulled a small digital recorder out of her purse and handed it to me. "What's going on?"

I hit the record button and slid the thumb-sized piece of technology into my shirt pocket. "I can't tell you," I said. I adjusted my jacket to cover my pocket, trying to find a balance between hiding and smothering.

"You're going to do something stupid, aren't you?"

I smiled my calmest smile and said, "Nothing stupid. I promise. But I need you to stay here and trust me."

She nodded without saying another word.

I stood, took a deep breath, and walked into Briggs's office.

Six moves ahead.

Briggs sat behind his desk, waiting for Niki and me, his desktop cleared of any distractions. He'd been preparing for this meeting—but so had I. He looked confused when I entered alone.

"Where's Vang?"

I closed the door. "She's not coming."

"What do you mean she's not coming?"

"I mean that this conversation is between us and will remain that way—if you're smart."

"Are you out of your mind? Do you have any idea how much trouble you're in? And you dragged Niki into the mess with you." He slammed his hand on the desktop. "Go get her and bring her in here now!"

Briggs's reaction made me smile as I remembered how Sun Tzu wrote that an enemy who makes a lot of noise, clanging his sword against his shield, is showing that he is weak. "No, Briggs," I said calmly. "Niki stays out of this."

"You can't—just who the hell do you think you are?" Tiny drops of spit sailed from Briggs's mouth as his anger climbed toward a full-blown conniption. "I know what you've been up to, Rupert. I know all about it."

"Yeah, and what have I been up to?"

"You've been snooping around in your wife's case again." His lips tightened against his teeth as he seethed. "I'm going to go to Chief Murphy and recommend that Detective Vang be reprimanded and that you be suspended—and after this show of insolence, I may change my recommendation to termination. Now go get Vang or clean out your desk."

"Are you done?"

"That's it, Rupert. I've had all I can take." Briggs picked up the phone hit the top button of his preset numbers, a line that would connect him directly to Chief Murphy's office.

"Did you go see Dennis Orton this morning?" I spoke my words like a man asking nothing more than what time it was. He had no idea that I was leading him toward a battlefield, one that I had selected. This fight would be on my terms, not his.

Briggs hung up the phone before the chief's assistant could answer. He looked like a man who'd just walked into an invisible wall, his eyes blinking hard to wipe away the confusion. I could see him trying to move game pieces around in his head. What did I know about his visit to Orton? How could he explain it away?

"Are you accusing me of something, Detective?"

He didn't answer my question, so I didn't answer his. "Tell me, Briggs, have you been involving yourself in my investigation?"

"What investigation are you talking about?"

"The minivan case, as you called it. Have you been sticking your nose into things you shouldn't?"

"I'm the one asking the questions, Rupert. If you have any desire to remain a detective here, you'd better remember who you are and who I am."

I pulled a folded piece of paper from my pocket, a printed shot of Briggs leaving Orton's hospital room, a souvenir given to me by my new friend, Dan Clark at HCMC Security. I moved in slow, deliberate motions as I unfolded the picture and slid it across Briggs's desk.

At first, Briggs leaned away from the picture like it might be radioactive. Then he picked it up, squinting to get a better look.

"Recognize that face?"

He didn't answer.

"Because I do and so will Chief Murphy—and my friends at WCCO."

"Where did you get this?"

"Why did you go to see Dennis Orton?" I ask.

I must lock him in on his lies. Cut off all of his escape routes before making the final attack.

"I didn't. I . . . I went there to see if he was still intubated. I wanted to see if you were lying to me again. It's your penchant for lying that—"

"You didn't talk to him?"

"No. Why would I talk to him?"

"That's right. What would you possibly have to say to a guy like that?"

"I didn't say anything to him. I just wanted to see if you were being straight with me."

"So you didn't say a word to your buddy Dennis Orton?"

"My buddy? I don't know what you're talking about. He's not my buddy."

"You didn't go to college together?"

Now Briggs could see the trap coming. I wouldn't have that kind of knowledge unless I did my homework and already knew about the relationship. Briggs leaned back in his chair, cuing up his next lie.

He said, "Detective, you know damned well that Mr. Orton and I went to college together. You wouldn't be asking the question if you didn't know. But that doesn't change the fact that I went there to see if you were doing your job. You tend to get sloppy in your investigations when you're distracted by the past. But don't worry, Rupert. After you're terminated, you can spend all the time you want chasing your wife's ghost."

My chest tightened as thoughts of beating this man to a pulp flashed by. He was trying to provoke me. I refused his bait. Shoving my emotion aside, I got back to the game.

"You say you didn't talk to Orton, yet I have a nurse telling me he heard you having a conversation." A lie, but Briggs was off balance and I wanted to take advantage of it.

"I . . . I may have said hello."

"A conversation, Briggs. The nurse heard back-and-forth. I have video of you in that room for almost twenty minutes. That's not just saying hello."

"Okay, we spoke, but I never—"

"So you were lying just now when you denied talking to Orton."

"As I said, we went to college together. I only asked him how he was doing. That's all."

"No, that's not all. You told him to stop talking to me."

"That's a God-damned lie." Briggs tried to take the offensive. "I would never impede an investigation. And if you tell anyone differently, you're a liar. It's slander. If you utter a word about that to anyone, I'll sue your ass."

I smiled and lifted the digital recorder from my pocket, the one with Orton's confession on it. I gently laid it on the desk in front of me. "Are you sure that's the answer you want to stick with?"

Briggs tried to act calm, but the darting of his eyes, bouncing from me to the recorder and back, gave away his fear. I hit play.

Briggs turned ashen when he recognized Orton's voice. I watched his expression melt from anger to fear as we listened in silence. When the recording was finished, I turned it off and returned it to my pocket, along with the photograph.

"Orton's a liar," Briggs said. "That bullshit about WE Fest—I never—what kind of game are you playing here, Rupert? You violated *Miranda*. You got him to make up a pack of lies. What did you promise him?"

"No, Briggs. That's not going to fly. You can't spin your way out of this."

"You have nothing. The word of a murderer."

I reached into my pocket and pulled out the hard drive, holding it up for Briggs to see. "I have your voice," I say. "You give the location of the accident. It will be easy enough to get the accident reports from five years ago. You nearly killed some poor woman, and then you stand by and watch her get convicted of your DWI. Hell, you dodged a charge of criminal vehicular injury."

My bluff of the hard drive hit him hard, and I could see him floundering to find a way out.

"How are you going to prove that I was drunk? Go ahead and report it. The worst I'll get is reckless driving."

"You're missing the big picture here, Briggs. You interfered with a murder investigation, and you did it to repay a debt to Dennis Orton. The WE Fest accident merely corroborates Orton's version. You're screwed."

"It's the word of a murderer against mine," Briggs said. He was trying to come across as confident, but it wasn't working.

"I think we should test that theory," I said. "I'll turn all this over to the press, and we'll see how many people believe you. We could put a wager on it. Think about it, Briggs. The second in command of the Homicide Unit actively working to thwart a murder investigation as payback for a criminal cover-up. You were helping a murderer."

"No, I wasn't."

"You told him to shut up. You were looking for a way to get Orton out of trouble."

"Don't get carried away, Max. You have your back against the wall as much as I do."

"My back's to the wall? How do you figure?"

"You were investigating your wife's case. That's enough to get you fired. I'm willing to make a deal here. I'll turn a blind eye to your improper investigation, and you forget about that recording in your pocket. If you pull your trigger, you'll force me to pull mine. Let's call it a Mexican standoff and walk away."

"Mexican standoff?"

"You look past my mistake, and I'll look past yours."

I leaned into his desk and looked him in the eye. "The thing about a Mexican standoff—Briggs—is that it won't work if one of the men doesn't care if he gets shot. You figured me all wrong if you think I'd give a goddamn about getting fired. Your downfall, on the other hand, will be a spectacular thing—public and humiliating." My words bounced with laughter as I spoke. "You'll be torched in the press. This might even make the national news. Think about it, Briggs—CNN. You could become famous."

"You're bluffing. You need this job every bit as much as I do. You're nothing if they take that badge away."

"Wrong answer, Briggs."

I reached across his desk and picked up the phone receiver, punching the direct line to Chief Murphy. Murphy's assistant answered.

"Yes. This is Detective Max Rupert calling, is Chief Murphy available?"

Briggs snatched the phone from my hand and slammed it back to its cradle. He had no more cards to show. We both knew it was over. His voice quivered when he spoke next.

"You can't do this."

"What the hell were you thinking, Briggs?"

"I messed up. I'm sorry. Please don't—"

"Once the story's out, there's no police department in the world that would hire you. Hell, forget law enforcement. Any company that checks your name on the Internet will see the articles. You'll be a pariah—and all because of your damned ambition."

"Why are you doing this to me? Please, I'm begging you. Don't do this to me."

One of the most valuable lessons that I learned from reading Sun Tzu was that if your enemy is cornered, they may lash out. Instead of boxing them in, give them a path through which to escape and you can lead them to any place you desire.

"Okay, Briggs, here's what's going to happen," I said. "You will tender your resignation to Chief Murphy."

"I . . . I can't," His voice limped weak past his lips.

"You will, and you'll do it today—right now."

He stared at me in confusion, as if my words hung in the air just beyond his grasp.

"I'm giving you a gift here, Briggs. I'm letting you make up whatever lie you want to explain why you're leaving. You may even have a career in law enforcement down the road, but that career won't be here."

"This is not right," he said. "I worked too hard to—"

"Briggs." I spoke sharply to pull him out of his haze. "You need to start typing that resignation letter. I'm done talking."

"I . . . I can't."

I pulled Niki's recorder out of my pocket and wiggled it for Briggs to see before turning it off. "If you won't resign, then you leave no alternative. I'm heading down to Murphy's office." I stood. "When the dust all settles, just remember that I gave you a way out."

I turned and walked toward the door.

"Stop!"

Briggs had his eyes closed. His hands squeezed the arms of his chair. I waited. Then he slowly opened his eyes and reached for his keyboard, his fingers trembling as he clicked open his e-mail. He stared at the screen for a moment and began composing.

Briggs typed in spurts, pausing every few seconds to ponder. I suspect he was trying to find a way out of his predicament. The further he got into his resignation letter, the more difficulty he had breathing, at one point closing his eyes and heaving as if he'd just been punched in the gut. After typing for the better part of ten minutes, he turned to me and I could see the tears that clung to the red sags forming under his eyes.

"Please, Max. We can work this out. I have friends. Please don't do this."

"You have nothing to offer me, because you have nothing I want. Your friends won't impress me."

"But Chief Murphy is weak. I could make you the heir apparent. I can do that."

"Are you finished with that letter?"

"You could be the chief of police for the City of Minneapolis. Think about it."

"Let me read it."

Briggs slowly turned his computer screen to me. I could see that the e-mail was properly addressed to Chief Murphy with a copy to Human Resources. I read it out loud.

Dear Chief Murphy,

I am writing to inform you of my resignation from the Minneapolis Police Department, effective immediately. I know this is sudden, but for personal reasons I must tender my resignation. My reasons for this decision will remain undisclosed, and I will not partake in an exit interview. It has been my honor to serve such a distinguished organization, and I will always cherish my time here. Thank you for all that you have done for me over the years.

Sincerely,
Emil Briggs

When I finished reading it, I turned the screen back to Briggs and said, “Send it.”

“Please, Max, I’m begging you. Please. I’ll give you—”

I slammed my palm on the desk. “I said . . . send it.”

I watched as he directed his cursor to the send tab. He closed his eyes and clicked. The e-mail disappeared from his screen.

I had nothing more to say to Briggs. I stood up and left his office to the sound of a grown man whimpering and sniffling like a child.

Fucking politics.

CHAPTER 25

Up North

How many rocks does it take to keep a body at the bottom of a lake? I should know the answer to this. I've been trained on water deaths and handled at least five drowning cases that I can remember. Minneapolis, after all, is the City of Lakes. I try to revisit those trainings, but the knowledge that I'm looking for remains out of reach.

A body will sink if it is less dense than the water around it. I know that. It makes a difference whether the lungs have air in them or water. A drowning victim is more likely to sink than a victim who is killed somewhere else and later thrown into the water. But after a body sinks, the process of decay creates gasses, which will fill up certain cavities and bring the body back to the surface. So the question isn't how much weight would it take to send a body to the bottom of a lake, but how much weight would it take to keep him there.

In all my trainings, no one has ever answered that question.

I spread out the snowmobile cover at the edge of the lake and climb onto shore. With my foot I push snow to the side, sweeping my leg back and forth until my toe hits on something. Brushing snow away, I find my first rock, about the size of a cantaloupe. I have to hit it with my heel to dislodge it. Then I heave it about twenty feet, landing it in the middle of the snowmobile cover, and go back to sweeping my foot in search of another rock.

What are you doing? Nancy asks.

I know it's not Nancy—she died two years ago at her sister's house in Florida—but there's poetic logic to hearing my doubts animated by the one person who knew me before I became so sure of myself. I probably shouldn't, but I answer that voice in my head.

"I'm doing what I have to do," I say out loud.

My foot bumps against another rock, this one a little bigger than the last. I work it out of the frozen ground and weigh it in my hands. "About ten pounds, don't you think?" I ask that of Nancy, who, I know, is nothing more than a phantom of my conscience, a nagging vestige of my younger, more idealistic self—someone I thought I'd packed away long ago. The quiet must be getting to me. Away from the man and his ranting, my mind wants to pull memories out of the shadows where they've been hiding. I attempt to push them back with the sound of my own voice.

"Let's see . . . ten pounds for this rock and maybe eight for the first one. Eighteen. And how many will I need? Let's say I match his weight . . . I'm guessing a buck eighty."

Max, do you hear yourself?

"Yeah, one eighty, I'd say. Now I have eighteen pounds . . . and . . . that means . . ."

You're not going to go through with this, Max. That's not who you are.

"You don't know who I am," I say. I'm angry and at the same time a little unnerved.

I know you, Max.

"You left twenty years ago," I say to the air around me. "Hell, I was just a kid when you knew me." I find another rock, another ten-pounder, and toss it to my small pile.

I didn't feel like I was a kid when Nancy left, but looking back now, twenty years old seems so young. She moved out the day after Alexander graduated from high school. She'd fulfilled her unspoken promise to take care of me and my brother. With Alexander old enough to set his own course, she kissed us both good-bye and headed for warmer climes. Our father didn't show up to see her off. By that time, he was absent even when he sat in the same room as we did.

I find my fourth rock, and it is larger than the other three. I contemplate whether to take it. I question if it might cause a jam when I slip it through the hole. I decide that it will work, and I kick at it with my heel.

You can't kill him. You know that.

"I know no such thing," I say. I try to dismiss the memory. She knew me as a boy, not as a man. She's from that part of my past during which I lived in truths of black and white. Now I know that we live in a world of gray. We are the ones in charge of the balancing. We are the reckoners. The only question to be answered is: can one live with the aftermath? The men who killed Jenni had to understand that. They knew the rules. What this man had coming is nothing more than what he should have expected.

And that gives you the right to take his life from him?

I sit down to put my foot against the stubborn rock and push. It lifts out of its home, flat on the bottom, which will make it easier to fit it through the hole in the ice. I pick it up, struggle to my feet, and head toward the lake. "Yes," I say. "That gives me the right to take his life from him. It gives me all the right I need."

Would Jenni think so?

I stumble in the snow, falling headfirst to the ground, the rock sliding down the embankment and coming to rest on the edge of the lake. I don't want to hear those words, so I fill my head with the task of adding weights. "Twenty pounds," I say. I'm out of breath, and I start to cough as I roll onto my butt. "At least twenty pounds." I speak out loud as I add the weights together, hoping to shush the echo of that last question. "That was eighteen and ten . . . twenty-eight . . . and . . ." It's all a muddle. I can't keep track of the numbers. I haven't eaten since . . . when was it? Yesterday. And I need sleep. It's been too long.

I see the rock below my feet, and I slide down and pick it up. "Twenty pounds. That's right. Plus . . . um . . . what was it? Yeah, twenty-eight. That's about fifty pounds so far. About a third of the way."

I drop the rock with the others.

Would Jenni think you have the right to kill this man?

"Jenni's not here," I say.

I start a new path up the embankment and quickly find an outcropping of stones just the right size. "Ten pounds. Twelve pounds. Fifteen. That's, what . . . thirty-seven . . . let's call it thirty-five. Here's another fifteen. Now that's fifty, plus the fifty from before. One hundred."

Max, you know that's not an answer.

I don't want to think about it, because I know the answer. Despite my effort to keep the memory quiet, it pries its way past the numbers. We were watching a documentary on politics that day—Jenni loved to follow politics. In this documentary they played the famous 1988 debate in which Michael Dukakis was asked if he would support or oppose the death penalty if his own wife had been raped and murdered. A longtime opponent of the death penalty, Dukakis said that it would make no difference in his position. I made an off-handed remark that Dukakis answered the question wrong.

"How's that wrong if it's the principle he lives by?" Jenni asked.

I hadn't meant to stumble into a political debate, especially given her strong leanings on most issues, but I felt I was on good footing here. "I'm not saying he should give up his principles. But there are two parts to that answer, and he left out the most important part."

"Two parts?"

Jenni turned on the couch to face me, as if readying herself for a contest.

I took a breath and continued. "He should have said that, as a governor or president, the death penalty is wrong, because jurors are human and humans make mistakes. But at the same time, as a man, as a husband, if someone killed my wife, I'd have no qualms about sending that bastard to hell."

I expected Jenni to be impressed with my political savvy, coming up with an answer for Dukakis that would have both preserved his principles and give a voice to the primal need for revenge, a trait that, like it or not, lives in all of us. Instead of being impressed, she furrowed her eyebrows a little and asked, "Would you really?"

"Would I really what?"

"Would you really send the man to hell? Do you think you could end someone's life like that?"

"If someone killed you, yeah, I'd have no problem pulling the switch or plunging the needle into him."

I remember the sad look on her face when I said those words. I got the sense that I'd missed some important point, something so fundamental that it caused Jenni to rethink how she saw me. Then she shook her head and put a hand to my cheek and said, "Don't you see? It's not about the murderer. He's defined himself by what he's done. The question is: how do you define who you are? Vengeance is not justice. It's that simple. I would never want you to kill someone for me. I'd never want you to become someone bad because of me. You're a good man, Max Rupert. Don't ever lose that."

She looked so disappointed. I shrugged and nodded my agreement but made the mental note to myself to never bring up the subject again.

I lose count of my rocks, picking up two more, each a little over ten pounds, and I walk them to the pile. I add up a rough total in my head and figure I'm around one hundred and twenty pounds of weight now. How much weight do I need? One twenty seems like a lot, especially when I think about the burden of dragging those stones a quarter mile over the snow-covered ice. I decide I have enough rocks.

The snowmobile cover has a bowl where the canvass fits over the wind screen. It also has nylon straps to keep the cover secure when it's on a trailer. I put the rocks into the bowl and tie it off with the straps, making a tight bundle.

The toes on my left foot have grown numb from the moisture and cold that has seeped through the broken stitching. I get down on one knee and heave my bundle of stones onto my back, lifting it up as close to my shoulder as I can. It's heavy. When I stand up, my legs shake with exhaustion. But I know that it's not just exhaustion that saps my strength—it's the memory of Jenni.

I came to this frozen lake certain to the very core of my being that I would kill the man who killed my wife. Now, as I walk back to him, carrying these rocks, I also carry the weight of Jenni's words to me: *I'd never want you to become someone bad because of me.*

That memory presses me down and threatens to buckle my knees more than any bundle of rocks ever could.

CHAPTER 26

Minneapolis—Yesterday

The look on Niki's face, as I walked back to our cubicle, told me that she had heard the yelling coming from Briggs's office but didn't know who had won the argument. I smiled to let her know.

"What the hell happened in there?" she said.

I plopped into my chair and ran my hands through my hair, lacing my fingers behind my head. "Briggs resigned."

"He . . . he what?"

"He's out. You don't have to worry about him ever again."

"What did you do? How?"

I shook my head. "It's best you not know. There could be repercussions coming down the pike, and you need to stand clear of it all."

"Still keeping me out."

"Protecting you. It's not the same thing."

"What did you do in there?"

"We had a little come-to-Jesus. Briggs saw the light and decided that his time with us has come to its natural end."

"Why does this strike me as anything but natural? Did you make a deal with that devil?"

"Nothing I can't live with." I put my cursor back to the play button for the CD still waiting in my laptop tray, and steadied myself. "You ready to hear this?"

"Let's do it."

I clicked play and heard the judge speaking.

"Your name is Raymond Alan Kroll?"

"Yes."

The voice sounded right, but one word wasn't enough.

"You've been charged on a five-count complaint with assault in the first degree, assault in the second degree, assault in the third degree, and two counts of assault in the fifth degree. The maximum penalty for the top count is up to twenty years in prison and a fine of up to thirty thousand dollars. Do you understand the charges against you, or would you like to have the charges read aloud in open court today?"

"I understand. I don't want no charges read."

It was the same slow, rusty voice from the phone call; I was sure of it. I played the phone call on my digital recorder and listened to the recording of the Henchman.

Hello?

Yeah, it's me.

The boss said you'd be calling. What's up?

We have a job. I need you to lift a car. Keep it clean. No fingerprints. No DNA. Wear gloves.

I know what I'm doing.

We have to deal with someone right away.

Send a message?

No. Extreme prejudice. Hit-and-run.

Great. Another drop of blood and we do all the work.

This is serious. It's a cop's wife.

A what?

You heard me. She stumbled onto something she shouldn't have. If we don't move fast, we'll all be fucked. I don't like this any more than you do.

When?

Today. 3:00.

Where?

Hennepin County Medical Center. There's a parking garage on the corner of Eighth and Chicago. Meet me on the top floor. I'll fill you in there. I'm not sure if they have cameras at the entrance, so cover your face when you drive in.

"It's him," I said, turning to Niki. "No doubt it's him. He's the Henchman. It's . . ."

Niki's eyes showed horror, not excitement. Her mouth hung open on its hinge, and the rose of her cheeks had fallen pale.

"You okay?" I asked.

"I know that voice," she said in a cold whisper.

"I know. It's Raymond Kroll."

"Not him—the other man. I know his voice."

"The Planner? Are you sure?"

She nodded. "So do you."

"I do?"

"Reece Whitton."

I couldn't move. I stopped breathing. Words and thoughts flung around my head like leaves in a twister. Reece Whitton? That wasn't possible. It made no sense.

"It's Reece," she said. "I'm sure of it."

I remembered, the first time I heard the recording. Something in the Planner's voice sounded familiar, but I couldn't place it. I spoke to him just yesterday, but it didn't hit me. Why would it? It never occurred to me to look within my own circle for the men responsible. But now I heard it. I played the recording again and listened as Reece Whitton planned my wife's murder.

My world took on a spectral shift once I connected Reece's voice to the recording, as though I could now see wavelengths of light that had been hidden to my eyes. Things started to come together in a crush.

"Whitton was the investigator at the hospital," I said. "He would have gotten the call about the girl at HCMC."

"That's why there was no supplemental report in the file."

"And the photos taken by the responding officer . . ."

"Whitton has access to the Cappers system," Niki said. "He's the one who deleted the pictures. He wanted to erase any evidence that Zoya went to the hospital that day."

"But why? Who was Zoya to Whitton? And why kill Jenni?" My thoughts hummed and pinged with such ferocity that it made me dizzy.

Whitton, Kroll, Jenni, Farrah, Zoya—where was the connection? A cop, a thug, a social worker, an interpreter and . . . Zoya.

"Slow down," Niki said. "Let's walk through this."

I took a deep breath. "OK, let's review. There's at least three of them: the Boss, the Planner, and the Henchman. The two guys on the recording are the Planner and the Henchman."

"Whitton and Kroll."

I nod my head, still disbelieving that Whitton could have been involved, even though I heard it with my own ears. "The third person is the Boss. On the recording, Kroll says 'The boss said you'd be calling.' That means there's a third person."

"So Whitton went to HCMC on the morning of Jenni's death," Niki said, her eyes fixed on something far away as she worked it through. "He didn't send a detective; he went himself."

"He must have known about Zoya being thrown through the window before he got the call?"

"Makes sense, but how?"

"And when he gets there, Zoya sees him and shuts down—what did Farrah say?"

"She clammed up when the investigator walked in."

"Zoya recognized Whitton," Niki said.

"But Jenni called Ms. McKinney back. She wanted to set up another meeting for that afternoon, at three thirty."

"She would have called Whitton too," Niki said in a soft, sad voice, almost to herself. "Whitton would have known that Zoya was talking again."

"That's when he put this plan together."

My fingers tapped lightly on the desk, my outward appearance as calm as the ripples in a brook. In my head, however, I fought to see and hear. A scalding red rage drowned out my vision, and in my ears, I couldn't hear past my own thoughts: *I'm going to kill him. I will beat the life out of Reece Whitton. I will track him down and rip him apart with my bare hands and stomp the scraps of his skin and bones into the snow.*

"Max?" I felt Niki's hand on my arm.

"Huh?"

"I asked you a question."

"What?"

"I said, 'What are you going to do now?'"

"You know where Whitton lives?"

"Max, that's not—"

I hit my words harder the second time. "I said, 'Do you know where Whitton lives?'"

"In Kenwood."

"Give me the address." I started stacking the files together: Zoya's, Jane Doe's, everything. There'd be no trace of any of this left behind.

"I'm going with you."

"No, Niki, you're not. Your part ends here." I shove the files into my briefcase, papers stacked helter-skelter, sticking out through the mouth of the case. "If anyone ever asks you, you don't know where I went. You don't know anything. You can't go where I need to go."

"But—"

"Niki!" I barked like a man yelling at a beloved dog to stop it from running into traffic. It hurt me to do it. "I'm going alone."

Niki sat back in her chair, the hurt of my words apparent on her face. It was time for our trail to split into diverging paths. She had to know that I couldn't involve her in what would happen next.

I stood up as a million wishes and regrets swirled in my head. She was my only friend, the last to leave my side. And the time had come to push her away as well.

I turned to leave, feeling certain that I would never see Niki again.

CHAPTER 27

Whitton lived in Kenwood, a neighborhood on the southern edge of Minneapolis, where the houses ran on the more expensive side. His two-story Tudor stood on a fine corner lot overlooking Lake of the Isles. Not the kind of place one might afford on a civil servant's pay. My guess was that Reece came into some side money along the way.

It was just past five o'clock in the evening when I got to his house, parking down the block. Darkness had settled over the City of Minneapolis, and lights were blooming in the windows of the houses around me, random buds of white and yellow, vivid against the darkness. In Whitton's house, a light flicked on, filling the square of a picture window, another, dimmer, light bled from a room deeper in the guts. I didn't see his car, but it made sense that he'd have parked in the garage.

I pulled my Glock from its holster and chambered a round. He won't be expecting me. He doesn't know that I know. I slid the gun back into its holster. I wasn't sure what I would do when he answered the door. I trusted that something in his reaction, in his answers to my questions, would tell me what to do.

I walked down a sidewalk across the street from his house, the frozen Lake of the Isles over my shoulder, the crunch of ice under my shoes. Pausing opposite his house, I stood in the shadow of a streetlight and pictured his face when he'd see me, eyes wide with confusion, then squinting thin as he tried to figure out why I was there. I would pull my gun and be inside before he could put the pieces together.

I looked both ways before crossing the street, even though I knew I was alone in the darkness. Careful not to make a sound, I made my way up to his porch, pressing the doorbell and then resting my hand on the grip of my gun. I heard the muffled padding of someone approaching the door. The porchlight came on. I turned slightly to block the peephole view of my gun and waited.

A click of a lock. The door opened.

A woman stood on the threshold, looking at me with a mixture of curiosity and hesitation. She was stunningly attractive, with long, dark hair falling loose past luminous blue eyes that seemed to hold light. I tried to place her in Whitton's world. She appeared too old, and far too beautiful to be genetically entwined with that pig, so daughter was out. Wife? Girlfriend? Lover? Again, she was far too attractive to be any of those, either.

"Yes?" she said as a question.

"I, um . . . is Reece home?"

"Reece is not here."

She spoke in a heavy accent, Russian or something in that neighborhood. Why did that not surprise me?

"Do you expect him soon?" I asked, not knowing what else to say.

"Who are you?"

"I'm . . . just a coworker. I'll try back later."

I turned around and headed back to my car, muttering curses under my breath. I would wait until Whitton came home. I could be patient. Strategy, not reaction. Intellect, not emotion. That's what I told myself, but that didn't stop me from slamming my fists into the steering wheel as soon as I closed the car door. I thought about leaving, driving around the block. The woman might have been watching me from a window, calling Whitton and screwing up my plans.

I was about to start the car to move to a different vantage point when my phone buzzed in my pocket. I looked at the screen and saw it was Niki. I gave serious thought to not answering. How many ways can I tell her to give up on me? Leave me to my blindfold and my ledge. She was my last tether and she refused to let it be a simple cleave.

"Rupert," I answered.

"Oh, is that how it is now, *Detective*?" No sarcasm. Hurt.

"Yes, that's how it is."

"Well, I called because I thought you might want to know Zoya's last name."

"You know her last name?" I heard a note of excitement in my voice that I didn't mean to put there.

"Yes. It's Savvin."

I returned to my flat tone. "I appreciate that. How'd you find it?"

"I looked on Interpol and other databases for missing persons and had no luck. Then I typed in the name Zoya and Lida, the city you thought she might be from. I found a local website for missing Belarussians. There's not much on her. It says she and her sister left Belarus to take jobs in Canada. They disappeared from Toronto. I'll e-mail you the link."

"Thanks," I said.

I stopped talking and let the silence drag on.

"Max . . . are you okay?"

"I got to go." I ended the call without saying good-bye.

I turned my attention back to the house. Nothing had changed, and I decided not to move my car. I checked my watch. Five thirty. Any minute now.

My phone chirped to let me know that Niki's e-mail came through. I opened e-mail app. Might as well kill some time reading.

I scrolled past rows of Russian letters and words that meant nothing to me—of course it would be written in Russian—until I came to Zoya's picture. There was no question it was her, a little younger than the autopsy photos, and much more beautiful. A high-school class picture, maybe. She wore a mischievous smile, the smile of a girl with plans, the smile of a girl who couldn't fathom a path that would lead to a frozen dumpster in Minneapolis, Minnesota.

I shook my head and scrolled down, looking for more pictures of Zoya. Soon, another picture entered my screen, a face I recognized, but not Zoya. This was a different girl—a girl with luminous blue eyes. I had seen those eyes before. They were the eyes that had greeted me just now when I knocked on Reece Whitton's door.

I tried to understand the connection as I looked back and forth between the picture and the house, summoning my memory from only a few minutes ago. It had to be the same person—a little older now and packaged as a woman—but the same person. Who was she, and what was she doing in Reece Whitton's house?

I toggled to a pop-up at the bottom of the screen that offered to translate the page for me. I hit it and looked at the name under the picture. Anastasia Savvin, the sister of Zoya Savvin. The woman in Reece Whitton's house was Jane Doe's sister.

I grabbed Zoya's file from my case, stepped out of my car, and walked at a brisk pace back to Whitton's front door. Fragments of understanding floated around me, always in my periphery, like fireflies. I wanted answers. She would give me those answers.

The door opened, and this time I held up my badge. "I'm Detective Max Rupert. I need to talk to you."

She didn't smile or ask me in, so I stepped past her.

Her eyes lit with fear. "What are you doing?"

"I want to talk to you about your sister, Zoya."

Fear turned to confusion. "My sister? I don't understand."

"You are Anastasia Savvin, aren't you?"

"I am married now. But I was born Anastasia Savvin, yes."

"Sister to Zoya Savvin?"

"How do you know my sister?"

"I'm investigating her death. I—"

"You are wrong," Anastasia hissed. "You are a liar. Why do you say this to me?" She looked like she was searching my face for proof of my deception. "My sister is not dead. She is home in Lida."

Now it was my turn to search her face for deception. I saw none. This was not going the way I expected it to go. I opened my folder and pulled out the crime-scene photos of Zoya Savvin. I hesitated before handing them to her.

Her reaction started with a slight quiver in her lip. She looked at me as if I might tell her that it was a mistake, that it wasn't her little sister lying pale in that dumpster. Her hands began to shake as she looked again at the picture. Tears flooded her eyes, and the name Zoya escaped from her lips.

She dropped to her knees, her knuckles white as she gripped the picture with all of her strength. "Zoya!" This time it was a howl that filled the house. She collapsed inward, her stomach heaving her words out. "No! No! Zoya, no!" She rocked back and forth on her knees, the picture in a crumpled wreck on the floor. Her breath hammered out of her chest as she wailed in Russian, spitting out words that announced her pain with no need for translation.

I wanted to put an arm around her, comfort her, but I was afraid that any such movement might result in a fight. She was a wounded animal ready to lash out to ease her pain. Then she stopped rocking. Her breath calmed, and she looked up at me with such hatred that I froze.

"Get out," she snarled.

"I have some questions I need to—"

"I said get out!" She stood and grabbed a lamp off of a nearby sofa table.

I opened my mouth to speak, and she launched the lamp at my head.

I raised my arm and took the blow in the forearm. Before I could counter, she had a vase and sent it flying.

"Get out of my house!" she screamed.

I turned to the door as the vase hit me in the back. "Get out!" Her yowling sounded more like a wounded cat than a human. I made it to the door just as a candle stand crashed into the wall beside me. The door slammed shut, and I heard the deadbolt click. And then, from deeper in the house, I heard the animal wail again.

CHAPTER 28

Up North

I plod back toward my little nest in the snow, the bundle of rocks slung over my shoulder, pulling at my arms and wrists and fingers. Twice it slips from my grip and falls behind my heels. With each step I am bludgeoned with thoughts and voices, memories that cut through the fog of time. I start counting my steps out loud, losing track before I get out of double digits. When the bundle falls for a third time, I grip the edge of the snowmobile cover behind my back and drag it through the snow.

Why are you doing this?

Nancy's voice has a way of parting all of other thoughts and demanding attention. I still have a long way to go before I'm back at the nest, so I answer.

"Something has to be done to restore balance to the world."

You're restoring balance to the world? And how will killing this man do that?

"His death will be justice."

Justice? Or vengeance?

"He has to pay a price for what he did."

And you are the one to determine that price?

"He robbed me of my wife—my child. I think I have that right."

Did Mr. Yager have that right?

I shake my head as the memory comes rushing in—as if I could wave it away that easily. I can still remember the drop of sweat that glistened on Mr. Yager's upper lip as I told him that Kristen, his fifteen-year-old daughter, was dead. A tow-truck driver found the girl's body in the trunk of an abandoned car. It was a hot day, the temperature touching one hundred degrees, sweltering for Minnesota. When I told him that she was found in the trunk of a car owned by a man named Victor Nacio, I could see the recognition in his eyes, even as he told me that the name meant nothing to him.

I offered Mr. Yager my condolences and left, driving my car around the block to wait. Two minutes later, Yager came out of his house with a paper bag in his hand, a bag that swung as if it held something heavy—a gun, maybe. I followed him to a flophouse in North Minneapolis. When Yager stepped out of his car, carrying the bag, I debated whether I should stop him. I actually gave voice to the thought of letting his vigilantism be the last word on the death of his daughter. No courts. No judges. No plea bargains.

Yager walked up to the house and peeked into one of the windows. When he put his hand into the paper bag, I ran up and stopped him. I expected a fight, but Yager began crying instead. He fell to his knees, handing me the sack with a gun inside. He kept uttering the words, "He killed my baby. He killed my little girl."

"We'll get justice for Kristen," I told him. "That's our job, not yours. I promise, we'll convict Nacio, and he'll spend the rest of his life in prison."

I found Victor Nacio inside the flophouse, passed out on a couch. When I put him in handcuffs, he wouldn't shut up. He kept asking why he was being arrested. After I told him that I was taking him in for questioning regarding the death of Kristen Yager, he stopped talking all together.

But Nacio never went to prison because Victor Nacio didn't kill Kristen Yager. Rich Molitor, a man who was letting Nacio crash at his house, killed the girl. Molitor had slipped a few clonazepam into the wine that Nacio and Kristen shared that night. Victor Nacio slept in the bowels of a drug-induced blackout while his girlfriend was raped and murdered and stuffed into the trunk of his car.

Victor Nacio was an innocent man.

"I'm not Yager."

You don't make mistakes?

"I didn't make one here. I've come too far. I'm too close. I have to make it right."

You sound like your father.

"I'm not my father."

No, you're not, are you?

And just like that I'm back in fifth grade, crossing the playground to punch Hank Bellows in the nose. I was almost to him when I heard Nancy's words in my head: "You're the one who has to live with what you do." Her voice stopped me in my tracks, and Hank went home from school that day oblivious to how close he came to getting his nose broken.

I put the bundle of rocks down and crouched to catch my breath.

"There's got to be a reckoning," I say. "There's a great many things I can live with, but what I *cannot* live with is the thought of this piece of shit seeing another sunrise. I *cannot* live with the notion that men like him can murder and maim without repercussion."

And what if you're wrong?

"I'm not wrong." I pick up my bundle of rocks again. "He'll confess. I'll make him tell me that he killed Jenni."

My forearms are burning to the point that my grip fails and I sit in the snow to rest. Up ahead, I can see the shadow of the nest, but I can't see the man. He must be lying deep in the snow and out of sight. I'm still far enough away that he can't hear me, but I'm getting too close to keep talking to myself like this.

He wants a chance to defend himself.

I stand up and drag the bundle of rocks to where the auger lay. The wind is notching up, biting where my cheeks and neck are exposed. My left foot is starting to throb from the cold.

"Fine," I say. "I'll give him a trial. He'll lie to me and try to convince me that I'm wrong, but I'll give him his trial."

I wait for Nancy to answer back, maybe applaud my magnanimity or chide me for some unseen flaw in my offer. I wait, but I hear nothing other than the wind. She is gone from my head, and I can tell that she is gone for good. Her absence leaves me with an odd sense of loneliness, even though I know that she was never there to begin with.

CHAPTER 29

Minneapolis—Yesterday

"God dammit!" I pounded my fists against the steering wheel. This was not how it was supposed to go. All I managed to do was kick a pile of leaves and scare off my prey. I got nothing out of Anastasia, except bruises. She didn't know her sister was dead. No one can fake that kind of pain. I know. I've been there. The picture knotted her up inside, dropping her to her knees. That was genuine.

I sat in my unmarked squad car, trying to decide what to do next. I could wait here for Whitton to come home, or I could . . . I don't know. If Anastasia told Whitton about my visit, what would he do? I never mentioned Jenni. For all Anastasia knew, I was simply looking into Zoya's death. I had every right to question Whitton's wife about the death of her sister. Hell, maybe I should barge back in there and demand that she talk to me. I should treat her like any other witness—or suspect.

As I narrowed down my options, settling on a plan to get back inside, a light came on in the garage. After a minute, the garage door rose up and the brake lights of a vehicle shone out of the bay. Then reverse lights. The vehicle backed out of the driveway and headed up the street. I followed. The first few snowflakes of the evening sparkled in front of my headlights. I turned on the radio to an AM station, hoping to catch a weather report.

Anastasia drove her car fast, barely slowing for stop signs, pulling out in front of other cars. I considered the possibility that she was trying to shake me, but at one stoplight where she was forced to halt, I made it in behind her and she never looked in her rearview mirror. Her erratic driving had nothing to do with shaking a tail.

As I followed Anastasia into the city, I caught a weather report saying that they were increasing their snowfall estimation from six inches to eight—even more up north. Anastasia made her way to Hennepin Avenue and into the heart of the city's entertainment district. She pulled into a parking lot across the street from a block of bars and shops and one upscale strip club called the Caviar Gentlemen's Club.

I pulled into a tow-away zone near the front of the club and parked. With the snow coming and the cold wind picking up, patrol officers would be too busy with car accidents to pay attention to red zones tonight.

From my vantage point I could see Anastasia getting out of her car. She wore a thick down coat and carried a purse big enough to be a gym bag. She walked with a determined stride, crossing the street less than twenty feet in front of me. She never looked my way. As she neared the entrance to the strip club, she eased a hand into the purse. Whatever she had been reaching for, she found immediately, and she rested her hand in the bag as she opened the door to the club with her other hand.

I didn't like the look of it. I jumped out of my car, pulling my badge from my belt, and scurried the few feet to the door.

I had never been inside that club before. The guy at the door didn't ask for an ID; he barely looked at me. He was still watching Anastasia, who walked through the place like she owned it.

I stood in the doorway, waiting for my eyes to adjust to the dimness of the room. A single stage jutted out into the audience with a pole in the middle of the runway. A young woman in a red thong, and nothing else, swung lazily around the pole to "Wild Thing" by the Troggs. Five or six men lined sniffer's row with beers at their elbows and dollar bills in their fingers. Tables littered a hardwood floor between the stage and the bar, and four other girls in skimpy, tight-fitting attire roamed between those tables, offering lap dances and other forms of companionship.

At the far end of the room, a staircase with a wrought-iron rail led up to a balcony with what appeared to be private rooms or maybe offices. Anastasia had made it halfway to that staircase before a man from behind the bar scuttled out to intercept her. He stepped in front of her and was shaking his head. They argued. Anastasia still had her hand in her bag, nodding toward the upstairs offices. And the man shook his head with more vigor, not noticing the implicit danger of whatever might be in that bag.

I started making my way to Anastasia, brushing past a woman asking me to buy her a drink. I couldn't hear the argument, but I could see anger animated on the faces of both Anastasia and the bartender.

In a dark corner, near the bottom of the steps, I saw a man sit up and take notice of the disturbance. It was Whitton. He had a near-naked girl on his lap, and he held her by the arms as she continued to grind. He said something to the girl, and she stopped her act.

That's when Anastasia pulled her hand out of the purse, a small automatic pistol in her grip. Now the bartender understood the gravity of the situation. He grabbed the gun and pushed her hand up toward the ceiling. The gun fired.

The girl on stage screamed and dropped to the floor. Whitton threw the girl from his lap and stood up but made no further move to advance. I ran to Anastasia, getting there just as the bartender pulled the gun from her hand. I shoved my badge in his face. "Minneapolis PD!" I yelled. "I got this."

The bartender took a step back, more confused than compliant. I grabbed Anastasia by the arm and yanked her toward the door. Whitton took a step in our direction but stalled there, a look of utter bewilderment on his face.

As I got Anastasia to the door, I saw a man upstairs step out from an office and onto the balcony. He was early-forties, dark hair, and well dressed, with a thin beard. I suspected that he might be the owner of the club, and he too looked on with confusion as I pulled Anastasia out into the night air.

"What are you doing?" Anastasia screamed. "Let me go!"

I dragged her to my car, opened the door, and threw her in. "Stay!" I shouted, pointing my finger at her as if to suggest that I meant business. She nodded her capitulation. Closing the door, I ran to the driver's side and jumped in. As I pulled away, I could see, in my rearview mirror, both the bouncer and the bartender step out, followed by Whitton.

I headed for my house, a ten-minute drive from downtown. I didn't know where else to take her. I needed to talk to Anastasia, and if kidnapping was my only option, then so be it. She faced away from me, her forehead resting against the passenger window. I opened my mouth to ask a question but stopped when I heard the sound of her crying. I expected her to lash out at me or attack me, or maybe even to realize her plight and leap from the car. I didn't expect crying. I held off saying anything until her sobbing had run its course. By that time, we were nearly to my house, and it was Anastasia who spoke first.

"Where are you taking me?"

"You can't go home," I said. "You're in danger. I'm taking you to my house—just for a while, until we can figure something out."

"Why did you stop me? Why didn't you let me finish it?"

"I didn't stop anything," I said. "That bartender already had your gun. The only thing I stopped you from doing was getting wrestled to the ground and arrested. You're welcome, by the way."

I drove into the alley behind my house and into my garage, parking beside the Durango that used to be Jenni's car. Like everything else of hers, I couldn't bring myself to get rid of it. I shut the garage door and headed toward the house, with Anastasia following me.

"This is your house?"

I'm sure she meant her question to come across as small talk, but it landed on my ear with a hint of judgment. It was a hovel compared to her fine home in Kenwood. I felt a tinge of embarrassment as I walked her past the garbage cans outside of my back door.

No woman had been inside of my house since Jenni died, and I couldn't help but feel disloyal, regardless of the circumstances. We walked through the kitchen and into the living room, where Anastasia took a seat on my couch, sitting in the exact spot where Jenni liked to sit.

I handed Anastasia a tissue to touch away the tears on her cheeks.

"Thank you for getting me out of there," she whispered.

"Don't mention it," I said. "I was only trying to keep things from getting out of hand. Besides, I couldn't let you go in there and kill your husband. I'm a cop. It's kind of my job."

Anastasia stopped crying and looked at me, her eyes searching mine, as if looking for an answer to a question that she hadn't yet asked. "You think I went there to kill my husband? To kill Reece?"

"Didn't you?"

"No. I went there to kill Mikhail."

CHAPTER 30

Mikhail. Two days ago, that name meant nothing to me. Now, it meant a great deal. *Mikhail will kill me.* That's what Zoya said.

"Mikhail was at the club?" I asked. "He was there?"

Anastasia looked at me as if I should already know the answer. "Of course he was there," she said. "He owns the club."

"Mikhail who? What's his last name?"

"Mikhail Vetrov."

"Stay here." I ran up the steps to my lair and fired up my laptop. Once awake, I typed in "Caviar Gentlemen's Club" and went to news articles. The first hit was a story of a shooting outside of the Caviar from two years ago. I scrolled down the article, looking for a picture. I wanted to see the man's face. Finding none, I skimmed the story and came to a small paragraph stating that the owner of the Caviar, a man named Michael Vetter, had refused to comment on the story. I found no mention of named Mikhail Vetrov.

I brought the laptop down to show Anastasia my find. She sat on my couch, back rigid, knees together, hands on her lap, her eyes fixed on the floor in front of her. It struck me, in that moment, just how out of place she seemed, sitting where Jenni used to sit: too young, too pretty, her hair too dark, her lips too red, her eyes too blue. She had a vibrancy that stood in stark contrast to the gray and the dust that had settled throughout my house over the years—a color portrait leaning against a pallid wall.

I sat down beside her. "It says here that the owner of the Caviar is a man named Michael Vetter."

"Yes, he is Michael Vetter, but he is also Mikhail Vetrov. He is from Belarus, like me, but he came here when he was a very young boy. He lives in two worlds. In one, he is Michael Vetter, a businessman, respected. But to people from his other world, people like me, he is Mikhail."

I typed "Michael Vetter" and "Caviar" into Google and pulled up a screen full of pictures. At the top of the page was a face I recognized, the man I saw standing on the balcony just before I whisked Anastasia outside.

I pointed at the picture. "Mikhail?" I asked.

She nodded.

"His father was a bad man," she said. "They came here to escape many other bad men. One day, the men from Minsk found Mikhail's father. They killed him. Mikhail told me this story. He said that he was eighteen when they killed his father. Those men had a business proposition for Mikhail. Lots of money."

"Mikhail confided in you? You were close?"

Anastasia faced ahead, staring at nothing in particular as she considered my question. Then she swallowed hard and said, "I belong to Mikhail . . . or at least I used to. Now I belong to Reece."

"You belong to . . . ?"

"Mikhail brought me here when I was seventeen. He paid for my travel. He . . . he took care of me. I was his girl. And then I became his . . . I worked for Mikhail."

"You were his prostitute?"

"Yes."

"And your sister, Zoya? Did she also work for Mikhail?"

"She wasn't supposed to. He promised me—"

"She had a tattoo on her neck—the symbol of the ruble."

Anastasia continued to stare straight ahead, as if she hadn't heard me. I waited patiently. I could tell that she wanted to talk to me. I could also tell that her words came at a great personal cost, each revelation having to be wrenched up from some dark place deep inside of her. Then she lifted her hair back on the right side of her neck, exposing a small ruble tattoo behind her ear.

"You said that Mikhail gave you to Whitton?"

"Yes. Mikhail struck a bargain with Reece. I was part of that bargain. One day Mikhail came to me and said that from that day forward, I belonged to Reece Whitton. That was all there was to it."

"Anastasia, tell me about this bargain. What did Mikhail get out of it?"

She took a moment to size me up, her eyes staring into mine as if something deep behind my irises could tell her whether she could trust me. In the end I must have passed scrutiny, because she leaned back with a measure of self-satisfaction in her expression and said, "You have never heard of Mikhail before today, is that correct?"

"That is true."

"Yet he has been operating in this city for years. How is that possible? How can he do the business he does and never come to the attention of the police?"

"Whitton is covering for him."

"Who better to have as a partner than the man who would be in charge of the investigation—the man who made the decisions about who got attention and who got ignored?"

"And you were the price for Whitton's loyalty."

"I was only part of the deal. You've seen his house?"

"Not the kind of thing most cops can afford."

"I was a mere token in that deal."

"But you married Whitton."

Anastasia's eyes flashed with a sudden hatred. "I am his property," she said. "I am his payment—his reward. I am not a wife. I am a possession, and he treats me as such—no, he treats me worse than a possession. Me he hurts."

She opened her coat and pulled down the collar of her sweater to expose the tops of her breasts. "Look!" she demanded. "Look where he burned me." She showed me three button-sized scars, the likely result of hot cigarette ash. "And here . . ." She pulled her collar around to expose her shoulder blade. Again more small circles. "I have many more."

She closed her sweater back around her neck, and her eyes took on the faraway stare of someone replaying a memory. "My husband is my captor. Mikhail delivered me to him, and I went to Reece willingly. I wanted to prove to Mikhail that I would do anything for him—even this." Then she looked at me with incredulity. "You could never understand. You see only a whore. You do not live in my world."

"I'm trying to understand," I said. "But if you hate Whitton so much, why did you go to the club to kill Mikhail and not your . . . not Reece?"

"Because my sister is dead and it is Mikhail who will pay for that. You should not have stopped me. I would have killed him even if I had to tear out his throat with my bare hands."

"Why Mikhail? How is he involved?"

Her gaze turned suspicious. "You will not help me. You are a policeman, like Reece. You do not care for women such as me. You only get in the way."

"I'm a cop, that's true enough; but I am not like Whitton. I want to get these guys as much as you do. I want them to pay for their crimes. I understand what you want, I do, but I need your help. Tell me about Mikhail and about your sister."

"My sister . . ." I thought Anastasia was going to cry again. She tightened her lips and drew in a shaky breath. Then she asked, "When did Zoya die?"

"Four years ago."

Anastasia's breath halted in her chest. The answer caught her off guard. "Four years?" Her lips began to quiver, but she held it together. "How did she die?"

I hesitated, then said, "She was beaten and then drowned. We don't know exactly where it happened or how, but that's what the autopsy showed."

"And then?"

"And then they threw her body into a dumpster."

With that, Anastasia began to cry again.

"I'm sorry."

Her cry grew until she gritted her teeth and screamed into her fists. "God damn him." Hot breath shot through her lips in hissing bursts as she spoke. "I'm going to kill Mikhail. I don't care if you arrest me. I don't care about anything. I will kill him and no one can stop me."

"Please, Anastasia. I'm not here to arrest you. I'm here to help. You've got to believe me. We need to work together. We need to trust each other."

Again, she looked at me with suspicion in her eyes.

"I prefer Ana," she said. "Not Anastasia."

"Okay, Ana."

My phone rang. I looked at the number and recognized it. Reece Whitton. I answered.

"Yes?"

"Where's my wife, Rupert?"

I looked at Ana and put a finger to my lips to tell her to remain quiet. Then I switched the call to speakerphone. "Ana's here with me. We're having a chat."

"What kind of game are you playing?"

"Game?" I started to get angry, the memory of his voice planning my wife's death boiling up inside me. "You think this is a game, you piece of shit?"

Now it was his turn to hesitate. Then he said, "I think we should meet. Hash this out."

"I think that's a good idea."

"I'll be on the top floor of the LaSalle Court parking ramp."

How fitting that he would choose a parking ramp for our meeting, just as he chose a parking ramp to meet Jenni all those years ago. Quiet, isolated. The kind of place where one can do very bad things away from the prying eyes of a city. He couldn't have picked a better location.

The poetic justice of it all brought a slight smile to my face, and I said, "I'm on my way."

CHAPTER 31

Up North

He's not in the snow-nest when I get back.

I'm a dozen yards away when I see that he's gone, and a spark of panic flairs in my chest. I charge back to where I'd left him, dropping my bundle of rocks in the snow at the edge of the circle. My panic skitters to a halt when I see a path of matted snow about thirty yards long and leading to where he's lying on his back, writhing and covered in snow. He rolled to get away from the nest, and his trail looks like it had been laid down by a drunken walrus. I bend over to catch my breath. Without the rocks, my arms feel light enough to float away and my shoulders ease back into their swollen sockets.

He is facing away from me, unaware of my presence. I take a few steps toward him and squat to watch. His snowmobile suit is partially unzipped, which I think must have been loosened in his attempt to roll away. But then I see him working his hands up and down over his abdomen, his face creased by pain. I take a few more steps and he sees me.

"You fucking psychopath," he says. "I can't feel my fingers. I think I have frostbite."

I walk up and kneel down beside him, ignoring his insult. Even with his elbows strapped behind his back and his hands tethered together, he has somehow worked his coat's zipper down to his waist. At first, I'm not concerned, but then I notice that he's been sawing the cotton cord up and down against the zipper. The teeth of a zipper aren't sharp, but given enough time and enough motivation—and I suppose there's no shortage of motivation here—those teeth could cut a cotton cord.

I had doubled the cord when I tied his wrists, and to my surprise, he's managed to saw through one of his bindings and has notched a gash into the second.

"Impressive," I say. "I must have been gone longer than I thought."

"You're insane. Let me go, you fucking nutjob."

There's not enough drawstring to retie the section that he cut, but one strand should be enough to hold him—besides, I have the belt around the elbows as a backup. I'll just have to keep a better eye on him from now on.

I grab the collar of his snowmobile suit and drag him back to the nest as he curses and threatens me. Before I start to dig the fifth hole, I tug his zipper back up to his neck. "Wouldn't want you catching a cold," I say.

"How can you be so glib?" he asks with swelling anger in his voice.

I set the auger into the fifth starter hole and my body stiffens as it prepares to greet the pain. The first turn of the shaft awakens the tattered muscles in my chest and arms again. Four more holes to go. I'm only halfway done and it feels like I've been at this for days, not hours.

As I drill, the man works on me the way he's been working me the whole day: prattling on about the terrible mistake I've made, threatening to have my job, offering to forgive me if I stop now. His words fall into a thick, blurry hum, as if he's talking to me from the bottom of a swimming pool.

Pain radiates across my pectorals with each turn of the crank, but the sharpest aches are the spikes stabbing my forearms and the dull throb punching up from my toes. When I get about halfway to the water on this fifth hole, I stand and stretch my back. From the corner of my eye, I can see him twisting his shoulders and stomach, trying to reach the zipper again. I turn to face him, but he's focused on his escape plan, writhing and bending to try and reach the pull tab of his zipper. When he sees me watching him, he shoots me a scowl and stops his wiggling.

"You're working awfully hard to cut that rope," I say. "Not the actions of a man who thinks this is all a bluff."

"I'm tired of this," he says—and he does sound tired now. "You know you can't go through with this. You're a cop. It's not in your DNA."

"You have no idea what's in my DNA."

"If I did something, show me the evidence. Come on, asshole. Show me." He makes a point of looking around in mock confusion. "What? No evidence? I didn't think so. This whole Kabuki theater is because you have nothing."

"You're my evidence," I say.

"I'm your evidence? What does that even mean? That's bullshit. I'm innocent—innocent until proven guilty."

"No," I say. "You're not innocent until proven guilty. Not here. You don't have that right. But you want your day in court, so get on with it. I have three and a half more holes to cut. You have until I finish this circle to prove your innocence."

"Prove my innocence? How can I—?"

I start turning the auger again.

"I . . . I'm not even sure what I'm accused—"

"State your name for the record," I holler over the grind of the auger.

"What?"

"That's how you start a trial. Don't you know anything? If you're going to testify, you have to state your name first."

"You want me to—"

"What's your fucking name?"

"Christ, you're going to kill me, and you don't even know my name? I'm telling you, I'm not the guy you think I am. I didn't kill your family. I don't know anything about it. You have to let me go. You have to—"

"Shut. Up!" I stop the auger again so that he can see the seriousness in my eyes. "I said, state your name."

"My name is Michael Vetter—"

"What is your birth name?"

"What?"

"I'm not asking you what you call yourself now. I want you to tell me your real name—the name they gave you when you popped out of your momma's lady parts."

"I'm Michael Vetter, you sick bastard."

"You're lying already."

I see fear and understanding coalesce on his face. He's wondering how much I know. I start turning the auger again.

"I am Michael Vetter. I don't know what else you want. That's my name. That's always been my name."

"You were born Mikhail Vetrov. You were born in Minsk and came to America as a young boy. How am I doing so far?"

He doesn't answer.

I point my finger at Mikhail. "Mikhail Vetrov, you are here today accused of the murder of my wife, Jenni Rupert. You are also accused of the murder of her unborn child. You are a pimp and a destroyer of the innocent. These are a just a few of the many crimes for which you will pay today."

"Now I'm a pimp as well? Why don't you add some more bullshit to the list, maybe arsonist, or . . . I know, shoplifter. Honestly, Detective, you're not making sense. I never did any of that. I'm innocent."

I pull the blade out of the hole and jam the shoveled end into the ice near Mikhail's face, sending chips spraying into the air. "Don't say that!" I yell. "Don't fucking say that. If you tell me, one more time, that you're innocent, I swear I'll shove a glove down your throat. You wanted a trial, well, here it is. Say what you need to say, but this will be your only chance. Talk—don't talk—I don't care. But if you tell me again that you're innocent, I . . ."

I close my eyes and take a deep breath. Then I return to my project, lowering the auger back into hole number five. I shouldn't have gotten mad. I should have held my tongue, let him continue to deny his crimes. His lies make it easier for me. There's some truth to the notion that a person who is truly sorry for what they've done shouldn't suffer the same fate as the unrepentant. But that's a bridge I don't have to cross as long as he sticks to his script.

Mikhail's eyes study me for a while, trying to work out what I might know and how I know it, piecing together what he can and trying to figure out what he can get away with. We saw each other in his club. He has to know he can't deny that. He knows I left there with Ana. What did she tell me? I know his real name. What else did I know? What can he still deny?

Then he says, "I own a gentlemen's club. There's nothing illegal about that. I don't let my employees screw the clients. There's no prostitution. You're making assumptions. It's a strip club. Nothing more."

"I call you a murderer and a pimp, and it's the pimp part you want to argue about?"

"I want to argue about all of it. I am none of those things, and anyone who tells you otherwise is a liar."

"I suppose you have no ties to the Belarussian underworld either?"

"Do you hear yourself? You sound like a crazy man. Now I'm a mobster from Russia—?"

"Belarus—not Russia. Don't play games, Mikhail."

"My name is Michael."

"Keep it up, Mikhail. Keep stalling. Let's see where that gets you."

"I don't know what you think you know, but you're wrong."

Water bubbles up and out of the fifth hole and the auger blade slips below the bottom edge of the ice, getting caught there for a few seconds. My motor coordination is fading, and I jerk on the handle until the auger is free and pops out of the hole.

As I pause to catch my breath, before starting the sixth hole, I look at Mikhail and see in his eyes that our game has changed. Like a man discarding his checkers and resetting the board with chess pieces, he's calculating his moves with a whole new set of rules. He's upping his game. And I'm ready for him.

CHAPTER 32

Minneapolis—Yesterday

Snow was coming down in earnest when I headed for my car. Ana had argued to come with me to meet Reece, and I shut her down. In my pocket, I carried a copy of the digital recording of Whitton talking to Kroll. Whitton would answer for the recording—that much I knew. How he would answer remained obscure in my mind. He would be waiting for me, but did he have any idea why? He saw me drag his wife out of the club. He knew I was investigating ruble symbols and tattoos, but did he have a clue as to how close I was to the full truth? I doubt it. But then again, maybe that's exactly why he wanted to meet on the top of that parking ramp. Maybe he sees a way out.

I was familiar with the LaSalle Court ramp, one of those where you drive up the sloping floors but exit through a corkscrew. I remembered, from an investigation I'd done some years ago, that LaSalle had cameras at the entrances and exits, in the elevators, and in the vestibules outside the elevators. I also remembered that it had an opening in its side where the dumpsters were stored, and that that opening had no camera.

I parked on Eighth Avenue, behind the ramp and out of sight, should anyone be peering down from the top. A narrow alley cut down beside the ramp, and halfway down that alley stood the dumpsters. An eight-foot-tall chain-link fence protected the opening. That was easy enough to scale. I peeked into the guts of the parking ramp to see that I was past the entrance cameras. Thirty feet ahead of me was a security office. The lights were on, but it was unmanned. Beyond that was the corkscrew exit.

I walked casually across the two lanes for entering the ramp and started my trek up the corkscrew. As I neared the top, I slowed, inching my way up until I could see the darkness of the night sky where the corkscrew opened onto the eighth floor. Whitton would be waiting for me out there, but would he be alone? Everything about that meeting smelled like a trap.

I drew my gun out of its holster and eased to the mouth of the corkscrew entrance. A curtain of falling snow put a lacy white veil in front of me, but I could see Whitton's unmarked Dodge Charger about thirty feet out, facing down the entrance ramp, waiting for my car to come around that last bend. His lights and engine were both off.

I scan the shadows and edges, looking for an accomplice, and see no one through the darkness and thick snow. If I couldn't see them, then maybe they couldn't see me either. I dropped to my belly and low-crawled onto the parking ramp, the snow building up in piles against my forearms. His car was thirty feet out. He must have been lowering and raising the windows to keep them cleared of snow, because I could see inside the cab. A green dashboard light glowed bright enough that I could see Whitton's head in the driver's seat. No passengers. I crawled on my belly through the snow, my eyes watching for the slightest movement from Whitton.

Once behind his car, I slid up into a sitting position, leaning against the back bumper. I waited and listened. No radio. No talking. I again scanned the perimeter and saw no movement. I could see Whitton's tire tracks in the snow. The hazy lights on that top floor of the ramp gave off enough illumination to see that there were no footprints anywhere around the Charger. Whitton came alone.

I considered my next step. Frankly, I hadn't expected to make it this far without a throw-down. I could point my Glock in his face and demand he step out. But Whitton might already have his gun drawn, and where would that leave me? If he didn't comply, would I shoot him? I didn't know.

Another alternative—I rush the door, yank him out, and hope the element of surprise tips things in my favor. I drove the same model of

Dodge Charger, so I knew that the door would have unlocked when he put the car in park. That seemed like the better of my options.

I holstered my gun and slid to the edge of the bumper, where I took a breath to steady my nerves. Three . . . two . . . one. I jumped from my hiding spot, my feet digging to find purchase as I turned the corner, flung the door open and grabbed Whitton by the coat. He looked up at me as if I were a banshee from his worst childhood nightmare, come to steal his soul.

I pulled him out of his seat and sent him sprawling across the snow-covered concrete. It was then that I saw the gun. He must have been holding it on his lap, because it fell to the ground as I yanked him out of the car. I kicked the gun and it slid under the Charger.

"What the hell?" Whitton yelled as he rose up onto his elbows.

I kicked him in the ribs and he rolled twice over, ending on his backside. He started to scramble to his feet, getting to his hands and knees before he saw me pointing my gun at his head. "Don't," was all I said.

He sat back on his heels and held his arms out to the side. "What are you going to do, Max? Shoot me? What the fuck's wrong with you?"

"Why'd you do it?" I yelled.

"What?" He looked honestly confused.

"Tell me why you did it, Whitton."

"Why I did what? What are you talking about?"

"I will shoot you. You have to know that."

"Shoot me? Have you lost your mind? I see you dragging my wife out of a club and now you want to shoot me?"

"I'm giving you a chance to buy your life, Reece. Don't throw that away."

"Buy my life? Why would . . ."

A dark shift in his expression revealed that some new level of recognition had taken hold, and I watched as a tiny spark of understanding unlocked behind his eyes. He knew; I could tell, and I saw fear dig into the lines on his face. "I don't know what you're talking about."

"Don't say that, Reece! Don't you fucking say that." I took a step closer, the barrel of my gun just out of his reach.

He turned his face away and crossed his hands in front of the muzzle. "Stop, Max. Whatever you're mad about . . . I don't know what you think I did."

"Tell me why you killed her."

"Killed who? I didn't kill anyone. For God's sake, I don't know."

I reached into my coat pocket, pulled out the recorder, held it out in front of me, and hit play.

Hello?

Yeah, it's me.

The boss said you'd be calling. What's up?

We have a job. I need you to lift a car. Keep it clean. No fingerprints. No DNA. Wear gloves.

I know what I'm doing.

We have to deal with someone right away.

Send a message?

No. Extreme prejudice. Hit-and-run.

Great. Another drop of blood and we do all the work.

This is serious. It's a cop's wife.

A what?

You heard me. She stumbled onto something she shouldn't have. If we don't move fast, we'll all be fucked. I don't like this any more than you do.

When?

Today. 3:00.

Where?

Hennepin County Medical Center. There's a parking garage on the corner of Eighth and Chicago. Meet me on the top floor. I'll fill you in there. I'm not sure if they have cameras at the entrance, so cover your face when you drive in.

I stopped the playback.

Defeat pressed down on his shoulders. He can't deny his own voice. "I just want to know why, Reece."

Whitton's hands slowly lower to his sides. He fixed his gaze on some meaningless scuff of snow near my feet, no longer concerned about the gun pointed at his face. "Where'd you find that?"

"Does it matter?"

"No. I guess not." Then he shook his head and to himself, he muttered, "I should have known better." Then to me he said, "I have money, Max. Lots of it. And—"

"I don't want your fucking money."

"You can have Anastasia? She's—"

I stepped in and whipped the barrel of my gun across his face, sending him tumbling back into the snow. He curled as he rolled, mumbling curses at me, holding the side of his jaw. He maneuvered onto his hands and knees again, and when he spoke this time, the sound came through a broken jaw. "Christ, Max. I'm sorry. I'm sorry."

"Why, Reece? Why'd you kill Jenni?"

"What do you want, Max? I can't change anything. I wish I could. I really do. I can't tell you how many times I've put my own gun in my mouth over that one."

He began looking around as if searching for his gun. The kick must have disoriented him, because he didn't think to look under his car. When he couldn't find it, he dropped his head and asked, "What're you going to do with that recording?"

"You're not getting out of this, Reece."

Reece put his hands on his thighs, and shook his fallen head. "I had to do it, Max. I had no choice. I . . . I fucked up."

"We all have choices, Reece."

"I didn't. Just like I don't have a choice now." Reece slowly rose to his feet.

"Don't move. I will shoot you."

He held out his arms, "Please. Go ahead. Get it over with."

I tensed my finger against the trigger.

"You think I'm scared of your gun? I'd welcome a bullet. Come on, Rupert. Shoot me!" He walked toward me, his chest open and ready to take a bullet. When he got too close, I hit him in the head with my gun again. He fell to the ground, blood trickling down his cheek and neck. "That's what I thought. You don't have the balls to shoot me."

"I'm just not ready to shoot you yet," I said.

"Does Vang know about the tape?"

I thought about his reason for asking that question. I think he wanted to know how widely dispersed his crime had become. Was there a chance of stopping the spread—maybe by killing me and Niki?

"Niki knows," I said. Whitton wouldn't have believed me if I said otherwise. "So does Chief Murphy, the county attorney, and a couple of folks in the City Attorney's Office." I added to the list to protect Niki, just in case things went south for me in the next few minutes.

"Damn," he said. He rose to his feet again and brushed the snow from his pants. "Well, that's that, I guess." Whitton turned and walked away from me, shuffling his feet in a slow dirge until he reached the wall on the outer edge of the parking ramp.

"Don't do it, Reece. God dammit, don't you do it."

The wall had two parts, a concrete stub about waist high and a two-foot metal rail anchored atop the concrete. Whitton stopped at the wall, his chin resting on top of the rail. "I'm not going to prison, Max. And I'm not going to stick around to watch this all play out on the evening news."

Whitton climbed onto the wall, slipping one leg over the metal rail.

I put my gun away. "Reece, wait!" Now it was me with my hands out. I stepped closer to him. Reece had one leg on either side of the wall. "At least tell me why you killed her," I begged.

He looked over the wall, at the alley eight stories below. Through the snow I could see tears trickling down his cheeks. "I have parents," Whitton said. "I'm their only son, and they think the world of me. I know you don't care, and I don't blame you, but when I'm gone, you have no reason to tell anyone about this. For their sake, please don't . . ."

"Reece, come down off there. We can talk."

Reece lifted his chin into the slight breeze and stared at nothing. "No, I don't think so," he said. He paused and closed his eyes. I thought about rushing him, pulling him back from the precipice, but then he sat up and smiled at me and said, "You know, Max. I never did like you." With that, he leaned into the nothingness and disappeared from my view. I heard the pop of his body hitting the ground. I didn't need to look over the wall to know that Reece Whitton was dead.

Before walking back down the corkscrew exit, I retrieved Whitton's gun from under the car and laid it on the seat, making sure that a round was chambered. The snow was already starting to hide the evidence of our scuffle. With any luck, the investigation would conclude that Whitton went there to commit suicide, choosing to jump instead of shooting himself.

As I walked back down the corkscrew, I replayed those lasts few seconds of Whitton's life. I could have grabbed him, pulled him back to safety. I could have shot him to disable him. I could have told him that I wouldn't send the recording anywhere. I had all of those options in my head as I watched him climb onto that wall. There could have been a different outcome. But in the deepest recesses of my conscience, I didn't want any other outcome.

I left the parking ramp, climbing over that same chain-link fence by the dumpster, and entered the alley only a few feet away from Whitton's shattered body.

CHAPTER 33

It was strange to find Ana still sitting on my couch when I came home. Before I walked in, I peeked in through a small window pane on my back door. I could see that she was going through my investigation file on Zoya. She held the picture of her dead sister in her hand, pressing it against her lips. At the sound of the door opening, Ana put the photograph down and sat up, her attention focused sharply on me.

Neither of us spoke at first. She appeared to be reading my face, trying to ascertain what had happened at the parking ramp. I was stalling because I didn't know how I would tell her about Whitton's death.

It was Ana who broke the silence.

"You met with my husband?" she said in a flat tone.

"I did."

"And did he tell you what you wanted to hear?"

I opened my mouth to answer, but the words did not come out. I sat down on the couch next to her. If she had been lying to me about her hatred for Whitton, this moment would bring that lie to the surface.

"Ana, I have some bad news."

I paused, looking for a reaction. Her facial expression did not change.

"Reece is dead," I said.

She inhaled a small gasp. Then she closed her eyes and sighed, a slight smile edging up in the corners of her mouth. "How did he die?" she asked.

"He . . . jumped off the roof of the parking ramp. It was an eight-story fall."

"He jumped? You did not push him?"

I was taken aback by the question. This woman does not mince words. "No, I didn't push him."

"I would not have been upset if you had," she said. "Did he tell you anything about Zoya's death before he . . . jumped?"

"He didn't tell me all that much. I'm afraid our conversation took a bad turn right away. You think he killed Zoya?"

"Mikhail is the one responsible for Zoya's death. Not Reece."

"How do you know?"

Ana looked at the photo in her hand. "Nothing happens to one of Mikhail's girls without Mikhail's permission. She was not even supposed to be in this country. He promised me. We had struck a bargain. I kept my end of the bargain. He did not."

"I need to know everything you can tell me about Mikhail. I need to go to him tonight, before he finds out that Reece is dead."

Ana cast her eyes down and shook her head. "You will not find him tonight. He is gone. When he saw me in the club—and he saw you pull me out—he knows. He sent Reece to meet with you. They want to know what you know. They want to see how close you are to the truth about Zoya. By now, Mikhail is on his way to Canada."

"I don't think anyone knows that Reece is dead. They probably haven't even found his body yet. Mikhail can't know already."

"He will not wait to tempt fate. If there is a threat, he will run." Ana reached into her bag and pulled out a cell phone. She hit two buttons and laid it on the coffee table in front of her. It rang twice before someone on the other end answered.

"Caviar Gentlemen's Club. Dawby speaking."

In the background, AC/DC blasted out "You Shook Me All Night Long."

"Dawby, this is Ana. I need to speak to Mikhail. It's important."

"For fuck's sake, Ana. What the hell's going on? You 'bout got me fired."

"I'm sorry, Dawby, but—"

"You come in here with a gun and then some cop pulls you out? Mikhail's pissed. He got all up in my shit and threatened to fire me. What the hell was I supposed to do? Fight a cop?"

"Dawby, is Mikhail there?"

"No. He and Reece had a powwow upstairs for a few minutes.

Then Reece ran out of here like his ass was on fire. A little while later, Mikhail tells me he's gone for the rest of the week, maybe longer. Says I'm in charge of things. I mean, what the fuck. One minute he's firing me and the next, I'm the boss. What's going on?"

Ana hung up the phone.

"Where's he going?" I asked.

"North. He has a cabin in the Superior National Forest, just on this side of the Canadian border. He has friends who live in a cabin ten miles into Canada. When things get too dangerous, he crosses the border until it is safe to return. He will need to walk across the border, so he'll wait until morning. Then he will leave the United States. If he makes it across, we will never see him again—not after what happened to Reece."

"You know where his cabin is?"

"I know where it is."

I ran to retrieve an old atlas from the coat closet.

"I cannot show you where Mikhail's cabin is—not on a map. I only know what it looks like from the road. I have to go with you. It's on the Gunflint Trail. That's the only road name I remember."

"Well, that narrows it down to about sixty miles."

"I will know it when I see it. You must take me with you."

"Just until you show me where his cabin is. Then I'm dropping you at a resort. Is that agreed?"

"That is agreed."

I went into my bedroom to grab some winter clothes: gloves, boots, a coat, and a pair of thin gray ski pants, more for fashion than function. I also grabbed some sweaters that I thought might fit Ana. We'd be going through the heaviest band of snow, eight inches or more, and the possibility of sliding into a ditch was all too real.

My unmarked squad car, a Dodge Charger, didn't stand much of a chance in eight inches of snow, so we piled our supplies into Jenni's Durango. I rarely drove the Durango and hadn't started it for almost a year, so I had grave doubts that it would even turn over. I held my breath as I turned the key. It gave a short moan but then caught and started up.

Before pulling out of the garage, I went over my checklist of supplies: my gun, bottled water, winter clothes. I had a snow emergency kit in the car and a near-full tank of gas. What was I forgetting? A plan? That didn't seem to matter. Time mattered.

As I pulled the car out of the garage, a thought struck me, and I stopped the Durango, the back bumper sticking halfway into the alley.

"Let me see your phone," I said, pulling my own phone out of my pocket.

"Why?"

"Give it to me." I held the side button down on my phone until it gave the option to shut it down, which I did.

Ana hesitated but then gave me her phone. I turned on the dome light so I could see to pop the back of her phone off. I pulled the battery out, put it in my shirt pocket, and tossed the dead phone back to her. She wasn't expecting the toss and it hit the back of her wrist and fell between the seat and center console.

"Why did you do that?" she asked as she slid her fingers into the crack to retrieve her phone.

"Cell phones talk to towers. Towers leave a trail. No phone calls. No evidence. We never left the city."

"I would have shut it off."

"I'll feel better if I can hold onto the battery."

She pulled her hand up but she did not have her phone. Instead, something shiny dangled from her fingers. A bracelet—Jenni's bracelet with the engraved charms of her mother and aunt and grandmother.

"What the hell?" I grabbed it away from Ana, holding it under the light to make sure I wasn't seeing things. How did that bracelet get between the seat and console? Why wasn't it in the sewing box upstairs? I didn't understand.

Then I saw it—a charm brighter, more polished than the others. I counted. Where there had been six charms, there were now seven. The newest held no name, its golden surface unscratched, untarnished, waiting for a name to be engraved upon it.

Jenni knew she was pregnant.

Everything grew hot. My eyes filled with tears. All that I knew for certain was that I had to get out of the car. I pulled the handle and half fell out of the driver's seat, the bracelet twined around my fingers.

I ran toward the mouth of the alley where the glow from a streetlight flickered through the static of falling snow. I couldn't breathe. I couldn't see past the blur of tears in my eyes. The very air around me pulsed with an off-pitch ringing that I was pretty sure was only in my head.

At the base of the streetlight, I fell to one knee, holding the bracelet to my lips, a ball-peen hammer pounding in my ears. She was going to use the bracelet to tell me about the baby, wear it to dinner or maybe have it on her wrist when she curled up in my arms at night. I would have noticed the tinkling of the charms and asked why she was wearing it. She would have smiled and said nothing until the light came on in my thick head. That's how she would have done it.

Tears fell hard down my cheeks. My lungs heaved and stammered as I tried to catch my breath. I put one hand on the light pole to steady myself.

In that last second before the impact, in that moment when Jenni understood that a speeding car would rob her of her life, she knew about the baby. Her pain was shared. Her fear was shared. Her death would be shared. Her last thoughts would not have been for herself; they would have been for her child, a universe of love and hope and regret folding into her womb, cradling a baby no bigger than a single jelly bean.

Slowly, my grief began to harden inside my chest. The man who killed Jenni was fleeing north, hoping to never be seen again by the likes of me. With that I found a new hunger, a passion strong enough to unseat my memories of Jenni. I had prey to pursue and a commitment to keep.

I heard a scuffing in the alley and glanced over my shoulder to see Ana standing there, watching me. She must have thought that she'd thrown in with a mad man, the way I frothed and sobbed against that light post. I stood up, despite some objection from my shaky legs, and turned to face her.

I could see no readable expression on her face. I took that as a sign that she hadn't changed her mind about leading me to Mikhail. I slid the bracelet into my pocket and headed toward the Durango, which was still half in and half out of the garage.

"Are you okay?" she asked.

I was far from okay, but I nodded as I passed her, and she followed me to the car.

CHAPTER 34

Up North

By the time that I'm drilling my sixth hole, the clouds are almost gone from the sky. The line between low and high pressure systems is passing over our heads, and I can feel the temperature falling. It has to be well below zero now. Clear skies in Minnesota are the coldest skies. I ball my fingers into the palm of my shredded gloves to keep them warm. My fingertips touch against the tender skin and blisters on my palms. My pectoral muscles feel like they're clamped in a steel-jaw trap. I've gone past hungry to numb. Every turn of the auger takes focus and effort. My left foot is screaming in pain, and my right foot isn't too far behind. I try marching in place as I dig. I try hopping. Nothing seems to warm my feet. I can't stop now. I've come too far.

"Someone's been feeding you a pack of lies," Mikhail says. "You're being used."

"Uh-hum," I say.

Mikhail has to be cold, but he isn't showing it. Maybe he thinks I'll give up if I get too cold. If that's what he thinks, he's wrong.

"If I was doing all that," Mikhail says, "if I was running prostitutes out of my club, there'd be a record. Someone would have noticed and I'd have been arrested. There'd be some proof other than your belief. But I've never been arrested. I have a clean record because I've never done those things."

"You have a clean record because you're smart. You know how to cover your tracks."

"You'll choose to believe what you want to believe. I'll never be able to prove that I didn't kill your wife as long as you want to believe that I did. You have nothing."

"I have the words of Zoya Savvin."

"Who the hell is Zoya Savvin?" I can hear a slight shake in Mikhail's confidence. He pauses for a second to put this new piece in place before he continues. "I've never heard of her."

"Sure you have. She used to work for you. She was one of your prostitutes."

"Of course, she was."

"She wore your tattoo. You branded her." I tap on my neck just behind the ear. "Yes, Mikhail, I know all about the ruble tattoo. That's your brand, isn't it?"

"That's sick! How can you—"

"That's how you mark your girls."

"I don't have girls. If this Zoya is saying that I'm a pimp, then bring her here. Let her say it to me directly. Let me face my accuser."

"Zoya's gone."

"I suppose I killed her too?"

"I didn't say she was dead." I pause in my drilling to look at Mikhail. In his eyes, I see trepidation. "But, yes," I say. "You killed her too."

"Why would I do that—if she was my prostitute?"

I lean on the auger. "My wife loved her job. She loved trying to help people like Zoya. The officers found Zoya wandering down the street in a daze. She'd been beaten and thrown through a motel window. Of course, you already know that."

"I've never heard of the girl. I have no idea what you're talking about."

"The girl," I say slowly, letting his mistake sink in. "Not 'the woman'?"

"It's just an expression."

"My wife wanted to help the girl. She wanted to protect Zoya from you, and you killed her for it."

"And how, exactly, did I kill your wife? Knife? Gun? I'd really like to know how I did it."

"Oh, you didn't do it yourself. No, you ordered it done." I start drilling again.

"You are sounding more and more like one of those crazy conspiracy theorists, Detective. Now I have lackeys and hitmen working for me? I must be a regular gangster."

"Ray Kroll. You remember him."

Mikhail pauses, pretending to give my question some consideration. "Yeah, I remember Ray. He used to be a bouncer at the club. He quit some years back. Too bad. He was a decent bouncer. So you think Ray killed your wife?"

"At your direction. He and Reece Whitton."

"Reece Whitton? That name sounds familiar. I think he's a customer at the club. Spent a lot of money there. He was a cop, wasn't he?"

"'Was'? Past tense?"

"I . . . it seems I heard a news story on the radio this morning. Something about a guy falling off the roof of a parking ramp. I'm pretty sure they said his name was Reece Whitton—a cop. You a friend of his?"

I just shake my head.

"I think the guy on the radio said that Mr. Whitton was dead." Mikhail purses his lips, probably to keep from smiling. "So, let's see if I have this right," he says. "You're going to execute me because you say that I ordered my former bouncer and a cop to kill your wife. And the evidence that you have for this is a prostitute, who is dead, my former bouncer, who is dead, and the cop who fell off a roof yesterday, and he's also dead. Too bad the dead can't testify."

"Sometimes they can," I say. "Before you killed my wife, she left a voice-mail message with an interpreter." I watch as Mikhail's face goes slack. "On that recording, the girl you killed, Zoya, names you. She says that you are going to kill her—and then you did just that."

"That's impossible."

"I also have the blackmail CD Kroll made."

"What blackmail CD? What are you talking about?"

"The one where Kroll and Whitton are planning my wife's death. Kroll says your name: Mikhail Vetrov. I have the recording. I've heard it."

"That's a lie." Mikhail raises his voice in anger. "That's a goddamn lie, and you know it."

"You know, Mikhail, you're right. That was a lie," I say. "They never actually said your name. Of course, you knew that, because you listened to the recording."

"Okay, he played it for me," Mikhail says. "Kroll was in trouble for beating some guy up and he wanted money for an attorney. He said that he was going to tell the police that I ordered some hit if I didn't give him a hundred thousand dollars. I didn't know what he was talking about. It was all a lie. I fired him on the spot. I didn't know they were talking about your wife. I swear to God I didn't."

"God dammit!" I stop drilling and straighten up. "What are you doing?"

"What?"

"I'm giving you a chance here. You can't keep lying to me. You're hanging off a cliff, and instead of grabbing the rope I'm offering, you spit in my face."

"What the hell are you talking about?"

"Soon, you're going to beg me for forgiveness. You're going to want me to believe that you're sorry for killing my wife. I can't believe you if all you do is lie to me."

"I'll never ask for forgiveness for a crime I didn't commit."

"You killed my wife. And you're going to make me execute you because somehow you think you have cards yet to play. You think you can talk your way out of this. You've misjudged the situation."

"Don't you turn this around. If you kill me, that's on your conscience. Don't you believe for one second that this is my doing. You want to kill an innocent man, that's on you, not me. I had nothing to do with your wife's death. Kroll worked jobs for Reece Whitton. I had no part in what happened to your wife."

"You ordered it."

"Where's your proof? You want to believe it's true, but that's not proof. Kroll's dead. Whitton's dead. That recording never mentions my name. You have nothing except what you believe to be true. No prosecutor in the world would buy what you're selling."

"You're right," I say as I go back to drilling. "No prosecutor would buy this, but this isn't going to a prosecutor. You'll never see the inside of a courtroom. You're running out of time."

"And you're running out of bluffs. You have nothing."

"I have Anastasia," I say.

"You're going to believe the word of a whore?"

"Whore? She's Reece Whitton's wife. You say you barely remember Whitton, yet you feel comfortable calling Mrs. Whitton a whore? Why is that?"

Mikhail goes silent again.

"Your lies are falling apart, Mikhail," I say.

"You think you know something, don't you?" he says with a slight shiver in his voice. "You think you've figured it all out, but you don't know shit. You've got it all backward. You're being played, and you can't see it."

I hear his words, but they fall numb on my ears. It's all a game to him. He's still trying to get in my head. I'm sore, and I'm tired. I haven't the energy to care about his bullshit anymore. I break through to the lake in hole number six, and I watch the water fill it up. The sun is growing weak in the west, and my shadow is growing long. I have two more holes to drill and only enough sunlight for one.

CHAPTER 35

Snowflakes attacked my headlights and windshield, obscuring the edges of Interstate 35 as we headed north. Ana hadn't spoken to me since my breakdown by the streetlight. That was at least an hour ago, and we hadn't even made it as far as Forest Lake yet, a drive that, on a clear day, takes under thirty minutes. I stayed in the passing lane but got bottled up behind those less intrepid drivers who preferred to jam up my lane as opposed to getting the hell out of my way. I was glad to have the all-wheel drive of the Durango, but I really missed my strobe lights.

I figured that Mikhail had a good hour's lead, maybe more depending on how soon after the strip-club ruckus he'd hit the road. He might have even gotten enough of a head start to be in front of the storm and the cluster-fuck of bad drivers stacked up in front of me.

A gap opened up as a minivan reconsidered its lane choice and moved over behind a semi. I eased on the gas, bringing the Durango up to thirty-five miles per hour. A cloud of white rose up behind the semi next to me, and I disappeared into the cloud, blind to everything except the truck's running lights to my right.

I felt the cushion of thick snow against my tires as I pushed the limits of safety. The truck encroached into my lane enough that it put me on the shoulder where a ridge of plowed snow hip-checked me into a slide. I twisted a few degrees clockwise and then another few degrees counterclockwise before regaining control.

"We won't get there if we're dead," Ana said. She was holding onto the door handle with both hands.

I maintained my death grip on the steering wheel and slowly moved past the truck.

"You should give me the battery for my phone. When you crash, I don't want to have to dig through the pockets of a dead man to call for help."

"No offense, but I've only known you for a couple hours. It takes me a little longer than that to sum up a stranger."

"Have I done anything to make you not trust me?"

"Other than try and kill a man? I guess not."

"And yet only one of us succeeded on that score."

I looked at her to see if she was serious or joking. In the dark I couldn't tell.

"You don't trust me," she said. "I understand that. I am, in your eyes, one of them. You think that my life with Mikhail and Reece ties me to their actions. They killed my sister. How could I be a part of that?"

"I don't know what you're a part of, Ana. I don't know much of anything. You say you're an innocent bystander; I'll buy that for now. But there's too much gray area."

"It is not gray. I want Zoya's killer stopped. You want that too. This is not gray."

She had no idea about Jenni and the real purpose behind our mission. I thought about telling her. That would have been the fair thing to do. Here she was, risking her life in a car that had nearly fish-tailed underneath the back tire of a semi, and she still thought this was about arresting Mikhail for the death of her sister. I opened my mouth, fully intending to tell her the truth, but I couldn't. Instead, I decided to fill in some of those gray areas.

"Tell me about your life with Mikhail and Reece. How does a girl from Belarus come to find herself in Minneapolis with a tattoo behind her ear?"

My words came out harsher than I wanted, and in my periphery I could see Ana retreat into her seat. I didn't expect her to answer. It was a dickish move on my part. I may as well have come right out and asked her what made her a whore.

I pulled in behind a convoy of travelers moving at a sluggish but consistent speed. "Slow and steady wins the race," I muttered under my breath.

"It's not the strip club," Ana said. "That's what you might think, but it's not. It's the cleaning company."

"The cleaning company?" I said.

"Mikhail owns a cleaning company as well as the strip club. He has some legitimate contracts to clean offices and houses. He runs the prostitution out of that company."

"And you worked for his . . . cleaning company?"

Ana pulled her knees up to her chest and wrapped her arms around her shins—cocooning herself as best she could around the seat belt. "I was a seventeen-year-old girl in Lida, my home in Belarus, when I met a man. He said that he could get me a job in Canada cleaning homes and offices. He said that after a few months, he could get me to the United States. He promised that once I got to America, I could do anything. He said that I was beautiful."

Ana turned toward the window as she slipped deeper into her past.

"I wanted, very much, to come to America. You don't know what it was like in Belarus. My father left us after Zoya was born. My mother did her best, but we had very little. We lived in a basement apartment. Pipes ran across the ceiling and dripped water onto our beds and shook with noise all night. We had no money. I wanted to help. I wanted to come to America to earn money to help my mother."

"Was that Mikhail who came to you in Belarus?"

"No. It was an associate, a man whose job it was to get the girls to Canada. I moved to Toronto and began cleaning offices. It was a good job. I made more money than I could ever have made in Lida."

"In Toronto, did you . . . were you . . ."

"Was I a prostitute? No. I only cleaned offices. I liked Canada. I was there for a year. That's when Zoya came over. By then, I was eighteen and she was sixteen. They got a passport for her saying she was eighteen. We lived in the same apartment. We were happy. Then I received word that I was to come to America. I told them that I didn't want to go. I wanted to stay with Zoya. But I owed them lots of money for my travel, for my apartment. They kept my passport. I had to do what they said."

"How'd you cross the border?"

"In a canoe. First, I was delivered to Mikhail's Canadian partners in Thunder Bay. Then the Canadians brought me to a cabin about ten miles north of the American border. From there, we carried a canoe into the woods and paddled across the border. We looked like any other tourists. When I arrived on the American side of the lake, I met Mikhail. He brought me to his cabin."

"The cabin we're going to now?"

Ana shuddered and wrapped her coat up around her neck. Her answer, a single word—"yes"—fell heavy from her lips, as if it carried the weight of years of regret.

"And the cleaning company, here in America?"

"That is how Mikhail hides everything. The girls are hired to clean. They go to a location. They perform the services requested, but the money came as a payment for cleaning services. The books are legitimate to anyone who doesn't know the truth."

"And no one ever slipped up? No one ever let it out that this cleaning company was a front for prostitution?"

"Mikhail's clients are carefully chosen. You don't come to Mikhail without a referral, and then he looks into your background. The clients must pass his inspection before he will permit his girls to go to them. Mikhail sells discretion, a very rare and expensive commodity for which he is greatly rewarded. His clients can be assured of the most beautiful women, but more importantly, they are assured their privacy. None of Mikhail's girls have ever been arrested. Secrecy and loyalty—that is what Mikhail values above all else."

"And Reece ensured that privacy?"

"Reece was important to everything. Reece kept Mikhail in the shadows. One time, a client was arrested for stealing prescription pills from his own pharmacy. He tried to cut a deal to keep his license and his job. He offered to hand Mikhail's operation over to the police if they would turn a blind eye to his theft. Reece heard about this man and what he had offered the authorities. Reece took care of it while Mikhail waited at the cabin, ready at any moment to cross the border. The pharmacist was later determined to be a liar."

"No one believed the pharmacist?"

"The pharmacist recanted, said he made the whole thing up. I suspect that the recantation saved the pharmacist's wife from a terrible fate. That's how Mikhail operated."

"And you know this because . . . ?"

Ana looked at me and shook her head, as if to warn me off a topic. "You must not confuse me with an innocent. I am not innocent—I have not been for a long time. I was innocent once, in Canada. Now I am . . . I am not sure what I am anymore."

"You could have walked away. You didn't have to go along with what they wanted you to do."

I tried to soften my words so that they didn't come across as condemning. I don't think I succeeded on that score. Ana again turned her gaze to her window. The darkness outside and the dim lights from the dashboard gave her an eerie reflection against the glass. After a few minutes, she said, "I will tell you what I am. You will judge me, I know, but at least you will understand."

CHAPTER 36

"I met Mikhail the day they brought me across the border," Ana said. "He was waiting for me in a clearing of pine trees. He was so American, wearing his plaid shirt and bright smile. I thought he was more handsome than any actor I had ever seen. He spoke Belarussian, and he kissed my hand like I was something more than just a cleaning woman from Lida.

"As he led me through the woods, he told me about the trees, showing me the difference between the many pines. He told me about the forest fires that swept through and cleared everything out, and about mushrooms and lichen that survive the fires to grow the forest again. He was so smart and caring, and when he held my hand, I felt like I was in a dream.

"He brought me to a cabin in the middle of the woods, two or three kilometers from the lake. He called it a cabin, but it was nicer than any house I had ever lived in. I remember thinking that if I could live in such a house, I would never leave. My bedroom was in the basement. He said that I would be staying in that room until it was safe for him to bring me to Minneapolis. He told me that he was putting me down there for my protection; but the door locked from the outside, not the inside."

"You were his prisoner?" I asked.

"I was his prisoner, yes, but I did not feel like a prisoner—not at first. He spent time with me in that room. He brought me food, fresh fruits, and wine. He would drink with me and tell me how beautiful I was. I had never felt so special. But he would also tell me that his friends from Canada had spent a great deal of money on me. He told me that he paid my debt to them, and that I now had a debt to pay to him. He would kiss me and tell me that he would help me, that I should trust him.

"It was wonderful at first, but as time went by, he changed. He would stop bringing me food—for days at a time. I could hear him walking on the floor above me, and I would scream to him, but he would not come down. Often he would wake me in the middle of the night and he would do things to keep me awake. He would not let me sleep. This went on for a long time. I did not understand why he was depriving me of food and sleep. But now I understand. He was changing the way I think, the way I saw who I was."

"He was breaking you down," I said.

"Yes. And when I thought I would go insane, he changed again. He became loving. He would come to me and hold me. He was protecting me, and I believed him."

Ana sniffed and wiped tears from her cheeks.

"That's when he started to make me do things . . . sexually."

"He forced you?"

"Force? No, he did not force me, not in the way you might think. It's hard for people to understand. He had become everything to me. I wanted to show him how much I loved him. When I did the things that pleased him, he showered me with love and attention. I felt like I was the most special person on the planet."

Ana's voice dipped to a sadder tone as she continued. "I know it sounds like I'm describing a dog that stays with a wicked master, but in a way that is how it was. That is how it is done—not with iron fists and beatings, but with velvet gloves and kisses."

"As time went on, he began to test me, to see what I would do for him. He brought me presents: clothing, jewelry, shoes. With each new gift, he would push the boundaries of what I had to do. He taught me how to please a man in ways that made me hate myself. I did things, terrible things, and I did them with a smile on my face because it made him happy. I wanted to show him that there was nothing I would not do for him. He would abuse me and I would smile and say 'see what I am willing to do for you?'"

Ana closed her eyes and leaned back in her seat, the corners of her lips tugging downward, stopping her from speaking. Whatever memory she was trying to summon had to be a painful one. She took a deep breath to regain her composure and then continued.

"One day, Mikhail came to my room with another man, a big man who smelled like rotting teeth. This man sat on my bed and looked at me in a way that ran needles up my spine. Mikhail told me that my next test would be to do everything that he asked of me, but I would do it with this man."

"I begged Mikhail not to make me do these things, but he slapped my face. It was the only time he ever hit me. He said that I had embarrassed him—I disrespected him in front of his friend. He called me a child—accused me of being disloyal because I would not do what he had commanded. He told me that I must prove my devotion to him by being with this man."

"I did what he told me to do. I had sex with that man—many times—because that is what Mikhail wanted. After that man left our house, Mikhail told me that I was his best girl and that I had passed all my tests. I was ready to go to Minneapolis. I was ready to dance in his club and tease the men and be with the men. That is when he brought me to the city and to his office. There, Mikhail etched the tattoo behind my ear—proof that I belonged to him."

She brought her hand up and touched the ruble behind her ear.

"I know it makes no sense to you, Detective, but it pleased me to get this tattoo. I was his girl. I lived for him. I would do whatever he asked of me. It sounds foolish as I tell you these things now, but, as I said, that is how it is done."

I didn't know what to say. How do you respond to a woman who's just told you how she was turned into a slave? In my periphery I could see Ana staring at the dashboard. She looked so much smaller than the woman I wrestled out of the strip club a few hours ago, her hands folded around her knees, her hair falling in wisps across her cheeks, some strands clinging to the wet paths of her tears. She must have thought me as much of a monster as Mikhail. She had let me in, peeled back her layers to expose the hardened marrow beneath, showing me her darkest shades, and I responded with silence.

"I'm sorry," I finally said.

"Sorry?" She raised her eyes to me and stared in puzzlement.

"We should have protected you. Whitton should have protected you. That was his job."

"Reece could do nothing for me. Mikhail had him tied up tight. Reece could not even save himself. It did not shock me that he took his life. It has been his only way out from the beginning."

"What do you mean?"

"Not long after Mikhail brought me to Minneapolis, I learned about Reece Whitton. Reece used to come to the club to watch me dance. He watched others too, but he preferred me. He wanted me to go with him to his house. Mikhail forbade it. Mikhail knew that Reece was a cop.

"Then, one day, Mikhail brought me into his office. He told me that he had been looking into Reece Whitton. There were rumors. Other girls were telling stories of Reece. They said that he would hire them and when he got them alone, he would show them his badge. He would make them do things—bad things. He was cruel to them. And in the end he would not pay them. He would tell them that their payment was their freedom. The word was getting around, and soon no one would go near him.

"That's when Mikhail came up with his plan. One night I was dancing in the club and Reece came in. He took me to the private room and asked me to meet him later. I agreed. But I took him to my apartment, where Mikhail had cameras hidden all around. I let Reece do what he wanted. I did it for Mikhail. And before Reece left, I made sure that he told me that my payment would be my freedom.

"When Mikhail showed Reece the footage, Mikhail didn't ask for money. Instead, he offered to make Reece a partner. He brought Reece into the company. If Reece agreed, Mikhail would own him. Reece would never be able to deny Mikhail anything."

"So Reece Whitton became a partner in Mikhail's operation. And you?"

Ana looked at me like I had just insulted her. "You still think that I am one of them?"

"I don't know, Ana. I honestly don't know."

CHAPTER 37

Up North

"Ana's playing you, Rupert." Mikhail's words clatter across his teeth like falling bits of stone knocking together, his jaw clenching as he fights to hide the deep, frozen chill in his bones. The ice seems to have finally penetrated his snowsuit, and I can hear a new desperation in his voice, a trapped animal finally aware of the cage around him. "She lied to you," he says. "She set you up. She sent you here because she wants you to kill me."

"What happened to 'I have no idea what you're taking about'? What happened to 'I'm just a businessman'?"

Every part of my upper torso burns as I crank the auger with a renewed vigor. He's changing his tack again, retreating to his fallback position. He has no choice but to admit what I already know.

The sun is slipping beyond the hills in the west, the hue of blue and violet melting into night as the light passes over our little nest. I want to get this hole drilled before I run out of light. In the east, the clouds are nearly gone from view and the rays of a brilliant moon seep through the final wisps. The wind has picked up a notch, and it pinches the exposed skin of my face. Mikhail remains burrowed into the snow to keep out of the wind, but I can see him shivering despite his best effort to act tough.

"Ana runs the prostitution ring," he says. "She's the one who pulls the strings. I'm just a front man."

Now we're getting somewhere. "So there is a prostitution ring," I say.

"Yes, but it's not me. It's Ana."

"A couple hours ago, there was no such thing. You swore to God. You begged me to believe you. Now you want me to believe that the ring exists, but you're not involved? You see how this looks, don't you, Mikhail?"

"I swear to God—"

"I'm sure you do."

"Okay, I started it—yes, but I haven't been in control of the operation for years. It's been Ana and Reece Whitton. They've been squeezing me out. Now she's going to have you do her dirty work and finish the job. You kill me and she has it all. Don't you see that?"

"I see a man who will say anything to save himself."

"She knows the business. Hell, she was my top girl. She has the client list. That's all hers now. She's the one who kept the thing running."

"How do the women get here? Who brings them here? That's you, not Ana."

"It used to be me, yes, but not anymore. Ana knows all my contacts."

"What was Whitton's role?"

"Whitton was a customer. He used to come into the club and get hammered, then hit on the girls—offer them money or whatever. He was trying to get freebies in exchange for protection. He used to grab their tits and say that a cop can't do that if he was going to arrest them."

"So how'd he start working for you?"

"It was Ana's idea. She convinced me that we should take him up on his offer. Blackmail him. She went with him, got video doing some twisted shit. Ana really is a brilliant actress."

"You blackmailed him?"

"Less than you think. He was already ripe for the picking. We made him a partner."

"We?"

"Ana didn't tell you? She was a part of this from the very beginning."

"You're lying again," I say.

Mikhail smiled like someone who just got the punchline of a dirty joke. "She's gotten to you."

"Swing and a miss, Mikhail."

"You think she's innocent. Hell, she ran the girls. Whitton kept an ear out for police interference, let us know if anyone was sniffing around the setup. If things got hot, we'd shut down for a while until things cooled off again. In exchange, he'd get a nice payment every month."

"So you admit, you're a pimp. All this pretending to be a legitimate businessman was a waste of my time."

"That's the thing, Rupert. I *used* to be a pimp. They took that all away from me. I haven't been in charge of that for years."

"Poor Mikhail."

"No, I swear on my mother's life. I swear on anything you want. They pushed me out. Whitton and Ana came to me and said that they didn't need me anymore. They had my contacts in Canada and Belarus. They had Reece inside the police to watch things. Ana ran the girls for me anyway, so why did they need me? They told me that they were taking over the operation and that they would pay me what I had been paying to Whitton. I would be the front man for the cleaning company, but Ana took over day-to-day operations."

"You had the video of Whitton. If he turned on you, you could destroy him."

"No, I couldn't. Don't you see? Without Ana on my side, what good would that footage be? If Ana says it's an act—a married couple doing some role-playing—it becomes worthless. It's a husband and wife getting a little dark. That's all."

"Why are you lying?" I ask. My head hurts. My whole body hurts. The hunger in my stomach burns, and my arms feel as thin as button thread. I turn the auger, but I'm not sure it's digging down.

"I'm not lying. I swear, I haven't been the boss of the operation for years."

"You're going to make me kill you, aren't you?"

"No! I'm telling you the truth."

"In a little while, you're going to change your story again, and you're going to beg me to forgive you. You'll add a little more to your confession—who knows, maybe the next story will be the truth. But it won't matter; it'll be too late. Every time you make up another lie, you force my hand. I'll have no choice, because you've given me no choice. In the end, you'll repent and swear that you're a changed man, that you'll never harm anyone again. But I won't believe you. You're giving me no choice."

"I'm not lying! You don't have to kill me. I wasn't the one who killed your wife. Ana did it. It was Ana who ordered the hit. Ana was the boss."

I stop drilling, clench my fists, and scream, "GOD DAMMIT, SHUT UP!"

The lake goes silent except for the wind. The sun has closed its eyes to my little undertaking, and to the east, a full moon slips out from behind the billow of clouds, its light dressing the snowy surface of the lake in a sparkle of blue. Not far away, expanding ice sends up a moan, which almost makes me think that the lake itself is baying. Such a beautiful night for such an ugly endeavor. I'm almost through to the lake on hole number seven. I start turning the auger again.

"You can't kill me," Mikhail says. "I'm not the one you want. Ana killed your wife. She's the one who ordered it. I didn't know about it until after the fact. I only knew about it because they told me."

"They told you about it?"

"I swear. I told them both to get out. I didn't want anything to do with no murder. That's why I didn't know what you were talking about. They never told me the details. I never knew who they murdered. All they said was they had to kill a social worker because one of the girls was running her mouth. That's all I knew. I swear to God."

I break through to the lake. I only have one hole left to drill. I take a moment to chip ice from the tops of earlier holes, which have frozen over. As I do so, I lay Mikhail's latest story over what I already know. He's done a pretty good job of filling in blanks and explaining things, but, as with all lies, there are still gaps, mistakes. His fast thinking failed to account for one big flaw: if Ana was behind all of this, why would she kill her sister? Also, he doesn't know what Ana told me that morning. I will tell him soon, and by then, it will be too late.

CHAPTER 38

Ana managed to fall asleep around two in the morning, and slept through my stopping for gas in Duluth; I paid in cash, of course. I let her sleep until I turned onto the Gunflint Trail, heading west out of Grand Marais.

"Where are we?" she asked, in a groggy voice.

"Gunflint Trail."

She rubbed her eyes and looked around as if to get her bearings, but there were no landmarks to speak of. The trail, a two-lane blacktop road, snaked west for sixty miles into the heart of the Superior National Forest, running more or less parallel to the Canadian border. Driving Gunflint was akin to passing through a tunnel. Pine and birch rose like walls of a canyon on either side of us. And with the snow choking the headlights and the dark sky pressing down from above, the whole world seemed as small as the inside of a boxcar. At times I felt dizzy and a little claustrophobic.

"It is a long way down this road," Ana said. She leaned up against the dash, her gaze scanning the reach of my headlights.

I could see the impression of tire tracks under the new snow. There were tracks going in both directions, so I knew that we weren't the only ones crazy enough to challenge the storm. Somewhere under my tires were the tracks laid down by Mikhail—unless he had the good sense to pull over at a motel. I would know soon enough.

"What am I looking for?" I asked.

"It is a small path. It will go this way." She swam her hand to the right.

"Are there any signs?"

"I think so, but I can't remember. I've only been there two times."

"You've been there twice?"

"I went there when Mikhail brought me to America. I told you about that. I went there a second time, four years ago. I didn't understand the reason then. Reece told me that we were going there to get closer. He was acting like he wanted to be my husband, not just my owner. He called it a belated honeymoon. I should have suspected the truth."

"The truth?"

"I hated Reece Whitton. I loathed him. I was with him because of Mikhail, and he knew it. There was no marriage—not in my eyes and not in his. I went where he told me to go and did what he told me to do, but we had no marriage, so there would be no honeymoon. He brought me to the cabin to keep me from hearing about Zoya."

I started to understand. "Her death was in the news," I said. "We posted her picture on television. We were hoping someone might identify her."

Ana nodded her head. "That is what I assume. When I saw the file you had on Zoya, I understood why Reece brought me to the cabin. There is no television there. No newspapers. He kept me there for six weeks. I did not understand why. Now I know. They needed me in the dark until the story about Zoya's death faded away."

"You didn't know that your sister went missing? That was four years ago. What did you think happened to her?"

"At first, when Mikhail offered to bring Reece into the operation, Reece did not agree. He saw how the path could only lead to his destruction. But he also saw few alternatives. In the end, Reece agreed to Mikhail's proposition, but only if Mikhail gave me to him as part of the deal. I would become his wife on paper, a title that exaggerated my true role.

"I told Mikhail that I did not want to go. That's when Mikhail told me that he was bringing Zoya to America. The trip had already been arranged. Mikhail would do to Zoya what he did to me. I begged Mikhail not to bring her here. I promised him that I would go with Reece if he would send Zoya back to Belarus. I did not want her to suffer what I had suffered.

"Mikhail agreed. He said that if I went with Reece, he would send

Zoya home. I could never talk to her again, but she would be safe. He knew that my love for Zoya was my final strength. Mikhail knew that if he deceived me on that score, I would turn on him.

"I believed him when he made that promise. But Mikhail Vetrov is not a man of honor. He brought my sister here and did not tell me. I was told that she went back to Belarus to be with our mother. She sent me a letter. I believed it. But I know now that her letter was a lie. They must have made her write it—probably from the same locked room at the cabin where he kept me prisoner. Mikhail's people mailed the letter from Lida, but she was here in America, being murdered."

"You never tried to contact her?"

"I am not permitted to have contact with my family. I am not permitted to use the Internet. My phone does not have data. Reece spied on me for Mikhail, but it was not necessary. I promised to obey Mikhail if he sent Zoya back to Belarus. I kept my promise. Mikhail did not."

I slowed the car as I saw a set of tire tracks diverging down a narrow path to the right, their faint outline barely visible beneath the fresh snow. There were still other tracks that continued straight.

"Is that it?" I asked, coming to a stop at the mouth of the turn.

Ana sat up straight and looked down the trail, studying it for a good ten seconds. "No, that is not it. It is farther ahead."

At ten minutes before 6:00 a.m., the night still maintained its dark cloak, but it wouldn't be long before lighter shades of gray began to filter into the sky. We were running out of time. I lowered my window to let in some fresh air. I needed to wake up. My hands were cramping from holding the steering wheel so tightly. Had it really been over ten hours since we left Minneapolis? The Gunflint Trail hadn't been plowed yet and we'd been on it for an hour and a half but hadn't yet gone forty miles.

That's when we rounded a turn and came upon another thin road cutting to the north. Ana locked onto that road with the sharpness of a hunting dog approaching a pheasant. She held her hand into the air to signal me to slow.

"This is it," she whispered. "His cabin is down there, about a mile and an half. He will still be sleeping—or maybe he is getting ready to leave." She looked to the east as if to gauge the rise of the sun. "I don't think he'll leave before the sun comes up. The trail is very dangerous in places. It is very steep. We can catch him by surprise."

I kept driving.

"Where are you going?"

"I let you come along to show me where to find him. That's all. Your part is done. I'm dropping you off up here a ways."

I'd been watching the signs for a resort called the Gunflint Lodge ever since we turned out of Grand Marais. The turnoff to Mikhail's cabin was only ten miles from the resort. I needed a place to deposit Ana before I finished my hunt.

"You cannot do this," Ana shouted. "You have no right to do this."

"I can't have you with me," I said. "I'm going after Mikhail, and you're going to wait at this lodge up ahead. That's all there is to it."

"I will not—"

"This isn't up for discussion. You're not coming with me."

"You can't stop me."

"I'll pick you up after—"

"I will not be denied!" Ana screamed and grabbed for the steering wheel.

I shoved her back into her seat, gripping the front of her coat and holding her at arm's length. She tried to bite my wrist, and I pulled my hand back.

Her eyes blazed with hatred as she cursed at me in Belarussian. Then she said, "If you think you can get me out of this car, you're sadly mistaken. I will fight you. That man killed my sister."

"That man killed my wife!" I yelled.

I had blurted the words out before I had time to think. Ana stopped her attack cold. What had been hatred and rage in her eyes now melted into confusion.

"What do you mean?" she asked.

"Nothing," I said.

"Mikhail killed your wife?"

I didn't answer.

"Please." She reached across and laid her hand on my arm. "Please tell me."

I thought about the risk of opening myself up to this woman, a woman I'd known for a matter of hours. But then I thought about her tears as she told me about her life and about her love for her sister, Zoya, the girl who connected Mikhail to Jenni. In a way, I felt that Ana had earned the right to hear the truth. Somewhere in my sleep-deprived brain, it became important that I tell her about Jenni.

"Not long before Zoya was killed, someone threw her through a plate-glass window, sent her to the hospital. My wife, Jenni, was a social worker there. She took care of your sister, and Zoya told Jenni some things. She spoke in Belarussian, so my wife didn't know what she was saying. I know now that Zoya was trying to talk about Mikhail. I didn't know who Mikhail was until tonight."

"Why do you say that Mikhail killed your wife? Do you have proof of this?"

"Your husband and a man named Ray Kroll were instructed to kill her. They made it look like a hit-and-run, and that's what we thought it was. But now I know the truth. Mikhail ordered her death, and they carried it out. Reece is dead. Kroll is dead. And Mikhail . . . well, he's . . . I'm not going to let him make it to Canada."

Ana looked pale in the soft glow of the dashboard lights. She had sunk back into her seat, and all that fight she had a minute ago had drained away. I expected her to ask me questions, maybe demand proof of what I said, but she didn't. Ana turned her face to the window and didn't make a sound.

I pulled into Gunflint Lodge, a small complex of cabins and trails that funneled down the side of a hill to the main lodge at the edge of a lake. The soft light of morning had begun to bleed through the trees and spill out onto the frozen expanse that separated Minnesota from Canada. I parked the Durango and walked to the front door of the lodge, where a dim, yellow light glowed its welcome. Ana waited until I had gone in before she followed.

The door opened into a vestibule not much bigger than three paces in each direction. I crossed the vestibule and tried the next door. Locked. I looked around for a phone or buzzer to call someone to come and let us in. Then I noticed a sign on the inside door that read "Open at 7 A.M." I peered through the glass for any sign of life. Nothing.

"Fuck," I muttered. A topographical map of Superior National Forest hung on the wall, and in the dim light, I found the tiny *X* that designated the lodge. I backtracked to the trail where Mikhail's cabin lay and studied the terrain and distances to the Boundary Waters Canoe Area, to the Canadian border and beyond, doing my best to commit it to memory.

I reached into my pocket and pulled out my wallet, retrieving all of my cash. "Take this." I shoved the money into Ana's hands.

"No. I don't—"

"I don't have time to argue," I said. "You can stay here. They open at seven. It's heated here in the vestibule. When they let you in, get a room. I'll come back for you when I'm . . . just stay here."

I started to leave, but she grabbed my arm and pulled me back.

"Wait," she said. "I have to tell you something."

"I have to go. He's getting away."

"Please, listen."

"What?" I snapped.

Her eyes looked up at me, beseeching me to listen to her. "I know about your wife's death. I know what happened to her. I did not know she was your wife—I promise—not until just now. I know what they did to your wife. I need to tell you. You must know this before you go."

Ana eased me onto the pine bench by the wall, and there she proceeded to tell me the details of Jenni's death.

CHAPTER 39

The trail leading to Mikhail's cabin still held the faint impression of tire tracks under the snow. I drove to the turnoff with my headlights extinguished. The sun was close enough to the horizon to give relief from the darkness, but the snow fell in a thick, cottony wave that made it seem like I was driving through a curtain.

I parked at the entrance to the trail and slipped into my snow pants, removing my gun from its holster and putting it into my coat pocket so I could zip the pants shut. My boots and coat were high-end, but old, and I seemed to recall that one of my boots had a hole in it. Walmart-quality gloves and stocking cap finished my ensemble.

As I started down the hill, the snow thickened into a flurry so heavy that I could barely see twenty yards, but I could see the dip of the tire tracks at my feet well enough to follow them. Soon the tracks turned and disappeared into the forest. Through the trees I could make out the faint outline of a structure—and lights. He was there.

I moved into the tree line, crouching low to creep beneath the branches. The snow rose above my knees, and each step required effort to keep from tipping over. Ahead was the trace outline of the cabin, the pallid gold of a rough-hewn pine exterior filtered through the wall of snow. I removed the glove from my right hand and drew my gun out of my coat pocket.

I could hear a motor running. The sound seemed to be coming from the far side of the cabin. I entered a clearing and sidestepped my way along the trees until I came to a tool shed at the edge of the property. The door was open, so I peeked inside, my gun leading the way. It was empty except for the clutter of random items you'd expect in such a shack: life jackets, canoe paddles, rope, an ice auger, and gardening tools.

I moved downslope and rounded the back side of the cabin. This was not a cabin like my little hovel in the woods north of Grand Rapids. Through the snow, I could see a deck jutting out beneath an A-frame wall of glass, which rose up a good twenty feet, the sparkle of electric light making the whole façade glow in the burgeoning dawn. On any other day, this might have been the perfect setting for a Christmas card.

I followed the sound of the running engine along the back of the cabin, leveling my gun in that direction. I hadn't had my glove off for all that long, but already I could feel the cold filling the spaces in my knuckles.

Like an iceberg emerging from a fogbank, the source of the engine noise came into view. A snowmobile. I took a few more steps, and could see that it stood idling, unmanned. Someone had started it to let it warm up for a trip. A helmet lay on the seat, and the light dusting of snow on top of the helmet meant that Mikhail had laid it there within the past few minutes.

Suddenly, I sensed movement in my periphery. Before I could turn to look, a wedge of pine firewood smashed into the back of my wrist. Pain exploded in my arm, shooting needles of fire and ice up my neck, and sending my gun sailing, disappearing into a haze of white.

I turned to see a second log heading for my face. I lurched backward to dodge it, my legs getting twisted in the snow, and I fell back. Mikhail stood at the back of the house, next to a stack of firewood, where he picked up a third log and flung it at me. This one I was ready for, and I knocked it down just before it hit my chest. He picked up a fourth and chucked it blindly in my general direction as he began a mad dash for the snowmobile.

I got to my feet, grabbed the log that I'd knocked down, and heaved it at the snowmobile. Mikhail had climbed onto the seat and had his helmet in his hands. When my log hit him square in the back, the helmet went tumbling, and Mikhail fell forward. I charged toward him, closing to within ten feet before he popped the sled into gear and screamed away.

I looked around for my gun, but in my disorientation, I had no idea where to look. I gave a quick scan for holes in the snow where it may have fallen, but I had made a mess of the area with my thrashing about. I didn't have time.

That's when I saw the ax handle sticking out of the snow near the stack of firewood. I ran and grabbed it, expecting to have the whole ax, but it lifted light in my hand. It was only the handle. It would have to do. Mikhail was getting away. I put my glove back onto my bare right hand and began running.

I headed down the path laid by the track of the snowmobile, sinking into the snow with each step, but not nearly as bad as it would have been without the track. I ran at a full charge for the first hundred feet, but then reason began to replace adrenaline. He was on a snowmobile heading for the Boundary Waters Canoe Area, and beyond that, Canada. The snowmobile trail would end when he reached the Boundary Waters, and he would be forced to go it on foot. He'll have a head start, but in this deep snow, I would have the advantage of stepping in his tracks.

I could hear the scream of the snowmobile engine in the distance. It swung in great crescendos, dropping to near silence after each—hitting the gas hard on the short straightaways and breaking for the turns. Reckless.

I slowed to a jog, working to get into a rhythm that would keep my breathing down so that the air didn't burn my lungs. I just needed to keep my head and gain on him in small increments.

As the sound of the engine grew faint, I heard it suddenly die. I paused to listen and could hear nothing. He couldn't have been to the end of the trail yet. He hadn't gone far enough for that to be the cause of the silence. Something went wrong.

I picked up my pace.

The trail bounced up and down with some climbs, steep enough that I was nearly on my hands and knees. I slowed on those hills, half expecting an ambush. I had considered that Mikhail may have a gun, but I discarded that concern early on. He would have shot me at the cabin instead of throwing logs at me. He must have been in the final stages of preparation for his escape north. I caught him off guard.

As I approached my next hill, I could see a glint of yellow in the trees. I slowed to a walk and tested my grip on the ax handle. The buzz of bees that had filled my wrist after getting hit by that log was all but gone and my strength had returned. I charged up the hill with my weapon at the ready, only to find the abandoned snowmobile jammed into the craw of a group of saplings. Mikhail had been moving too fast to make the turn. I could see the holes in the snow where his legs carried him north. Here is where my advantage would begin.

Mikhail's tracks led down a gentle slope to a valley and up the opposite hill. I couldn't see him, but he had to be just beyond the crest. I stepped into his footprints and gave chase. The mechanics of cutting a fresh trail through snow is so much harder than walking in another man's tracks. I would be limited to his gait, but not his pace. I could go faster, maybe only slightly, but it would be faster than he was moving. Catching him would be a mathematical certainty, as long as we had enough distance to cover, and I knew that we had plenty of distance before he would find civilization on the Canadian side of the border.

I moved as efficiently as I could, using the ax handle as a walking stick on the uphill climb. I needed to keep from falling down, which was difficult. Every stumble cost me valuable seconds. I could see where Mikhail tripped as he scurried down the slopes, and his wild, flailing steps as he climbed them.

Slow and steady, I whispered to myself.

As I came to the top of the second ridge, the snowfall had ebbed to a fine glitter, the lake opening up below me, beautiful and white, maybe half a mile across. Partway onto that lake, a tiny red figure trudged forward, lurching from one foot to the next as he fought to get across the lake.

I took a moment to catch my breath, my hands resting on my knees as I sucked in oxygen, my eyes focused on the man in red. He stopped and turned. With my gray pants and brown coat, I was pretty sure he couldn't see me, but he picked up his pace anyway. The race was on.

I smiled and charged down the hill, stumbling only once but recovering quickly. Again I had to remind myself to keep a steady pace. I didn't want to be physically depleted when I caught him. I punched through the last of the pine and aspen and found myself on the edge of the lake. I could see him well enough to see his arm swinging wildly, trying to keep his momentum going forward.

He was mine.

I slogged ahead, doing my best to ignore the pain in my chest. The cold air sizzled and wheezed as it abraded the tissue in my lungs. Snot from my nose froze against the stubble of whiskers on my upper lip. Tears, born of the cold breeze in my face, ran down my cheeks, and I had to blink hard to clear my eyes.

I was gaining.

I drew close enough to hear him coughing. The chase was destroying him. He glanced over his shoulder every ten or fifteen steps to see me gaining ground. He had to know the futility of his circumstance. Yet he kept up his pace—and I kept up mine.

We neared the northern shore of the lake, and he began to lean forward with every step, as if he were trying to reach out and grab the air to pull himself off the lake and out of my grasp. He yelled something over his shoulder, gibberish that vanished into the dwindling snow.

I was fifty feet behind him, and he was almost to the shoreline. He looked back at me and I could see the fear and exhaustion in his eyes.

Forty feet. I heard him yell something that sounded like "Leave me alone."

Thirty feet. He reached the edge of the lake, pulling on a birch sapling to drag himself off the ice. Staggering forward, his head turning sharply to the left and right as if trying to find a path.

I used the same birch to pull myself off the lake, and now he was only fifteen feet away, his back still to me, his head swiveling in confusion.

I gripped my ax handle and raised it, charging with the last of my strength. He turned in time to see that chunk of hickory slicing through the air at his head. He raised his left arm to meet my blow, and I heard a crack of bone.

He screamed in pain and dropped to one knee. He fought to get back to his feet, and I raised the ax for a second blow. As I started my downswing, I saw the knife. He lunged. I jerked to the side and drove my ax handle into his head. This time he dropped down onto both knees, his eyes rolling up into his head as he fell backward into the snow.

I took a breath and raised the ax for the third blow, the one that would kill the man who killed my wife. And there, the ax remained.

CHAPTER 40

The last hole is the hardest to drill. The ice seems to have turned to stone, and I can't feel my fingers on either hand. My feet throb as if they are being crushed in a vise. My arms and chest are so cramped and gnawed by fatigue that I can barely turn the crank. Every few turns, I have to stop and rest, but resting only prolongs the suffering. The wind has picked up with gusts that push me into the auger. I feel like I may fall down at any moment.

A full moon is rising in the east, casting a dark-blue patina across the lake and rolling my shadow out ten feet behind me. I can see well enough to know that Mikhail is shivering violently, his words rattling as he speaks. "You can't do this," he says. "This is wrong—it's murder."

I gave him his trial. He could have come clean. No one—not even Nancy—can say I didn't try. Lie upon lie upon lie. He had all day to do the right thing. I gave him every opportunity, and I feel half dead from the effort. He knew what was coming; he chose this path.

I can no longer push down on the auger with my arm. It hurts too much. I lean forward and rest my forehead atop my hand on the cap of the auger. As I turn the crank, I use my neck muscles to press the auger into the ice. The sounds and vibrations pulsing up through the shaft fill my skull with noise. I welcome it because it helps to block out Mikhail's pleading. But I can still hear him. Like a runner at the end of a marathon, I push until I think I will collapse. But I don't break through and I have to rest. I'm so very close.

"Please, I told you, it was all Ana. You can't do this; you can't live with this. For God's sake, listen to me."

I don't want to talk to Mikhail, but I ask a question that, he has to see, is his last chance to purge his sins. "Tell me about Zoya," I say. My words are cracked and weak as they climb from my tattered throat. "Tell me how she died."

"She's dead?"

My shoulders slump with disappointment. "Come on, Mikhail. We've come too far for you to pretend now." I try to swallow, but I have no spit left. "Tell me how she died."

"I don't know. I swear to—"

"I know . . . you swear to God." I shake my head. "You've sworn to God so many times today. And every time that you said that, you were lying to me."

He's gritting his teeth to keep them from chattering and doesn't answer me.

"Haven't I been fair, Mikhail? Don't you want to save yourself? I'm going to ask you one last time . . . and I want you to answer as though your life depends on it—because it does. How . . . did . . . Zoya . . . die?"

"I . . . I don't know what you're talking about. I had nothing to do with her death."

I smile. "That's right. You're an innocent man. You don't know how Zoya died. You weren't involved in my wife's death. This is all a big misunderstanding."

"I told you what happened. That's the truth."

"Well, I'm sorry to hear you say that, Mikhail."

I stand back up and go back to drilling my last hole.

"This is wrong," he yells.

My auger catches and breaks through to the lake.

"You're doing this because of Ana," he says. "She's manipulated you, and you can't see it."

I have eight holes, each one six inches in diameter, making my oval forty-eight inches around, big enough to fit this man through. Each hole is separated from its neighbor by a wall of ice about as thin as a pane of glass. With the head of the auger, I stab into each hole at an angle, chipping away those final impediments.

"You can't do this. Please . . . please, I beg you, look at the facts. It's not me. It's Ana. You're being used."

As long as I keep my shadow behind me, I can see well enough by the moonlight to finish my pit.

"Think about it. With me dead . . . and Reece Whitton dead, she has it all to herself."

When I cut through the last wall, the chunk of ice in the center lifts in the water and floats a few inches higher than the rest of the icy surface. I know that I am too weak to heave it out of the water, so I use the auger to push it down. When it clears the bottom, the chunk turns sideways and knocks against the underside of the lake ice. The pit is open, jagged and dark and cold.

"You're insane," Mikhail says. He's working the cord against his zipper. In the moonlight, his eyes seem as big as hen's eggs. I have my hands on my thighs. I am exhausted. I begin to cough, and it feels like my lungs are tearing free of my chest.

When I catch my breath, I search through the darkness until I find the loose end of the rope. I'm breathing as if I'd just summited Mount Everest, and I curse at my poor condition. It won't be much longer.

"Listen to me," Mikhail pleads. "You can't do this. You have no proof. I'm telling you the truth. It was Ana."

I tie the sack of rocks to the rope around Mikhail's legs, three feet of slack between his heels and the bundle.

"God dammit! Stop!" Mikhail's voice carries up and seems to fill the entire sky. "Would you just stop?"

I finish tying Mikhail to the rocks, and I crawl up to sit beside him, my elbow in the snow near his head. "I've given you a chance to come clean," I say.

"But I'm telling you—"

"No. Don't say another word. I want you to be quiet and listen to me now."

Mikhail is breathing heavily. I can see the fear in his eyes, but he stops talking.

"Before I came here, I was with Ana. You saw me at the club, so you know this already. But she told me a story, and I want to tell it to you now."

I think back to that moment when I was about to leave the lodge and Ana held me back. *I have to tell you something*, she said. *I know about your wife's death. I know what happened to her.* In that brief conversation, Ana handed to me a final piece of my puzzle, a nugget of proof that has been here on the lake with us the entire day, hiding, waiting to be unveiled.

I speak. "Four and a half years ago, Zoya Savvin was beaten by one of your clients and thrown through a motel window. A patrol officer found her and took her to Hennepin County Medical Center, where she met my wife. Because her assault appeared to be related to prostitution, the Vice Unit was called. Reece Whitton took the call himself and went to the hospital. Zoya must have known that Reece worked for you, because when Whitton showed up, Zoya got scared and wouldn't say a word."

"No, you're wrong," Mikhail says. "I don't—"

I slap my hand down on Mikhail's broken arm and give it a squeeze. He lets loose a howl that tears open the night sky. I probably squeeze a bit harder than I need to, but I really want him to shut up and listen.

A faint green light, like the smoky flame of burning copper, is pulsing above the crown of the Canadian hills. The Aurora Borealis—the Northern Lights. I pause in my story for a moment to take in the beauty. In some weird way, that glow makes me feel warm inside. But that could also be hypothermia setting in.

"I'm guessing you thought you were in the clear," I continue. "Maybe you thought Zoya would be a good soldier—keep her mouth shut after she saw Whitton. But that didn't happen. Zoya talked to my wife. She said quite a bit once she thought she was safe from Whitton. The problem was that Zoya spoke in Belarussian. Jenni wrote the words down in a notebook, not knowing that those words would lead to her own death."

"I had nothing to do with her death."

I take the glove off my right hand and pull the fillet knife from my boot. Then I wrap the glove around the knife handle.

"Please, no. I swear. Don't you see? It was—"

I use the knife handle to shove the glove into Mikhail's mouth before he thinks to close it. He bites down and growls his rage and pain.

"I told you not to talk. You've had your chance. Now you're going to listen."

I pull the knife back out and put my left hand over the glove to keep it in place. In my right hand I brandish the knife, swiveling it slightly to catch the glint of the moon as I continue my story.

"Jenni sounded out some of those words to Reece Whitton, who understood full well what Jenni was saying—what Zoya was saying. Zoya was not being the good soldier, so Whitton called you. You needed Zoya out of that hospital and you needed to burn those notes. You, Mikhail Vetrov, ordered Reece Whitton and Ray Kroll to kill my wife."

Mikhail begins slinging his head back and forth, the muffled "no" barely making it past the glove in his mouth.

"You told them to make it look like an accident—a hit-and-run. Make sure Jenni had the notes with her in the parking ramp. Kill her. Bring the notes back to you."

I lay down the knife so my hand is free.

"When the time came to kill her, Kroll sped down the ramp where Whitton had lured Jenni. Whitton shoved her into the path of the car. Then he collected the notebook and walked away."

I climb onto Mikhail's stomach. I can feel his body tremble against my thighs.

"Ana told me something else this morning, something that I'd missed completely."

I reach for the zipper of his snowsuit, my fingers too cold to grasp it, so I hack at the zipper with the side of my hand until I work it open.

Mikhail starts to twist and flail. Beneath his coat, he's wearing a winter cycling jacket. He'd dressed well for his journey to Canada. I try to unzip the jacket, but the zipper is too small and my fingers are useless, so I bend down and grip the zipper in my teeth. He's bucking and trying to dig his chin into the top of my head. He knows what I'm looking for. I lower the zipper as far as I can.

"Kroll said something in that conversation with Whitton that I didn't pick up on. He said 'another drop of blood and we do all the work.' I thought he was just trying to sound cold, like he's killed before, and this is no big deal."

Under his cycling jacket, Mikhail's wearing a thermal undershirt. I pick up the knife and cut it down the front.

"But that's not the case, is it Mikhail? He wasn't just playing at being a stone-cold killer. He was talking about you, about the tattoo on your chest."

I rip open his shirt to expose a dagger tattoo in the middle of his torso, the handle up and the blade pointing down.

"This is the salute you give to your bosses in the old country—your record of accomplishment. Ana told me all about it."

Mikhail is yanking his head from side to side, trying to spit out the glove, but I hold it in place with my left hand as I trace the tattoo's blade with the point of the fillet knife. At the bottom of the dagger on his chest are four drops of blood inked to look as if they are dripping down his abdomen.

"Ana said this first drop of blood, your first kill, is for a rival that you had to dispose of for your bosses. Kind of a good-faith initiation."

I slide the blade of the fillet knife down his skin until the point rests on the second droplet tattoo.

"But this one . . . this one is for my wife. That's the drop of blood that Kroll mentions in the recording—your mark of achievement. He was complaining that he and Whitton would do the murder, but you would take the credit."

I move the point of the blade to the next drop of blood.

"This . . . is for Zoya, I presume. And this," I touch the fourth drop, "I'm betting this is Kroll."

I move the tip of the knife back up and rest it on the skin beside Jenni's mark.

"But you made a mistake," I say. "You didn't just kill my wife that day."

I move my left hand from the glove in his mouth and instead use it to hold the knife upright and in place.

"You also killed my child."

I raise my right hand above the handle of the knife, the heel of my palm exposed like a hammer head.

"You're missing a drop."

I start to bring my palm down on the knife handle with all the force I can muster. I envision the blade punching though his stomach and spine, embedding itself into the ice beneath him. His eyes go wide as he screams through my glove. But at the last second, I hold up. Then I smile, and with two fingers I tap the knife just enough to break the skin with the tip. A single drop of blood seeps out of the wound.

I look in his eyes and whisper, "I don't want you going to your grave with an incorrect body count."

CHAPTER 41

"Please, God, I'm sorry!" Mikhail yells. "I didn't know she was your wife. I swear. Don't kill me—not like this."

I should have left my glove in his mouth, but my fingers were turning brittle from exposure. With both hands safely ensconced in the tattered gloves, I climb off of Mikhail's chest and kneel beside the bundle of stones.

"You can't do this. Stop! Please!"

I'm too weak to pick the bundle up, so I shove it toward the hole with my feet, pausing the stones at the edge of the precipice. I clear my head of all his pleading, and I listen, waiting for some argument against what I am about to do. I expect to hear Nancy in my head, or maybe even Jenni's voice, but all I hear is the wind. I push the stones into the water.

The bundle isn't heavy enough to drag Mikhail across the ice. I didn't expect that it would be. I know that I will have to feed the man into the lake. He's on his back, twisting from side to side, trying to work the ax handle out of his pant leg. He's yanking at the cord that binds his wrist. He is helpless, and has no choice but to fight like hell.

I sit down in the snow above his head, put my boots on his shoulders, and shove. He slides a foot closer to the hole.

"For God's sake, stop!" he screams.

I think about Jenni on the table in the medical examiner's lab—the day I had to identify her body. I think about the bracelet in my pocket and the baby who never got the chance to take a breath. I shove again. His feet are now over the hole.

"I killed her," he says in a flurry of panic. "Okay? I admit it. I ordered Whitton and Kroll to kill her. I'm sorry. I swear I'm sorry." He sounds like he's crying. Giving the performance of his life.

I won't be able to get him into the hole while he's on his back. I move to his side and try to turn him over, but he's bucking and twisting too much and I can't get a good grip. I take off my gloves to get ahold of the man's snowsuit. My fingers don't want to obey. They're too frozen. I zip my coat down and shove my hands under my arm pits, keeping the wind at my back.

"Please don't kill me," he bawls. "I'll give you anything you want. I swear. Anything. I'm sorry."

My fingers aren't warm, but I've worked enough blood through them to make them somewhat useful. I grab his arm and roll him onto his stomach, and when I do, the cord that binds his wrists together breaks. He is still bound by the belt that tethers his elbows, and he immediately starts to shake his arms to try and slip them free of the belt.

I stand up and take a second to catch my breath. The belt is tangled in the folds of his snowmobile suit, but he whips his arms frantically to get free. The toes of his boots are dangling over the mouth of the hole. He tries to bend his knees to get his feet away from the hole, but the ax handle that I shoved down his leg gives him very little wiggle room.

"Please, you've got to believe me. I'm sorry. I swear to God, I'm sorry. If I could take it back—"

"Tell me about Zoya," I say. My next move will take all of my remaining strength, and I need a moment to summon what I have left.

"What?"

"You killed Zoya. Why?"

"I don't know anything about—"

I put my foot on the back of Mikhail's heels and lean down to grab the waist of his snow pants. In one last depleting effort, I heave his hips up while at the same time I stomp his feet through the opening in the ice. Frozen water splashes and overflows as he drops, up to his hips, in the water. He is bent at the waist, his chest flat against the ice, his gloved hands clawing to find purchase against the weight of the stones pulling him down.

"FUCK!" He yells at the top of his lungs. "OH MY GOD! STOP!"

"Tell me about Zoya," I say again.

"You can't do this! God! No!"

"Why'd you kill Zoya?" I grab his shoulders and begin to lift.

"Okay! Yes. I killed her. Pull me up! Please!"

"Why?"

"I'm slipping!"

"Tell me!"

"She wouldn't listen. She wanted to find Ana. I told her no, but she wouldn't listen."

"How'd you kill her?"

"I can't feel my legs."

"I said, 'How'd you kill Zoya?'"

"I . . . fuck! I drowned her, okay? Now get me out of here. I'm burning. It hurts!"

"Keep going. How'd you drown her?"

"I shoved her face into a toilet. I didn't mean to kill her, I swear. I just wanted her to listen to me. It was an accident. Please!"

I stand over him, panting, my exhausted breaths shooting into the night sky. This man killed Jenni. He killed Zoya—drowned her in a toilet because she wanted to see her sister again. Only Zoya's true killer would have known that she had been drowned.

"God—dammit! P—p—pull me up!" His words are punctuated by short gasps of air.

I grab the shoulders of Mikhail's snowmobile suit and lift him off the ice—enough so that he can see my face.

"Thank you," he whispers. "Thank—God."

My chest burns as I pull against the weight of the rocks. That little bit of effort is almost more than I can take. I don't have the strength to pull him out, not with a hundred pounds tied to his ankles. I give another tug but stop.

And it's in that moment of pause that my universe shrinks to the size of a pinhead—my every thought orbits around one simple truth. It's not the pain that stops me from saving this man, nor the weight of the rocks tugging Mikhail downward. I could save him if I wanted to. I could end this ordeal with both of us walking off the ice, him going north and me heading south. I have what I came for. I have his confession.

But Jenni's words come back to me as I hold Mikhail's life in my hands. *Vengeance is not justice*. She was right about that, but those ideas are not strangers to one another either. They're born of the same mother, one sired by virtue, the other, the bastard son of vice. I used to think of them as standing back to back, facing opposite horizons, but I understand now that sometimes they can face the same path, the same end.

He looks at me, and in his eyes I see both hope and doubt. But deeper, behind it all, I see guile. I see the monster.

Vengeance is not justice. But on this frozen lake, under a sky ablaze with the Northern Lights, vice and virtue collude to deliver Mikhail Vetrov to the only grave he will ever know.

I'm holding him up by the lapel of his snowsuit, and he's watching my eyes as I hesitate.

He knows.

I tip his chest up enough so that he slides deeper into the hole. He lets loose a scream and claws at the ice, his hands able to reach out to his sides just enough to catch the wall of the pit. With that little bit of leverage, he manages to press his shoulder blades against the back edge and stop his slide into the lake.

"NO!" His words sputter through muscles turned thick by the cold. "I told you . . . what you wanted . . . I confessed . . . you can't . . . do this . . . you're . . . a cop."

I sit on the ice in front of Mikhail. "No," I say. "I'm not a cop. I'm a man—a man whose wife and child you killed."

Mikhail is breathing in hard spurts. I can hear a gurgle of spit churning in his exhales. He slips down a few more inches and jerks his head back to keep his chin above the water. His fingertips are barely holding on.

I look him in the eye and say, "In the end, it comes down to this: You're an evil sonofabitch, and the world is a better place with you not in it."

I climb onto my knees and move in so that I am only a foot away from his face. His eyelids are heavy, and I can tell that he is struggling to keep them open. He begins to grunt as the weight overtakes him.

"You may want to get right with . . . well, with whatever God you may believe in."

He speaks and I can barely make out the words. "Go . . . to . . . hell."

I shrug. "Maybe."

His hands slip, and I hear the final gasp as he sucks in a breath before he is swallowed by the water. I watch the pale glow of his face disappear into the darkness. I wait until I see the bubbles of his last breath break the surface.

He is gone.

CHAPTER 42

I fall onto my back, lying in the same hole where Mikhail had spent most of the day. Above me the Northern Lights are in full flare, green and white, pulsing like a wildfire above my head. I'm mesmerized by the dance.

If I don't move, my toes don't hurt as badly, the crushing throb is replaced with numbness. I shiver in waves that break at the base of my neck. I breathe in shallow puffs because I am certain that a deep inhale would rip my lungs open. Cold from the ice at my back radiates up through me, and I feel as though I am becoming fossilized in ice. I look at the aurora, and all of my concerns take on a lilt of insignificance. It fills me with peace. The lights above my head are so beautiful, I can barely keep from crying.

I am tired. I close my eyes and think of Jenni. I can feel her hand on my cheek and the tickle of her breath on my throat as she curls up with me. I am floating on a warm tide, and I can smell the sweet scent of sugar cookies. We are on the floor, in front of that fireplace. I touch the tender curve of her cheek. The nearness of her soft body causes my skin to tighten, and I remember the pleasure of that ache.

She kisses my neck, and her lips move up until they brush the lobe of my ear. She is whispering to me, but I can't make out what she is saying. I strain to listen. It sounds like a song, but not any song I've ever heard before. I listen more closely and hear it again. The sound is soft, quiet, not from a whisper but from distance. It rises and holds, hitting a sharp crescendo before trailing off.

I can't smell the cookies anymore. I reach for Jenni and she is not there. My hands hurt again, my chest hurts. The throb in my toes has returned. I hear the sound again and realize that it's the howl of a wolf. I open my eyes. The aurora continues to light the surface of the snow, casting a green haze across the lake.

I try to roll to my side, but my defiant muscles won't listen to me. Everything hurts. I want to go back to my dream. I want to feel Jenni at my side again. I curse the wolf whose lonely, selfish wail brought me back to this lake. I could try again. I could close my eyes and bring her back to me—this time forever. I know what I'm doing. It's my choice. I try to conjure up those memories, but the wolf howls again. She won't let me go.

I grit my teeth, hold my arms to my chest, and roll onto my left side. The effort causes me to cough, sending a jolt of pain through my rib cage and down my spine. I feel like I'm breathing glass shards. I work my hips up until I am on my knees. I shouldn't have rested. That was a mistake. I should never have let my energy settle away like that. I needed to get up, get moving.

I put one foot under me, then the other, wincing as the blades of pain reawaken my feet. With one last effort, I stand. The cracking of my back and shoulder muscles is almost audible. I look around the nest.

Nothing remains of my deed except the knife in my boot and the auger, lying beside the hole. I drop both through and watch them disappear into the black water. In a couple of hours, the ice will reclaim the hole, the lake skimming a new layer of skin over its wound. In a day or two, the blowing snow will hide the nest. There will be no evidence of my being here—beyond the dead body anchored to the bottom of the lake.

I start back to the cabin, the path lit by the full moon and the waning surge of the Northern Lights at my back. My snow pants are stiff with ice, having been glazed with lake water as I fought to shove Mikhail Vetrov through the hole. The wind catches the bare skin of my neck with the sharp edge of a guillotine, and I lift my hood over my head. When I get to the trees, I pull myself up the bank, pausing on my hands and knees to catch my breath. Just standing back up is like lifting an oxcart filled with bricks.

I climb the first hill, using the aspen scrub to pull myself along the portage. The snow grips my legs. I stub my frozen feet on rocks as I try to get a foothold, and the pain is so jarring that it spikes throughout my entire body and seems to settle beneath the roots of my teeth. *One step more*, I tell myself. *Just one step more.*

I crest the hill and see the valley beyond. I know that the snowmobile is at the top of that next hill. If I can make it to the snowmobile, I can make it back to the Durango and safety, but I am convinced that I cannot make it to that next hill. In the moonlight I can see the skeletons of the aspen and birch, black against the moonlit snow in the distance. It is too far.

That's when I see a shadow moving on the path ahead of me. I stop, my heart thumping hard against its frozen shell. The shadow has halted about thirty feet away, low and dark. She turns, and I can see the eyes of the wolf. I expect them to glow as they do in my dreams, but they look tired, resigned, forgiving. We stare at each other.

I open my arms and tip my head back, exposing my throat. I expect to hear a snarl as she launches at me. I hurt so badly, I just don't care anymore. Maybe this is how it all should end anyway. I am afraid, but somehow, this seems fitting.

I wait, and nothing happens. When I open my eyes, she is gone. I listen and can hear nothing except the wind. I start walking again, certain that one of only three things can happen: I will succumb to the cold; I will be eaten by wolves; or I will make it to the sled. *One more step. One more step.*

The valley seems longer and deeper, and the path far more narrow than when I had crossed it last. Tree branches tug at my arms and cast shadows that play tricks on me. I step cross-eyed onto fallen logs or jutting rocks that knock me to my knees. I don't stay down, though. With my nubby hands, I push myself back up and press on.

I try to fill my head with thoughts to distract myself from the pain, but they evaporate before becoming fully formed. I try to think of a song, something easy to remember, something with a marching cadence. The only one that comes to mind is "My Girl," by the Temptations. I can't sing that well on a good day, but as I start my climb out of the valley, I shove that song into my head, whispering the words as I pull and clutch my way up the hill.

I trip on a root and face-plant into the snow. The song plays on.

I lift myself up, making it back to my feet as the song tells me about the month of May. I push on, keeping the song playing in my head. At times, I get too winded to whisper the lyrics, so I let the rhythm of the bass guitar drive me forward.

I'm on my third rendition of the song when the snowmobile comes into sight. I'd forgotten that I turned it around when I parked it on the hill. I give a silent prayer of thanks to the fallen saint or random flair of synapse that had put that idea in my head. I'm fairly certain that I would have died trying to lift it now.

I straddle the sled, start it up, and take off.

The wind in my face fills my eyes with tears. I have to blink hard to see the path. A couple times, my eyelashes freeze shut and I force them open by raising the muscles in my forehead and under my eyebrows. In no time at all, I am back at the cabin, and I park where the snowmobile had been idling when I first came there. I leave the motor running and the headlight on so that I can search for my gun.

I see the divots where I'd been standing when Mikhail caught me in the wrist with that first log. I drop to my knees, feeling under the snow in the shadow of a pine tree. I can't leave my gun here. It's the only proof of my connection to the man who ordered my wife's death.

My fingers are numb, and I begin to question whether I'd be able to feel the gun if I brushed across it. I'm so close to being finished, so close to the safety and the warmth of the Durango, yet, I can't feel a thing beneath the snow.

Then suddenly the light above the cabin's deck bursts to life.

I am in the shadow of the pine tree, on my hands and knees, and I stop all movement. I hold my breath to listen. It might be a motion sensor. It has to be. Then I notice that the lights of the cabin are off. Total darkness on the other side of the glass. Those lights were on this morning. I remember.

I hear the glass sliding door open. Although the light blinds me from seeing who is on the deck, I know that I am not alone. A small figure steps into the light, a woman. Her arms are stretched out in front of her as though she might be holding a gun.

I shake my head. “For fuck’s sake,” I mutter. “What next?”

“Mikhail?” Ana calls out.

“No, not Mikhail. Max.”

CHAPTER 43

I close my eyes and wait for the sound of the gunshot. I don't move. I'm not sure if I am even able to move.

With my head down, I don't see Ana's ghostly silhouette slip out of the light. I don't hear the movement as she slides the deck door shut. The next thing I hear is the basement door opening. I raise my head to see her standing at the door.

"What are you waiting for?" she asked. "Come in."

I climb to my feet once more and stumble toward her. Ana is wearing the same clothes I'd left her in, except now she is wearing a pair of men's galoshes and has a blanket draped around her shoulders.

"What were you doing out there?" she asks. "You scared me to death. I thought it was Mikhail coming back."

I can't talk. I feel like my body is starting to shut down. I'm not sure what I would say if I could speak. I can't tell her the truth. Finally I manage to say. "Mikhail's gone." I won't explain what that means. For all she knows, Mikhail made it into Canada and is on his way to some other country with no extradition treaty with the US.

Ana leads me up a staircase and to the main room of the cabin. She guides my shoulders until I am sitting on a large sofa. She kneels at my feet and tugs at the frozen laces of my boots. I want to shoo her away, but I know that my fingers would never be able to grip something as small as a shoelace. My feet scream to life as she slides the boots off. Then she gently peels my socks off of my swollen feet. She lifts each foot to inspect it. Then she reaches up and unbuckles both my snow pants and my jeans.

"Take off your clothes," she orders before walking to the kitchen. I can see her putting water into a kettle as I start stripping down. She reaches into a cupboard and pulls out a fistful of tea bags, opening the kettle and dropping them all in. Then she retrieves a spice jar and adds several spoons full of something red to the concoction.

I wriggle out of my coat and shirt. I have to lay down to get out of my snow pants. They are so stiff they can stand on their own. My jeans are also wet, and cold, but not frozen. When I am in my underwear, I begin to shake violently. I fall onto the couch, and Ana is at my side again, tucking a thick, down comforter around me. My shivering tugs at my shoulders and back. My jaw rattles and the muscles in my neck cramp up.

Ana climbs under the comforter and wraps her arms around my chest. She lays her head against my cheek and twines her legs around mine. She stays there until the shivering stops. Neither of us say a word. When my breathing returns to normal, she looks up at me and smiles.

The whistle on the kettle shrieks to life, and she slips off the couch. She pours the boiling mixture into a large pot, the kind that can hold a dozen roasting ears or more, and adds tap water, sticking her finger in occasionally to test the temperature. When she seems satisfied, she carries the bowl to the couch, laying it on the floor.

"Sit up," she says.

I do, and she lifts my feet into the bowl. The warm water hurts and I clench my teeth to bear it. I ask, "What is this?"

"It is tea and cayenne pepper. It will shrink the swelling and help with the healing."

The chemicals in the water swirl around my toes, and I start to feel sensation—painful at first, but sensation nonetheless. She folds the comforter around my chest, making sure that no part of my skin is exposed to the air other than my ankles and my face. I lean my head back and close my eyes.

I can hear her moving around the kitchen again, opening cupboard doors and shuffling things around, all in a muffled attempt to be quiet, probably for my benefit. I must have fallen asleep briefly, because the next thing I know, she's nudging me awake. She has a bowl of soup in her one hand and a glass of water in the other.

"You need to eat," she says.

"Thank you," I whisper.

"Shhhh."

I drink almost the entire glass of water and put the remainder on a small table beside me. I place the soup bowl on my lap and lift the first spoonful to my lips. Chicken-noodle soup. The salty, hot liquid rolls down my throat like some miraculous elixir, healing the burn and bringing life back to parts of my body that had shriveled to dust over those many hours on the lake. As I eat, Ana lifts my feet from the warm bath she had created, drying each with a towel.

She has a tube of something and squeezes a dollop of the lotion onto her hands, rubbing her palms together. Then she starts massaging the lotion onto my feet, paying particular attention to my toes.

"What is that?" I ask.

"Aloe. You have blisters from frostbite."

Her touch is soft and comforting. A warm bliss inches up my legs and into my chest. She wraps my feet in gauze and strips of a cotton T-shirt. When she is finished with the bandages, I thank her, hand her the soup bowl, and lay back on the couch. I wait for her to come back. I expect that she will want to know what happened to Mikhail. I close my eyes to think of something to say, and I promptly fall asleep.

I awaken in a heavy darkness splintered by spikes of moonlight riffling through the naked shoots of the birch outside, the rays tipping the walls and furniture into crooked angles. I rise onto my elbows to look around and am reminded that I am in Mikhail Vetrov's cabin. Everything comes rushing back to me.

I wonder if there had been a dream that jolted me awake, some night terror that sent me scurrying back to consciousness before the pain became too much to bear. Had I been visited by Jenni, or the wolves? Or had some new memory, a vestige of my day on the ice and my unspeakable deed, come in the night to haunt me? I touch my temple and feel no sweat. No heart palpitations. No remnant of a nightmare. This time, I had simply awakened for no reason, good or bad.

I stare at the unfamiliar shapes and shadows amassed around me and wait for the wave of regret. I am in his house, lying on his couch. His bandages bind my wounds. His food nourishes my broken body. And he is dead at my hands. I looked him in the eye, and I executed him. I should be torn apart by this fact, rending my clothing and sweating with guilt, but there is nothing there. I do not feel sad. I search for it as a child may search for that one talisman of comfort, the teddy bear, the favorite blanket, that touchstone that calms them in their darkest moments. I search for my remorse, the proof of my own virtue, but find nothing.

It is the absence of the thing that makes me sad. I know what I should be feeling, but it is not there. There is no grain of regret to be conjured, despite my best efforts. I didn't expect this. I had braced myself for a maelstrom of emotional repercussions, but no such violence has come. I feel fine.

I look for Ana, and I find her lying at my side. She had lined up three cushions from another couch to make a small makeshift bed beside the sofa where I had fallen asleep.

I roll onto my side so I can see her better. In that soft blue luminescence, her face seems to radiate its own fine glow. Strands of her hair crisscross her eyes, and the subtle rise and fall of her chest as she breathes is almost feline. I can see her sister's features in her face, and it reminds me that the man I dropped through the hole in the ice had drowned Zoya by shoving her face into a toilet. He pulled the strings when Reece Whitton pushed my wife into the path of an oncoming car.

I roll back over and stare at the patterns on the wall until I fall back asleep.

CHAPTER 44

The next time I wake up, sunlight fills the cabin. I rub the sleep out of my eyes and sit up. Where Ana had been sleeping the night before lay my clothes, washed and folded. I can hear the muffled clacking of movement in the kitchen. Then Ana stands up on the other side of the island, a frying pan in her hand. She looks my way and smiles.

"I am sorry," she says. "I was trying to be quiet."

"What time is it?"

"Almost noon. You must have been very tired."

"Noon?"

I stand in my underwear, a little wobbly on my tender feet, and begin putting on my pants. Ana watches from the kitchen.

"There is very little food here," she says. "Nothing fresh. Only canned goods and some fish in the freezer. Do you like fish?"

"Huh? Fish? Sure, I like fish." I pull my flannel shirt over arms so sore that I can barely move them.

"Good, because I have thawed some to have for breakfast."

"You really don't . . ." I start to beg my way out of breakfast but stop when I see the hint of disappointment in her eyes. I feel like I'm in a hurry, like I need to make an escape from the scene of the crime. I rethink my answer. I have nowhere to go. Not anymore. "You know, fish sounds perfect."

I sit back down and unwrap the bandages from my feet. My toes are red and tender. I can't feel anything in my left pinky toe or in the tips of any of the others. My socks are warm and dry, and I feel like I'm dipping my foot into warm butter when I pull them on.

In the kitchen, Ana is wearing an oversized Vikings jersey and I think shorts, but I can only see her thighs. She's also wearing men's socks rolled down to her ankles to work as slippers. Walking to the kitchen, I'm about to make small talk about the fish when I see my gun on the island countertop.

"My . . . gun?" I pick it up and inspect it. There is still some moisture inside the barrel, but the rest of it looks as good as new. "Where . . ."

"I went out to where you were rutting around last night. It is much easier to find things in the daylight."

"I thought I told you to stay at that lodge."

"I had no choice but to come here. There were things that I needed to find. To get them, I would have walked far more than ten miles. The cold and snow were a small price to pay."

"What kind of things?"

"You would not understand."

"I can be a very understanding man. Try me."

She gives a glance over her shoulder, as if to size up my sincerity. The fish lay on a plate, and she pats them dry with a paper towel. Then she leaves the kitchen, heading to a room that I can see is a bedroom. I think she is ignoring me. When she comes back out, she's carrying a small paper sack. She hands the bag to me and returns to her cooking, lowering the fish into the hot oil.

In the bag, I find a stack of passports held together with a rubber band. I pull the top few from the stack and begin thumbing through them. Women—young girls, really—all with Russian-sounding names and Greek-looking letters skittering across the papers.

"What are these?"

"They are Mikhail's girls. They are the ones who wear his ruble tattoo behind their ears."

I shuffle through a few more and find Zoya's passport and then Ana's. I count fifteen in all.

Ana turns to face me, letting the fish fry unattended. "If we have no passports, we cannot run away. We cannot go home. We are here illegally and must do as we are told."

"What will you do with these?" I put the passports back into the bag and slide it to Ana.

"I will find the women. I will send them home—if they will go. I want to help them, if they will let me."

"That's very good of you," I say.

"They will be like me and refuse to listen at first. They are here because of Mikhail. They will be loyal to him. They will not want me to interfere with their lives. But soon, they will come to realize that Mikhail is . . . gone. They will be fearful and they will feel alone. That is when I will be able to help them."

"Do you need help? I know some people—"

"I will be okay. I am strong. I have been through much, and it has made me strong. You have freed me, Max Rupert."

"I wouldn't say that. I—"

She turns back around to her fish, flipping them over and sprinkling basil and rosemary and garlic salt on them. The aroma fills the cabin, and my mouth waters its approval.

"And what will you do?" she asks. "You will go back and be a detective?"

"No," I say. "I will not be going back."

She looks surprised and a bit saddened by my answer. "Then where will you go?"

"I have a cabin north of Grand Rapids. It's been in my family since before Minnesota was a state. I'll take you back to the city, and then I plan to go there and sit. I don't know what's going to happen beyond that, and I don't care. I may just live out the rest of my life in that old cabin. I guess I'll have to wait and see."

Ana dishes up the fish. "You do not have to take me to Minneapolis. I will drive Mikhail's car back and park it at his house. I will be careful to not be seen."

"You've thought this through."

"I have. And before I leave, I will clean this cabin. I have experience in doing a proper job of cleaning. When I am finished, there will be no proof of our being here." She looks at me with eyes chock full of complicity. "We never left Minneapolis, remember?"

After our lunch, she gathers the dishes and stacks them in the dishwasher, then shoves the bedding we'd used into the washing machine and starts it. For my part, I pace around the cabin, trying to think of what I might be overlooking. When I am satisfied that I have accounted for every trace of my being there, I pull on my coat and fold my snow pants over my arm.

"I'm going now," I say.

Ana walks with me to the front door, tucking her hair behind her ear like a schoolgirl as we stop to say our good-bye.

"Thank you for what you did for me last night," I say. "You may have saved my life."

"If I saved your life, then we are even," she says. She reaches up and cups her hand on my cheek. "Maybe someday . . . if we ever see each other again . . ."

I let my eyes fall to the floor. I can feel the wilt of her palm against my cheek.

"I'm sorry," she says. "I forgot who I am."

"No," I say quickly. "It's not that at all. Please." I hold her hand in mine and bring it to my lips. "I have to be alone. That's all. I'm no good right now. I don't know if I'll ever be good again. I need to be by myself for a while to . . . to figure things out. After that—well, who knows. Maybe we'll find each other again."

"I would like that," she says.

I lift her face and kiss her softly on the lips. It is the first time that I have kissed a woman since Jenni's death. I'd forgotten how sweet and soft a woman's lips could be. I let the kiss linger longer than I had intend, but without regret. Then I kiss her again, this time on her forehead. I give her a smile and leave.

CHAPTER 45

I don't turn my phone back on until I am within a mile of my family's cabin, a Lincoln Log hovel compared to the palace Mikhail Vetrov called a cabin. The logging road that leads to my place is invisible under the snow, and a four-foot ridge of crushed ice lines the side of the highway, left there by the county plows. I can't make it back to the cabin in the Durango, but I am pretty sure I can jam the SUV far enough into the snowbank to be off the pavement. I line the vehicle up crossways on the highway and make a run at it with all the Durango can muster. I hear plastic crunching as my nose shoots up, the snow exploding around me.

I lay on the accelerator until movement is replaced by the high whine of spinning tires. I'm far enough off the highway to be out of the way, and I call my friend, Sheriff Voight, the man tasked to keep the peace in this sleepy part of the woods, and tell him I'm at the cabin. I don't need him sending someone out to investigate my abandoned SUV.

I had stopped by a grocery store in Grand Rapids and loaded up on supplies, enough to last a few months, maybe longer if the fishing goes well. It takes me a couple hours to haul everything down the logging trail and to my cabin. I light a fire in the fireplace and watch as the flames grow and dance around the pine logs.

I wait until the cabin is warm before I check my phone. I find eight text messages and three voice-mail messages from Niki. I also see two missed calls from Chief Murphy. I decide to call him first. He doesn't answer—a stroke of luck.

"Chief, it's Max Rupert. I guess you're probably wondering where I am. Sorry I missed my shift. I needed some time off to think. I want to thank you for all you've done for me over the years, but I am calling to let you know that I am resigning. I'll make arrangements to turn in my badge, gun, and car. I'm sorry for the short notice, but . . . I need to call it a day." I hang up.

I go to the text messages from Niki.

WTF. Whitton committed suicide last night. Call me.

Where are you? Things blowing up here.

You're late. U OK?

Murphy's looking for you. He's not happy. Call me.

Starting to worry. What's going on?

Please call me. Are U OK?

Murphy's pissed, FYI. I'm getting scared. Call me ASAP!

Went by your house 1 a.m. where are you?

I don't bother listening to the voice mail. I know what the messages will say. I hit Niki's name on my phone and send the call.

"So you are alive," she says when she answers. "Where the hell you been? Murphy's threatening to hang you from the rafters."

"If he wants to hang me, he'll have to come up to the cabin to do it."

"The cabin? In January? What's going on?"

"Niki, I just called Chief Murphy and turned in my resignation. I quit."

The phone goes silent. I wait.

"Why would you do that?" Her tone holds a faraway sadness, the questioning of someone who didn't see the slap coming.

"I had to quit, Niki. I know you don't understand, but I had no choice." I should have prepared better for this conversation. "I need to step out of that world. I don't belong there anymore."

"What happened?"

"I . . . I can't . . ." I shake my head and pull it together. "Nothing happened. It's time for me to do something else, that's all."

"Does this have anything to do with Whitton jumping off the top of a parking ramp?"

I don't answer.

"It's a mess here. A million rumors floating around."

"Just keep your head down and let the rumors swirl. It'll pass."

"Max?" She pauses, as if trying to find the words she wants to say. Then, "Will I ever see you again?"

"I don't know." I'm pretty sure I'm lying to her.

"Are you . . . content?"

"Content?"

I know what she's asking. She wants to know if I tracked down Jenni's killer. She wants to know if I found a way to put to rest those ghosts that have been haunting me for the past four and a half years. "Yes," I say. "I am content."

She doesn't ask any further.

"I'm going to miss you, Max."

"Back at you, Niki."

I want to say so much more. I want to tell her how important she has become to me; how, after all that I have lost, she is the one person still there for me. I want to say all that and more, but instead I say, "I gotta go. Good-bye, Niki."

"Good-bye, Max."

I kill the connection and shut my phone off.

I am alone now, more alone than I have ever been, but I feel awash in calmness. It wasn't supposed to be like this. I wasn't supposed to be okay with what I'd done. Where was the anguish, the regret? I wait for it, but nothing happens. The snow starts to fall again in big, popcorn flakes that swirl in lazy swoops past my front window. It is beautiful and it makes me want to smile—so I smile.

The impact of what I did out on that frozen lake may visit me at some point. There may come a day when the darkness inside of me roils up in my chest to scream its damnation at me—but that day is not today. I lean back in my chair and close my eyes, letting the aroma of the burning pine take me back to my house in Logan Park, to a day when Jenni was at my side. The wolves are gone, and for now, I am at peace.

Acknowledgments

I would like to thank Sgt. Robert Dale, Detective with the Minneapolis Police Department, and Special Agent Ann Quinn of the Minnesota BCA for their insight into the criminal world in Minnesota. I would also like to thank John Filliman and Sheryl Hindermann for their expertise in the north woods.

I would like to thank my wife, Joely, for her patience and help. Thank you, Nancy Rosin and Terry Kolander for your editorial assistance with this book. Thank you, Amy Cloughley, my agent, for your sure-handed guidance. Finally, I would like to extend my heartfelt gratitude to Dan Mayer and Jade Zora Scibilia, my editors, as well as to Jon Kurtz, Jill Maxick, Cheryl Quimba, and everyone at Seventh Street Books for everything you have done for me.

About the Author

Allen Eskens is the bestselling author of *The Life We Bury*, *The Guise of Another*, and *The Heavens May Fall*. He is the recipient of a Barry Award, a Minnesota Book Award, a Rosebud Award (Left Coast Crime), and a Silver Falchion Award, and he has been a finalist for an Edgar Award, a Thriller Award, an Anthony Award, and an Audie Award. His books have been translated into twenty languages and his novel *The Life We Bury* is in development for a feature film.

Allen is currently working on his fifth novel, the sequel to his award-winning and bestselling debut novel, *The Life We Bury*, due out in 2018. He lives with his wife, Joely, in Greater Minnesota and is represented by Amy Cloughley of Kimberley Cameron and Associates Literary Agency. To learn more about Allen or his books, visit him at www.alleneskens.com.